QUEEN OF THE DOME

Copyright © 2023 Amizah R.

All rights reserved. No part of this book may be reproduced or used in any manner without written permission from the copyright owner, except in the case of brief quotations in a review.

To request permissions, contact the copyright owner at authoramizahr@gmail.com

Content/Trigger Warning: this book contains strong language, graphic violence, sexually explicit scenes, and discreet references to sexism

Table of Contents

Chapter One	7
Chapter Two	15
Chapter Three	25
Chapter Four	32
Chapter Five	36
Chapter Six	41
Chapter Seven	48
Chapter Eight	65
Chapter Nine	68
Chapter Ten	77
Chapter Eleven	83
Chapter Twelve	92
Chapter Thirteen	100
Chapter Fourteen	104
Chapter Fifteen	118
Chapter Sixteen	123
Chapter Seventeen	126
Chapter Eighteen	135

Chapter Nineteen	**144**
Chapter Twenty	**149**
Chapter Twenty-One	**151**
Chapter Twenty-Two	**154**
Chapter Twenty-Three	**165**
Chapter Twenty-Four	**171**
Chapter Twenty-Five	**178**
Chapter Twenty-Six	**185**
Chapter Twenty-Seven	**194**
Chapter Twenty-Eight	**198**
Chapter Twenty-Nine	**202**
Chapter Thirty	**210**
Chapter Thirty-One	**215**
Chapter Thirty-Two	**226**
Chapter Thirty-Three	**231**
Chapter Thirty-Four	**236**
Chapter Thirty-Five	**245**
Chapter Thirty-Six	**253**
Chapter Thirty-Seven	**257**
Chapter Thirty-Eight	**264**
Chapter Thirty-Nine	**270**

Chapter Forty	**278**
Chapter Forty-One	**288**
Chapter Forty-Two	**295**
Chapter Forty-Three	**303**
Chapter Forty-Four	**315**
Chapter Forty-Five	**319**
Chapter Forty-Six	**326**
Chapter Forty-Seven	**330**
Chapter Forty-Eight	**336**
Chapter Forty-Nine	**343**
Chapter Fifty	**353**
Epilogue	**358**

Chapter One

"The dumb brute and the deceiving bitch," the voice cackled from behind him.

Cade closed his eyes and took a deep breath, praying for this interaction to be over soon.

He was by no means dumb and the three idiots approaching his workbench knew as much. He did speak, just not a lot. He didn't see the need in opening his mouth if not for anything important. That sentiment didn't apply to Lia though. With Lia, he spoke freely, but one could argue that it was only because she didn't let him get away with his usual one-worded answers and quiet mumblings.

The lady in question stood up from where she had been sitting on the ground, skinning rabbits from this morning's round.

"Reporting for duty, sir!" she barked with a hand to her head, pulling a serious face.

Cade turned around, ready to watch this play out but reluctant to get involved. He knew Lia could handle herself.

"Is that so? Want to make yourself useful? Get on your knees." Theo smirked, taking a step forward, clutching his groin. Tag and Bron laughed beside him.

"Ooph," Lia winced, appearing apologetic. "I swear I would, but I have super strict requirements." She gestured at her forehead before slowly drawing out her hand clean over Theo's head. The pout she gave him was beyond patronizing. "Maybe next year. I'm sure you would have sprouted by then."

It was all Cade could do not to smile.

Lia was already a woman of tall stature, standing at five feet and ten inches. But head to head with Theo, who just barely passed her chin? The way she dwarfed him was almost comical.

His best friend always chose to escalate these run-ins, but Cade remained silent as usual. He would enjoy the show, but he didn't have to indulge her.

Theo took another step closer to Lia, face turning red, snarling. "Why don't you go back to the forest, you foundling whore!"

Lia only smiled. She'd heard it all before. But Cade could hear something dangerous in Theo's tone. He never took insults well.

Slightly on edge, Cade shuffled forward, ready to haul Lia into the house if things got out of hand. It wouldn't have been the first time he had to.

He was briefly reminded of an altercation that he had to stop a few months ago. It had started the same way and ended with Lia on top of one of the townies in the muddy grass, giving him the beating of his life. He'd promptly pulled her off him and carried her over his shoulder back into the house. Cade loved Lia to bits but her fearlessness often unsettled him, scared him even.

She could definitely hold her own against Theo, but all three of them were a different problem. Besides, he knew who would hold the blame if word got to the councilmen about another dispute.

Suddenly, Lia stiffened. Her head flew back, face to the sky, and she began shaking, eyes rolling to the back of her head. Theo, Tag, and Bron immediately began backing away, but Cade cocked his head at her in amusement.

Here we go again... he thought.

Cade knew what a real vision looked like, and this wasn't it. He was well aware that Lia's little displays wouldn't do her any favors with the people in their sector but he wasn't in a rush to stop her fun. It wasn't as if they didn't deserve it, even if it was mean.

Moments later, Lia dropped to her knees on the grass with her head down, startling their unwanted guests. All the while, Cade leaned back on his workbench, legs crossed, observing. He wondered how far she would take it this time.

Shivering, Lia lifted her head, dark curls falling to either side of her face. "A vision..." she whispered. "Theo... it's your mother," Her face twisted, feigning sorrow.

Had he not known Lia so well, he would have been just as anxious as the rest of them.

Theo blanched, fear leaking into his anger and shock. "W-what about her?"

She silently beckoned him forward, a solitary tear making its way down her face. Slowly, warily, Theo made his way to her, looking more apprehensive with each step.

In a flash, Lia stood up and threw out her hand. Even Cade flinched a fraction. He looked to Theo just in time to catch his yelp and watch him jump back as bloody rabbit skins splattered across his face and slid down his torso.

Lia doubled over with laughter and this time, Cade allowed himself to join in, unabashed by their current company.

Through their laughter, Cade heard Theo's outraged barking as Tag and Bron dragged him away. "I'll fucking kill you, Seer! You too, you bastard!"

When he finally sobered, Cade looked at Lia as tears of laughter shone in her eyes. "One of these days, they'll string you up," he said, shaking his head.

"Ah, let them," she snorted. "At least then I could haunt you and you'll never be rid of me."

Cade stared at her, an easy smile falling over his face. "As if I can be rid of you now."

He woke that night to the familiar sounds of whining and light tapping on the wall behind him. Cade swiftly drew the furs back and stood, padding over to the room that shared a wall with him.

Upon entry, he didn't startle at the scene before him. He'd seen it many times before.

Keeping his steps soft, he walked to the edge of Lia's bed and gently cradled her shaking body, maneuvering himself so that she laid back into his chest, before sinking onto her mattress.

He absently noticed that this one lasted longer than usual but made no move to get up. Just slowly rocked her, looking over her glazed, white eyes, murmuring into her ear as a bead of sweat dripped down her forehead.

After some time, she woke, blinking groggily, drawing herself from Cade's gentle hold. He gave her a second to catch her breath and refrained from asking questions, allowing her to fill him in when she was ready.

A lot of the time, Lia's visions didn't seem to make much sense or she deemed them as irrelevant, but Cade was always there if she wanted to talk about it or needed help interpreting them.

After several deep breaths, she sat up and looked back at Cade apologetically.

Sensing what was on the tip of her tongue as Lia opened her mouth, Cade shook his head. "Don't."

She nodded absently, visibly trying to piece together what was going through her mind.

Many people in their sector believed that seers manipulated the future through their visions to bring harm to others and if he had never met Lia, Cade probably wouldn't have known any better either. But he'd watched his best friend over the years, plagued by these visions, tormented by the guilt of not being able to prevent some events. He'd witnessed the hysteria and the confusion that followed the visions. He knew that they were far from voluntary or malicious and would never allow her to be sorry for something as menial as checking on her when she was in distress.

Tension began to wind up in Cade's chest as Lia's eyes began widening, darting around the room.

Patience forgotten, he softly asked, "What is it?"

She looked up, finally meeting his eyes with an urgent look in hers. "Enforcers from The Dome," she hissed. "Maybe a dozen, headed for the Western Council lodge."

For goodness sake.

Cade stood immediately and made his way to his room knowing Lia would probably follow him.

"Where do you think you're going?" she demanded as her feet slapped unsteadily across the wooden floors behind him.

He was right.

If she hadn't sounded so drained he might have ignored the question considering his mood, but she deserved an answer after the night she'd had.

"Council lodge," he said, slipping a shirt over his head.

Lia sighed, digging her fingers into the band of her nightcap. "You don't think it's time for them to quit this stupid game?"

"Of course, I do," he snipped back, dressing as he made his way around the room.

"Then let this run its course. For whatever they've done this time, I'm sure they have it coming," she stressed, throwing her arms out.

He knew who she was talking about without her having to utter their names.

For the past few years, Cade's father and younger brother had been formulating some ridiculous plot to take over The Dome and overthrow the queen to steal her power and riches. He understood their frustration. Of course, he did. The Dome was a hub of wealth and technology thriving right in the middle of Terra. Meanwhile, the surrounding sectors grew poorer by the day and were forced into manual labor in hopes of bartering with The Dome to get by.

If that wasn't bad enough, there was no such thing as fair trade. Everyone knew that the trading officials from inside The Dome were nothing if not greedy. They knew that they could get away with paying outsiders less, they didn't need the resources as much as the outsiders needed the money.

There wasn't much Cade or anyone else could do about it though. The Dome was swimming with the gifted. Seers, witches, psionics, empaths, azraels, and all of the like. This was exactly why he needed to stop his father before he did something that he couldn't take back.

"You know, you can come with me if you want," he tossed over his shoulder placatingly, heading for the door.

She narrowed her eyes. "Have you heard a word I've said?" she asked, voice growing dangerously high in pitch.

"Each one," he said dryly.

"Then why is your hand on the fucking doorknob?" she exclaimed, cutting through the relative calm.

She was agitated now but he knew that she was only scared for him. For what he might be walking into.

Lia was well aware of the state of Cade's relationship with his father so it was no surprise that she would be reluctant for him to go back to the Council lodge. Back to his childhood home.

He walked back towards her and framed her face with his hands, staring into her eyes, speaking softly. "I know, okay? I know that nothing good will come from me being there, but at the very least I have to see what's going on. They're my family." *Only family,* he added mentally. "Come with me."

Though her face hadn't changed, he felt the moment she conceded and fought a smile. After a few seconds, she rolled her eyes, blowing out a breath.

"Fine, but I swear to the Gods we are not staying for more than an hour. No offense, but your father makes me want to take up murder as a hobby."

His smile beamed from ear to ear, masking his own anxiety. "Me too."

Chapter Two

Cade didn't live far from his childhood home, but the journey took longer than usual due to the lack of daylight.
This wouldn't be the first time he had been back since he moved out, however, that didn't do much to stop the memories that assaulted him of his last night there as he approached the eroded steps of the Council lodge.

The door flew open.
Cade was startled out of his sleep. Blinking rapidly, he looked up to see his father storming around his bedroom, leaving only destruction in his wake. Flipping chairs, emptying drawers, even pulling the very blankets from Cade's half-alert body.
"Father," he called carefully, slowly standing as if confronting a wild animal.
"Where is it?" His father didn't even look at him as he continued his search.
"Where is what?" Cade asked, on edge.
"Your coin," he spat as he lifted the corner of the mattress.

Cade stiffened.

"And don't lie to me, boy! You were gone throughout the day so you better have something to show for it."

He took a steadying breath. "It's mine," Cade said, just loud enough to be heard in the silence of the dark room.

His words hung in the air for several seconds before his father finally paused his search and turned to him, staring deep into his soul with a look that would make lesser men quiver.

"What was that?" he said in an undertone.

"It's mine," Cade repeated, louder this time. "I earned it-"

He had barely finished his sentence when his head snapped to the side with a brutal blow. Cade had just about recovered when a second blow hit his ribs sending him to the ground, clutching his stomach.

"Who do you think allows you to live in this lodge?!"

A kick to the side.

"Huh? What have you earned?"

A knee to the head.

"You haven't even earned the clothes on your back and you want to clutch your coin and sleep soundly in my home?" he hissed bitterly.

That wasn't true. As hits and kicks rained down on him, Cade realized that he hadn't ever slept a peaceful night in the lodge. Especially not since his mother passed.

Cade closed his eyes and traveled far away in his mind. To his quiet place. It almost brought him peace when his father would get like this. Walking on eggshells around him was far more painful than the beatings. This, he could take. The sweet serenity of falling as opposed to the chilling anticipation of walking along the edge of the cliff. Despite the pain, it nearly felt good. It felt like letting go.

He didn't fear his father, not anymore. At sixteen he grew well past six feet, surpassing his father, but still to this day, two years later, he had never raised a hand against him. Not that he'd never wanted to.

Finally, the room went still and the silence stretched for what felt like years.

Long after the final blow, Cade stood shakily, though his body screamed at him to stay down.

He just wanted this to be over, and if that meant that his father would beat him to death this time, then so be it.

So with his last strand of defiance left, he looked into his father's eyes and wiped his bloody nose on his sleeve. Something deep down told him that this would be the last time.

"CADE!"

Cade flinched at the pained screech and subtly leaned sideways to peer around his father and out of his window.

Lia.

At the front gate of the lodge being held back by two men attempting to stop her entry.

For her to come at this time in the night, Cade knew that she must've had a vision. A vision of what had just happened.

He was grateful for her presence, he always had been, but he prayed that she hadn't seen too much. He didn't want her worrying about him on top of her own problems.

"Let me in! Cade!" she yelled, her anger warring with concern.

Not waiting to see how his father would react to Lia's arrival, Cade turned and began picking up his clothes that were strewn about the place, grimacing as he felt that familiar ache in his muscles.

Picking up two satchels, he filled them with anything he could grab, acting as if his father wasn't even in the room.

Once satisfied he staggered past his father to reach his chest of drawers. Locking eyes with him, Cade glared silently as he placed both palms on the edge. He grunted as he pushed it out and to the side. He never let his gaze fall as he bent and retrieved the bag of coins strapped to the back.

His father's face soured even further, but Cade paid him no mind as he started out of the room, down the stairs, and through the door, ignoring the griping from behind him.

"Oh my Gods, Cade!"

Finally free of the men holding her, Lia ran and embraced Cade only stepping back an inch when he winced from the contact with his bruises. His father walked down the steps and right over to him, completely ignoring Lia's existence.

He eyed the bag in Cade's hands, knowing that he couldn't make a scene in front of his men. "Tomorrow, if you have nothing to show for a day's work, do not return," *his father gritted out.*

So he didn't.

"Cade, are we going in or not?" Lia drew him from his thoughts, one foot on the steps, looking back towards him.

Cade shook his head and cleared his throat. "Yeah, I'm coming."

⊲▷

Knock, knock.

"Head Councilman Alden! Cade Alden and Eulalia Sambor have come to see you," called out his father's second in command.

Cade held back an eye roll at Young's use of his full name. As if his father wouldn't know it was him.

While he and Lia waited with Councilman Young, he allowed his eyes to drift down the corridor toward his old bedroom. His brother's room was only one door down from his and he wondered if he had been awake that night eight years ago, wondered if Cassian had heard what occurred the night he left. Regardless of his relationship with his brother, he hoped not.

He didn't have much time to wonder though as his father called out from behind the door in his gruff voice, "Enter."

Young opened the door and then there Cade stood, only a few feet from his father.

Drake Alden.

Giving him a quick once-over Cade attempted to gauge what kind of mood he was in. By the look on his face and the annoyance radiating from him, he wasn't hopeful.

While he quietly shuffled into the room, Lia strutted in, barely sparing the Head Councilman a glance as she took a seat at the round table without being asked.

Cade simply shook his head and sank into the seat beside her, briefly flicking his eyes to his father, who stared at them expectantly.

Tension quickly filled the room.

"To what do I owe the pleasure?" Drake asked, bored.

He would've thought that his father would at least pretend to be interested in his well-being considering his standing in the community and the fact that Cade had not visited his childhood home in months. Drake was nothing if not a showman but evidently, he was less than willing to extend their meeting with pleasantries tonight.

"What have you been doing on the western border?" Cade asked, just as plainly, ignoring his question.

His fathers' eyes flashed to his with a hint of surprise before his expression settled. "So, now you have an interest in the council's business?" he returned. "Finally fallen off your high horse?"

This again.

He was so tired of this false narrative.

"Is it so self-righteous to have a mind of my-" Cade cut himself off and sighed. He didn't have time to entertain his father's pathetic effort at deflection.

Knowing the reaction with which his next words would be met, he sat straighter, steeling his spine. "Lia had a vision," he murmured. One would think his chair had caught fire with the speed that his father stood. "Get out!"

"Father..."

"No! Leave. You have disgraced this household for years and I have allowed it, but I will not have you bring your lies and witchcraft under my roof!" he spat, turning to look at Lia with only disgust in his eyes.

Allowed it?

As if Drake didn't take every opportunity to remind him of how much of a disappointment he was.

Cade was surprised that Lia had held her tongue this long, but she quickly stood at Drake's derisive gaze.

"Hey! If you would just shut your mouth for two seconds and listen, you would see that he is trying to help you against his better judgment and my own advice."

"Do you think that I'm stupid enough to believe anything out of the mouth of a seer?"

Lia let out a condescending laugh. "We have no reason to lie to you and quite frankly, I hope you don't believe me. That way, when you don't listen, you get your ass put in the ground by whoever is on their way here now." She raised a hand when Drake tried to interrupt her. "But that's just me. Cade, however, doesn't want you dead for a reason that I am yet to figure out and I wouldn't be here to help you if it weren't for him. So, sit! Down!"

The look on Lia's face was one that Cade had seen many times. She wasn't necessarily quick to anger but when it came, it was never anything short of petrifying.

The Head Councilmen emanated pure rage, probably from the way he had just been spoken to, and a hint of fear at the potential repercussions of his arrogance. Still fuming, he sat.

Lia's patronizing smile did nothing to settle Drake's anger. "Thank you. Now, what have you been doing on the western border?"

"Nothing that concerns you," he retorted.

Lia and Cade simultaneously rolled their eyes.

Did his self-preservation not outweigh his pride?

"Is that so?" Lia cocked her head to the side. "Well, I think you would change your mind if I told you your son is about to be arrested and you won't be able to do anything about it without my knowledge."

Cade whipped his head to Lia. She hadn't told him that part. He knew she wasn't referring to him though. She'd never voluntarily refer to him as Drake's son.

His father cursed under his breath, closing his eyes, but he abruptly opened them once again as the door creaked.

In the doorway stood Cassian.

His brother was only eleven years old when he left, but now as he stood in the doorway at nineteen, Cade couldn't get past how different he looked. In appearance and demeanor.

Cade could practically feel the arrogance coming off of his brother as he stared at him down.

While they were both quite tall, Cassian was more lean, like their father, whereas Cade was built and toned from his years of hard labor. Honestly, the most similar thing about them was the thick dark blonde hair, though Cassian's was significantly shorter, that they both inherited from their mother, and while Cade had his mother's forestry green eyes, his brother had Drake's watery blue ones. Not that Cassian would remember much about their mother, he was so young back then.

Though irked by his brother's next words, Cade was grateful when Cassian spoke up, stopping his thoughts from going down that dark road.

"What's going on? Why are *they* here?" Cassian looked at the duo with contempt.

The room was silent, all of them seemed reluctant to tell him what he had just missed.

It was his father that broke the silence. "Eulalia has had a vision... She thinks that you will be arrested tonight."

Lia scoffed at the implication that she might be wrong.

Cade was slightly startled by the fear, denial, and desperation wafting off of his brother.

He had definitely done something. Something bad.

"And you believe her? Father, since when did you ever trust the words from the mouth of a seer?" Cassian exclaimed defensively.

At this point, Cade stood too and took a step toward Cassian, growing angry at the remark towards his friend. He didn't hold the same disdain for Cassian as he did for his father, but his brother's incessant need to gain their father's favor had caused a rift between them, even before he'd left the 'family home'.

Drake took a deep breath. "It's too close to be a coincidence," he whispered, looking up at his youngest son with worry.

Curiosity getting the better of him, Cade looked intently at his brother and spoke slowly. "What can't be a coincidence?"

Cassian kept his lips tight.

"Tell them," Drake said, his face downcast.

Cassian's eyes flicked back and forth between his father, brother, and Lia.

Impatient as ever, she snapped her fingers in front of his face, startling him. "Cassian! I don't know how much time you have, only that it'll happen soon and we can't change what we don't know. Start talking, if you want to sleep in your own bed tonight."

Cassian conceded.

Clearing his throat, he stared down at his feet. "Two nights ago... We-uh, we were waiting in the trees. On a trading route. A-and the truck we'd been trailing... we managed to stop it with the blockade and we were going to just grab the weapons and get out, I swear." he sputtered, looking at his father pleadingly.

Hearing the desperate tone in his brother's voice had sympathy slipping into Cade's body as Cassian continued.

"W-we were just going to sneak on while they were distracted, grab the guns and go, b-but when we were leaving they saw us and they just- we didn't have time to-"

"Alden!" The door flew open as Young came stumbling into the room.

"What is it?" Drake responded in a defeated tone.

"Twelve enforcers at the gates. By order of the queen." Young panted as if he'd been running.

As Cade saw the blood drain from Cassian's face, he looked to Lia and prayed to the Gods that his brother hadn't just gotten himself killed.

Chapter Three

Lia's heart began to pound as her eyes darted around the room, taking in the scene unraveling before her.

Most of her visions were difficult to interpret or she could never work out the importance of them, but this? It was as if time was repeating itself, like she was stuck in an endless loop with the most unsettling sense of déjà vu falling over her.

I shouldn't be here.

She wasn't present in her vision, but she let Cade drag her out here. It was all wrong.

The lights, the guns, the shouting, and the stomping of heavy boots amplified on the wooden floors.

She slid down the wall, curling into a ball, willing herself to calm down, to breathe.

It was too overwhelming.

Blood still rushing through her ears, she looked up to see at least ten enforcers standing in the room, guns pointed in every direction.

At last, the noise died down.

One man stepped forward, decked out in protective gear.

Upon looking at the letters sewn into his jacket, she recognized the man instantly.

'HEWN'

Despite his agedness and graying hairs on the sides of his face, he had a commanding air about him and she knew that he must've been the leader, especially when he spoke. Low yet clear, he said, "Head Councilman Alden, step forward."

For a few seconds nothing happened, but then, slowly, Drake stepped forward, hands in the air.

"Are you Drake Alden?" the enforcer asked.

"That's right," the Head Councilman replied, inclining his head.

The enforcer lowered his gun a fraction and spoke aloud for all to hear. "Two nights ago, a Dome trading vehicle was ambushed resulting in the murder of four officials. We have reason to believe that the culprits belong to this community after reviewing body cam footage clearly showing your family crest on a navy blue jacket." He tapped on some sort of bracelet on his wrist which promptly projected a blurry image of the Alden crest.

Three trees, a wolf's head engraved on the middle one.

Blocking out her wonder at the sight of an image coming out of the man's wrist, Lia whipped her head towards Cassian in shock.

Murder.

She knew that Cade's father and brother had never been up to any good but she would have never guessed that they were killing people now. She even had trouble believing it until she saw the look of sheer terror on Cassian's face.

Lia didn't like the guy by any standard but her heart squeezed a little at the thought of what was going to happen to him. He was so young. But there was no coming back from this.

Then her eyes found Cade's. He was staring at her too with a look that she couldn't quite decipher.

Not fear, not anger. Maybe... regret?

But why? He didn't do anything.

Before she had a chance to figure it out, the same enforcer spoke again. "Two of the three males caught on tape have been apprehended and will be tried for aggravated robbery. The other, for the murder of the four officials that were in the vehicle. If you are responsible or know who is, speak now. Your cooperation would be appreciated." His words were robotic as if they had been rehearsed and repeated many times.

"Tried? You mean slaughtered!" Drake snarled, evidently becoming fearful for his son who stood in the corner shaking.

"We have been authorized to use lethal force should you not cooperate. If you are responsible or know who is, speak now," Hewn reiterated.

Cassian still hadn't stepped forward and Lia's apprehension grew. Her vision hadn't gone like this. They should have arrested him already.

Drake took a step closer to the enforcer, outraged. "You come to my home thinking you can just take my-"

All of a sudden, Drake was on the floor with a thick boot pressing into his back, a gun pointed at his head, and an angry red mark on the side of his face from where he had been struck.

"Dad!"

As Cassian cried out Lia felt numbness seeping into her. She'd never liked Cade's brother, for obvious reasons, but seeing him cry out for his father, she tried and failed to muster up any sympathy in the moment. Not anymore. He may be young but his actions had consequences. He needed to face them.

"For the last time! We have been authorized to use lethal force should you not cooperate! Now, if you are responsible, or know who is, speak!"

"It was me," she heard quietly from the other side of the room.

Lia breathed out a sigh of relief, glad for this to be over, and instantly felt guilty for it. She shouldn't take relief in the fact that Cade would lose his only brother, even if she wasn't fond of him. Suddenly a sense of unease started to crawl over her spine as she looked at the corner of the room, expecting to see Cassian being advanced on. No one made a move towards him but the sight before sent her heart to her feet.

It wasn't Cassian who had spoken.

It was Cade.

"Cade?"

Cade turned his head to find Lia staring at him, eyebrows furrowed in bewilderment.

He repeated himself, louder this time. "My name is Cade Alden. It was me." His eyes found his brother who simply stared at him in shock.

"*Cade Alden, you are under arrest for the murder of four trading officials...*" The enforcer continued while another was already hauling Cade to the center of the room.

"Cade!" Lia shouted trying to get his attention, but his eyes stayed on Cassian.

He was frozen.

"*You will be transported to The Dome where you will...*"

Cade wasn't listening anymore. He already knew his fate.

For those unlucky enough to reside on the outside, all crimes against The Dome were punishable by death under the Prima Act.

Tuning them out, he finally turned his eyes back to his best friend as his arms were twisted behind his back painfully, cuffs roughly slapped onto his wrists.

"He didn't do it! He's lying!" she screeched, her panic growing, eyes widening.

When none of the enforcers acted as if they'd even heard her, she whirled on his brother. "Cassian, tell them!" she demanded. But Cassian just opened his mouth only to close it again.

Cade didn't blame his brother. He didn't expect him to scream from the rooftops that he was a murderer.

"Lia." He tried to get her attention while her eyes darted frantically around the room, looking for someone to do something. "Lia!"

Even his father's face was impassive. Not in the slightest bit ruffled at the prospect of his own son being put to death. Cade absently noted how all of the fight that his father held for Cassian had quickly dissipated when it was his life hanging in the balance. He barely even met Cade's eyes.

"Lia!" he called out, finally catching her gaze.

Feeling a tug at his arms, he allowed the two enforcers holding him to walk him backward while he spoke to Lia in low tones as she followed them out the door. "I'm sorry. I had to."

"Cade, don't!" She was shaking her head vehemently. "He's old enough to know better, he killed people!" she whisper-shouted.

"He didn't mean to, you know he didn't. You saw him, he was practically pissing himself in there."

Lia was shaking as she started mumbling to herself. "I shouldn't have told you. I should never have told you, this is all my fault-"

"Stop that!" he hissed, drawing her from her spiraling. Lowering his voice he tried again. "Please, talk to him." If this wasn't enough of a wake-up call, Cade only hoped that Lia could be the one to steer him away from his father. He obviously couldn't. "Do whatever you have to do, but get these stupid ideas out of his head. Don't let this be for nothing."

"Don't say that." Tears spilling over, she begged, "Cade, please…"

The head enforcer opened the door of the vehicle waiting outside with the driver already in the front seat. The enforcer behind him pushed Cade's head down so that he could climb in.

Lia ran up to the window of the armored truck the second the door shut.

Cade leaned forward through the small space as far as he could to press a gentle kiss to her forehead while her shoulders shook.

"Please, don't let my father get him killed," he told her firmly.

He wished he could've heard her say something, anything at all, but as he leaned back into the vehicle, the engine revved and with a jolt backward, they began to move.

Cade watched his childhood home in the rear window as it grew smaller and smaller. His brother, father, and other councilmen were now standing outside, watching him. It was the picture of a grim farewell.

Just before they broke through the tree line, he looked through squinted eyes to see Lia march back towards the lodge, wind up a fist, and send it flying into Cassian's jaw. She looked like she might leave it there before turning back to him and throwing a knee into his gut. Drake quickly moved to stand between Lia and Cassian, snarling in her face. Unfazed, Lia hissed something back before spinning on her heel and leaving the compound.

Cade thought that he must have lost it because, despite the circumstances, he let out a low laugh.

He was in deep shit.

Chapter Four

As the trees flew by, Cade stared out of the window in absolute awe of the place he'd called home all his life. He'd never been in such a vehicle before, it was as if the whole of the western sector was moving in slow motion before his eyes.

Though he kept to himself most of the time, when he did visit the town, the hustle and bustle of the place had always been discomforting to him, but seeing how the trees stood still, undisturbed even by the night's wind, brought him a great deal of peace.

That was what struck him as odd. The peace. The calm. The numbness. Surely a death sentence should evoke something fearful or desperate in person.

But nothing.

He didn't regret it either. The only thing that brought him close to feeling was the memory of Lia's anguished face as her figure retreated into the horizon.

Will she be okay?

Will she be angry?

Will she look after Cassian?
Subconsciously, Cade's hand came up to fiddle with the ring hanging from the chain around his neck. Thinking about his brother and why he had stepped forward for him, Cade was reminded of the words he'd sworn ten years ago.

"Mom, I'm sorry," *Cade repeated over and over again, tears streaming down his face.*
His mother looked up at him warmly, her face thin and pale, nothing like it used to be. "It's okay, my boy. It's okay."
Cade shook his head. "No, it's not. I'm sorry. I'm so sorry, I-I tried." *His voice broke off on the last word.*
All he could do was let the tears roll down his face while he clutched his baby brother to his chest. His baby brother who would never even get to open his eyes.
With his free hand, he aggressively swiped away his tears, conscious of the fact that his father was only in the next room. Crying wasn't acceptable and Cade wasn't looking to learn that lesson again.
His mother shifted on the bed in front of him and grasped his hand shakily. "Listen to me, it was not meant to be. There was nothing you could've done except be with me, and you were. I've never been more proud of you. But you promise me right now, promise me that you will look after your brother," *she implored him.* "You know how your father can be and Cassian will need you."
Understanding washed over Cade. His baby brother wasn't the only person he would lose tonight. "Mom... No-"
"Cade," *she cut him off firmly.* "Promise me," *she said, each breath taking more effort than the last.*

Eliza Alden was nothing if not selfless. Even on her deathbed, her husband in the next room pretending as if he didn't hear her cries, she wasn't thinking of herself. Even when he refused to have a midwife come to her aid out of shame that she would birth him a dead son, she was more concerned for the fate of her living children.

If she could do that, then Cade could give her this one last thing.

He took a shaky breath. "I promise," Cade said in a surprisingly steady voice.

At her nod of appreciation, he held her hand, listening to her shallow breaths, and waited until the room went silent.

As Cade felt his world begin to crumble around him, he didn't leave her side. Not even hours later when the men came to 'deal with them', as his father told him.

Cade was sitting out in the dirt, numbly watching her burial when someone settled onto the ground beside him. He didn't need to turn, he already knew who it was.

The silence dragged out before she finally spoke.

"Thank you," Lia said softly.

Cade kept looking ahead as the men began to fill the hole. "For what?"

Lia sniffled. "For sharing her with me. For letting her be my mother, too"

He wanted to respond but a lump formed in his throat.

"Here,"

He finally turned to Lia to see her hand outstretched, a small ring in her palm.

"Why?" he asked, not understanding.

"It was hers," Lia whispered. "She gave it to me years ago." She sighed before righting her tone. "Most nights she'd sneak food into the school so I could eat, but I think Drake caught on to what she was doing and the meals stopped coming. The next day though, she handed it to me after class and told me to sell it and use the money." Her thumb rubbed the band. "I didn't have the heart to." Cade took the ring out of her palm, feeling it between his fingers. "It's a beautiful ring. I have no idea where she got it but I think you should have it."

Cade inspected the ring closer. The thin silver band was encrusted with clean-cut diamonds. Nothing like the jewelry one would find in his sector. His mother had probably found it. Maybe she'd stolen it.

As Cade turned it over in his palm, something on the inside caught his attention.

An engraving.

~My Liz~

Liz? As in Eliza?

His father would never have gotten her such an expensive gift.

As quickly as the possible explanations came to mind, Cade pushed them away. No matter how she'd gotten it or who'd given it to her, she was gone now. Nothing could mar what he thought of her and all he could do was hold on to who she was to him.

A mother.

A friend.

A teacher.

A protector.

Chapter Five

Yesterday...

Deianira could practically feel her blood boiling as she watched the bright bursts of light and listened to the spray of bullets.
"Stop," Deianira commanded.
Officer Hewn obeyed, stopping the video that was projected all around the room.
"How many officials were killed?" she asked evenly. Now was not the time to lose her cool. The time would come.
"Four, Your Majesty."
She considered it for a moment. "Hewn, take your unit out tonight. I want them here by morning. Alive."
"Yes, Your Majesty."
And with that, Hewn and his two enforcers vacated the room.
After some time, Deianira fixed her gaze on the last person in the room, her sentinel, with an 'I told you so' on the tip of the tongue. Salem spoke before she had the chance. "I know."

"I told you that this would escalate," Deianira gritted out, her knee bouncing.

"You were correct," she said plainly. "But I still stand by my actions because it was highly improbable that the incidents were connected. I couldn't let you act based on a feeling when your reputation is at stake as it is. The trust of your people too."

Deianira stood slowly, her voice ice cold. "Let me?" she questioned, head tilting. "Let me?! I am your Queen!" she spat.

Salem stood too, but more gracefully. "And I am your second. That means I tell you when you're not acting in the best interest of The Dome. And you weren't. The incidents were spread across all four sectors and you were out for blood. These were a few children stealing off the back of trucks. Despite what the people might think, you are a leader, not a dictator and if I have to remind you of that every day, I will. It is my duty to do so," she said with no inflection of tone.

Salem was right and Deianira knew it. The robberies were random and arresting every poor soul that stole because they were cold or hungry would only be to make an example of them. Murder, however, was different.

It had been a while since there were any executions and though Deianira knew it was twisted, she silently relished the thought of ending these men who tested the extent of her mercy.

She swept her hair over her shoulder, toying with the ends. "They stopped being children when they killed four of my men."

"And they will be punished well for it, but as I said, I do not regret asking you to withhold your hand," her sentinel said, face straight.

Deianira stared into her fierce eyes for a second. She'd always been the most pragmatic of the two of them. Even when they were kids,

Salem was all logic and little emotion. It was one of the reasons she'd chosen her as her highest member of council and protector. Salem was the closest thing she had to a friend but sometimes, her intelligence and approach aggravated Deianira. She didn't like being wrong.

It wasn't all bad though. Salem's orderly nature had its advantages. She was the first person Deianira would go to when handling an uncomfortable matter. Her sentinel always tackled the issue head-on, unburdened by emotion or the need to appease others. Deianira wished she could be more like her sometimes. Blunt and unfeeling. But she wasn't. In fact, she felt too much and often needed an outlet for the excess.

Deianira flicked her hand in the direction of the door, opening it as she walked through, not bothering to look back. "Notify me when they arrive. Not a moment sooner. I wish to be left alone."

On her way to her training room, Deianira allowed all of her emotions to come back up and consume her. The missing cargo, the random robberies, and now, an ambush.

Four trading officials.

She was furious. This was not a coincidence. Only a hundred years into her reign and she could already smell mutiny.

Well, they would learn, and those who did not learn would pay for it.

Turning left into the training room, she spotted Jude straight away and felt instant relief. No matter what the day was, no matter what had occurred, she always had Jude.

Being her mother's twin brother, 'uncle' would've been the more appropriate term, but it didn't feel like them. As a very powerful psionic and her only living relative, he had counseled her throughout her reign from the age of thirteen. They were so in tune that she didn't even need to talk for him to know what was on her mind, and by the way he looked up and met her eyes, she could tell that he already knew what she needed as she marched through the doorway. Ever alert, Jude quickly stood and sidestepped as Deianira's fist just missed his jaw. He grabbed her offending arm and twisted it behind her back, attempting to get her into a hold. He was too slow though. She brought her knee high up and swung her foot back into his shin causing him to lean forward giving her just the right position to pull him over her back. As she brought her arm down again, ready to deliver a right hook, Jude rolled from beneath her at the last second and hopped back up to his feet.

"I'm assuming you heard?" Deianira said, righting her stance. Jude tried to catch her off guard with a jab, which she swiftly ducked. "I did. So, what are you going to do about it?"

"I've already sent Hewn's unit. They'll be here by morning," she replied absently as she deflected a blow sent to her side.

Something she couldn't recognize passed across Jude's features at her words before he sobered his expression. She used the opportunity to throw a flat palm chest, winding him while simultaneously swiping his right leg from beneath, sending him falling to the ground.

Before he had the chance to get up, she dropped down, pressing a knee into his chest with a satisfied smile on her face. "And even without shadows this time," she said, feeling proud of herself.
Jude let out a breathy laugh. "Whatever." His humor faltered momentarily. "But you didn't answer my question. What are you going to do with them?"
Rolling her eyes she got up off of him and walked to the other side of the room, re-tying her long black hair in its ponytail. "I said I'm bringing them here."
"You know that's not what I mean."
She turned to face him. "What the law states. I'll kill them," she said, her face devoid of emotion.
"Good girl."
While Salem always tried to keep her above ground, to keep her from falling too far, Jude was the only person that encouraged her to embrace the darkness inside of her. He taught her that it was nothing to be ashamed of and that being ruthless only made her a better leader.
It was the balance she needed.

Chapter Six

The truck rocked, jolting Cade awake.

As his eyes adjusted to the light, he wondered how long he'd been asleep. They must've been traveling all night.

He looked through the windshield and all that calmness that had settled over him quickly fled.

The Dome.

He'd only seen it from afar before.

Once, Cade had accompanied Lia to hunt when they traveled further than usual. They didn't pass The Dome's outer border but he was close enough to be amazed by the sheer size of it. That was nothing compared to driving towards it at full speed.

He wondered if the driver would slow down at some point.

He didn't.

Cade's heart began to speed up and he closed his eyes as they drew closer and closer, still not slowing. Any second now he would feel the impact.

Nothing happened.

Huh?

Cautiously, Cade opened his eyes and peered out of the window. He was inside.

Inside The Dome.

What?

Turning his head to look through the rear window, his attention caught a gap in The Dome, maybe ten feet tall, receding on itself. In the center stood a small man, arms raised. And as if it had never been there, the gap closed in on itself.

Cade turned back around, discreetly flicking his eyes from one enforcer to the next, trying to see if anyone else had just witnessed what he had, but they all appeared unfazed.

He shook his head and sat back in his seat.

After a few minutes, the truck rolled to a stop but Cade didn't have much time to take in his surroundings before doors were slamming and he was swiftly hauled out of the truck. Quickly scanning the room, he spotted many other parked vehicles and noticed that the door behind them didn't swing closed. It lowered with a mechanical whir.

Shifting his eyes, his gaze quickly stopped on the guns. Each enforcer with a free hand had a gun trained on him.

Did they really think he was a danger to them?

As far as they knew, he wasn't gifted. It was very rare for a gifted person to be born outside of The Dome. Even so, being an empath wouldn't do much for Cade in a room full of guns pointed in his direction.

A nudge from behind forced him to find his footing and walk towards what appeared to be an archway. He shuffled through with at least six enforcers. In front of him, at his sides, behind him. Their boots drummed in a synchronized beat on the concrete, barring

Cade's careful footsteps. He jumped slightly as the light above him flickered on. As they continued to walk, the lights above them continued to turn on in succession.

He didn't know what he was expecting inside The Dome but it wasn't this. Long bright hallways, doors with small windows, and lights that turned on as soon as you walked under them. It was all so strange.

It didn't take long for him to see other people. They were milling around, carrying trays and baskets, but they quickly froze as Cade was marched through. He was staring back at them, just as curious, when he noticed that they were all wearing the same sort of clothing.

Was everyone in The Dome made to wear a uniform?

With each step he took, more heads popped up, glaring in his direction. It wasn't anything new to him but still, he didn't like the attention. He never had. He was thankful for the reprieve he got when they turned down an empty hallway with a single door at the end.

Approaching the door, the head enforcer in front of him, with the name 'HEWN' sewn into his jacket, flicked his hand lazily, and just like that, the door disappeared.

Cade guessed that he was a warlock. He knew of the gifts that were present in The Dome, but seeing it in action was an entirely different thing. The only other gifted person he knew was Lia. Thinking about her caused a small ache in his chest at the fact that he would never see her again. But he knew she would be okay, Lia didn't break easily.

She was much braver than him and the day they met was a testament to that fact.

At the age of six, with her wiry legs and wild hair, she'd found him hiding in his mother's classroom during recess and claimed him on the spot. He didn't have any arguments, but that was probably due to the fact that he didn't speak a word until he turned nine. Cade was anxious as a child and though he could understand people perfectly, speaking wasn't something that he liked to do. He still held the same sentiment, but it wasn't due to anxiety anymore. It was more out of habit. It was one of the many reasons father despised him, disowned him. Though that didn't stop Lia from dragging him around everywhere with her and filling the silence.

Cade was wary approaching the arch where the door had been, but one by one, the enforcers walked through without issue, so he did too.

If he hadn't been paying attention he would have missed the sudden drop as they began descending stairs in the narrow hallway. The further they stepped down, the dimmer the lights seemed to get until they were on flat ground again.

Peering from side to side, Cade noticed the plain rooms. The outer wall on each one was made completely of glass, with only a small bed and toilet in them. They didn't even have doors.

That's when it dawned on him.

These weren't rooms. These were cells.

Each was empty until they neared the end of the aisle.

His eyes widened as he looked to the right to find Theo sleeping on a low cot in one of the cells.

Theo from the western sector.

Theo whom he had only seen two days ago.

And in the cell next to him was Bron.

Of course.

They were with Cassian during the raid. Of course, it was them. Seeing them brought an uninvited wave of anger over Cade. They had been with Cassian and did nothing when he started shooting officials. Cade was under no impression that his brother was innocent, but to think that Cassian's so-called 'friends' stood idly by while he made such a terrible decision irked him.

The walking stopped at the next cell down. Officer Hewn waved his hand again and the glass wall of the last cell disappeared.

"In." The enforcer behind him gave him a push.

Cade cooperated knowing that any resistance would be met with violence and would make no difference to the outcome. He knew he was going to die, but he'd much rather go out peacefully.

After entering his cell, the glass reappeared and the enforcers began to leave.

He was slightly surprised that they left so promptly but he wasn't sure what he was expecting.

For them to read him his rights?

To execute him on the spot?

Apprehension filled him as he slowly took a seat on the small bed, but right now, he was more concerned with the two people in the cells next to him.

He didn't know what came over him but before he could stop, he found himself calling out. "Theo."

Silence.

"Theo," he said, a little louder.

He heard a muffled groan.

"Theo, it's me, Cade."

"Cade?"

He rolled his eyes. "Yeah."

It sounded like he was walking to the front of his cell. "What the fuck are *you* doing here?"

He heard some more movement, closer this time. "Cade? Is that you?"

Bron.

Cade ignored their questions. "How long have you guys been here?"

It was Bron who responded shakily. "I don't know, maybe a couple of hours."

"Wait, since when did you talk?" Theo snorted.

Cade sighed, but he should've known not to expect anything productive from Theo at a time like this.

Of all the people he could've been locked up with.

Cade shook his head.

"What do you think they're going to do with us?" Bron sounded petrified.

Wait.

He *sounded* petrified.

Cade took a deep breath to focus his senses, but no matter how hard he tried, he couldn't get a reading.

Wherever they were, he wasn't able to use his gifts.

He shook the thought off. It wasn't as if he would be able to do much with them anyway.

Quietly, he replied to Bron, "They're gonna kill us."

Bron almost choked on his breath. "What do you mean they're gonna kill us? Don't we get a trial or some shit?"

Cade stared at the blank wall in disbelief. "You didn't think to learn the laws before committing a crime against *The Dome*?" He thought about ignoring his stupid question but found himself responding anyway. "That only applies if you're born here. You don't get a trial. Besides, you idiots got caught on camera."

Theo spoke up again. "Which brings us right back to my question. Why the fuck are you here? Where's Cassian? He's the bitch that got trigger-happy and landed us here."

Done with talking, Cade sat back in his cot and inclined his head to the ceiling, ignoring Theo's snarky words and Bron's anxious questions.

He was ready.

Chapter Seven

The people had already gathered by the time Deianira made her entrance. Those who feared her, revered her, and those who were required in the city center.

Ignoring the murmurs, she sauntered down the stone walkway, head held high, to the platform in the middle of the square where her throne sat. Her sentinel stood behind it, her face impassive.

Lifting her hand, Deianira summoned a shadow beneath her feet and propelled herself onto the platform to take her seat. She heard the loud whispers of shock and awe. Her people had seen her do things like that before but it didn't take away from the spectacle.

She knew her kind was rare. Azraels, beside herself, hadn't been seen for hundreds of years. It was believed that their power was too great, too dangerous for one to wield. The power to give and take life.

It was only her sharp mind and discretion that allowed her to make it past the age of ten, when she presented, without bringing attention to her gift. Even as a child, she knew what would've become of her if anyone had found out. It meant death, a swift and humane one but a death all the same. That didn't matter anymore. She was Queen now. No one could do anything about it.

Taking her throne and crossing one leg over the other, she receded her shadow and looked out into the crowds.

Silence had fallen and everyone waited for her cue.

"Bring them," she said, not needing to raise her voice to be heard.

Murmurs grew again as the crowd began to ripple. Deianira spotted Hewn and his unit walking through those gathered, unabashed by the looks, with the three men in tow. They were chained at the arms with bags over their heads.

After being marched to the front of the platform and brought to their knees, she waited for silence again.

At her look of impatience, the sound ceased and she turned to Hewn. "Take off the hoods."

One by one Hewn removed the hoods from the three young men. The first man was quite small. Small and angry by the looks of it. The way he glared at her held pure detestation. Deianira had seen men like him before. Wrong and strong. Uncompromising, but not in a good way. She instantly decided that he would be the first to die. The next man was slightly bigger, but this one was shaking from head to toe. Though not from regret or remorse, from fear. Like all the ones before him who only regretted being caught but would commit the same crime again in a heartbeat. Coward. Snake. He would be the second to die.

The third was the largest of the three. At least a head and a half taller than the second with taut muscles lining his arms. Not buff from lifting weights but defined. Defined enough for his biceps to stand out under his dark shirt. She knew a hard worker when she saw one.

It seemed as if time slowed down as the third hood was removed. The first thing she noticed was his skin. A warm ivory hue, clashing against the icy air around him.

Next were his lips, a pale shade of pink, full but pressed firmly together. As the hood lifted further, her interest grew until it reached his eyes.

His eyes were closed.

Everything else forgotten, she was swept by a refreshing wave of anger.

He'd stolen from her and killed four of her people. She recognized that he was the one holding the gun that night on the footage from the blonde hair just touching his shoulders. And he dared to close his eyes when brought before her? He would learn.

She stood abruptly, her stance menacing.

"Open your eyes!" Deianira bellowed, her voice laced with icy rage, causing many in the large crowd to startle.

Slowly, as if defiant, the third male opened his eyes and she was hit with the most alluring shade of green. Better yet, shades. Even from a distance, she could make out the emerald from the spring green with a small turquoise ring around the iris.

Despite his defeated expression, his eyes held all the vibrance of a thriving forest in the springtime. Lively and bold. But as her gaze explored the rest of his face, that vibrance warred with pain and anguish. That much was expected considering his circumstances.

A throat cleared to her right causing her to stop her perusal and look to Salem. Her sentinel raised an eyebrow at her.

Everyone had seen her staring at him.

Averting her gaze, Deianira took her seat again, letting her eyes drift over the three men once more.

With a single nod to Hewn, their day of reckoning began.

"Open your eyes!"
Cade thought that he might have had more time. After riding in this morning and only a few hours of being in his cell, the enforcers were back, dragging him through hallways again, but this time, with Theo and Bron in front. He didn't know why they bothered to cover his head though, he'd seen it all yesterday. Maybe it was something to keep the criminals on edge. A scare tactic.
If so, it didn't work. Cade had already accepted his fate.
But as he opened his eyes and met the gaze of the queen, his judge, something shifted. It was strange. As if something inside of him fixed itself, something he didn't know was broken.
From the sharp leather bodice of her corset down to her tight leather pants, she was encased in deep crimson. A red deeper than blood. The only thing that contrasted it was the silver cuff snaking up her right arm.
Her hair was so dark, the color black didn't sum it up. It seemed more like it was absent of color altogether, beautifully complementing her smooth pale skin. And her eyes. Staring into those dark orbs, he almost thought he could see his reflection. Like looking into a dark lake only lit by the moon.
At the last second, she broke eye contact, looking over to the head enforcer and giving him an almost imperceptible nod.

One of the men from Hewn's unit started towards them and Cade couldn't help the way his heart began thumping as he took his place in front of Theo. He didn't want to go last, to watch Theo and Bron die only to share their fate. It wasn't as if he liked either of them but he couldn't think of anything more disheartening at that moment. The executioner just stared at Theo and it didn't take Cade long to realize what he was doing. He was reading him.

Shit.

Just his luck.

The enforcer was an empath. He was the true judge. Not the queen. The man turned to look back at the queen and inclined his head, silently telling her something that Cade couldn't understand until she stood. With all the gracefulness and agility of a cat, she stepped off the platform and drifted over to Theo.

Cade blinked. He'd gotten it all wrong.

The enforcer was not the executioner. She was.

A shiver ran through him, and it wasn't because of the cold. He was well aware that the queen was not merciful, but he'd always thought of the monarchs of The Dome as figureheads.

He couldn't have been more incorrect. The dark look in her eyes told him everything he needed to know. Queen Deianira, evidently, didn't mind doing her own dirty work.

Theo, on his knees, stared straight at her the whole time she advanced on him with hatred and disgust in his eyes. Only seconds later, that hate and disgust were washed away and replaced with fear. His eyes widened as he realized that she wasn't slowing down. Cade stopped breathing as he watched the beguiling woman, whom he had just been perusing, smile as she placed one hand behind Theo's head, and the other just under his jaw.

Twist.

She didn't even hesitate. The distinct snap could be heard miles away as Theo's limp figure slumped to the ground, his head facing up while his body lay forward.

Without realizing it, Cade had honed in on Theo.

Excruciating pain. That was all that he could feel.

Oh, Gods.

He was still alive.

Not for long though. Cade's mind pulsed as he felt the life leave him seconds later.

Manically looking around, he watched some of the civilians' reactions in the crowd. Some looked at the spectacle in horror, some excited, but he couldn't hear anything over the ringing in his ears.

Theo was dead.

By the time Cade had tried to wrap his mind around it, the enforcer had already taken his place in front of Bron. He was shaking almost violently now, a glossy sheen of tears in his eyes.

"Please…" Bron whispered harshly. *"Please!"*

Cade whipped his head in the direction of the queen, searching deeply for any sign of sympathy or pity. He found none.

It was as if Bron hadn't even spoken because once again, the enforcer looked back at her and nodded.

As much as Cade wanted to close his eyes, to look away, he couldn't bring himself to as he watched shadows emerge out of thin air and encase Bron's limbs, holding him in place. And again, without hesitation, the queen stepped closer, putting a steadying hand on his shoulder. Pulling her arm back, she thrust it forward, sticking her hand into his chest. It was a fluid, effortless movement executed as if it had been done many times before.

Cade wanted to be sick as he watched her wrench her hand back. In the cold winter air, he could see the steam rising from Bron's beating heart as she let it roll from her fingers and onto the concrete, landing at the same time as his lifeless body.

Cade's heart was beating in his head. He absently saw mist coming from his mouth and realized that he was hyperventilating. But that didn't deter his executioner from moving to stand in front of him now.

Everything was happening so quickly.

Just yesterday he'd been at home, in his sector, with Lia. Now, he was about to meet his end, and in a horrifying way at that, if Theo and Bron were anything to go off of.

Cade had been expecting a clean death. A bullet in his head or even a hanging, but this was barbaric.

Despite his fear and rising sense of dread, he lifted his head and met her eyes once again, kneeling still, simply waiting for the enforcer to sentence him. She looked right back at him too. The smile that had been dancing on her lips only seconds ago was gone. Her gaze wasn't as cold anymore. It was deep and assessing.

Her head tilt was almost unnoticeable but Cade saw it. He saw it and held her gaze unrelentingly, examining her just as she was examining him. Cade had never liked the attention being on him. It should have made him uncomfortable, but it didn't. Her eyes weren't judgmental, they were curious.

Seconds passed that felt like hours before the enforcer looked back at the queen and Cade knew it was his time.

But the enforcer didn't nod at her.

He leaned over and whispered something into her ear.

She cocked her head to the side, staring at Cade for a moment longer before jerking her head to where Officer Hewn was standing without taking her eyes off him. The enforcer walked over and said something to Hewn in a low voice.

Cade didn't know whether to be relieved or disappointed. He didn't want his death to be anything like Theo's or Bron's, but he certainly didn't want to draw it out either.

After the short interaction with Hewn, the queen waited as the enforcer came back with a handkerchief. Holding Cade's gaze, she wiped her hands, her face betraying no emotion, before turning and making her exit back into the building, quickly followed by the sentinel.

Cade was so focused on her, he didn't notice the guards behind him before they dragged him up off the ground and began marching him back the way he came. His eyes darted everywhere. At the civilians shouting, making their displeasure known. At the lifeless bodies on the floor, mere meters away.

His heart fell again.

No one deserved a death like that.

As he was hauled back inside, Cade had so many questions but kept quiet. It wouldn't be smart to push his luck. He didn't know whether his life had been saved or extended so he didn't say a word for fear that they might take him back outside as they guided him to where he assumed he would be thrown back in his cell.

That was until they took a wrong turn. Alarm bells instantly started going off in his head.

Were they going to kill him in private?

As they walked down the unfamiliar hallway and stopped at a door, Cade noted that Hewn didn't use his gift to open this door but instead, he used the thin bracelet on his wrist. The same one that had projected his family crest the night before.

The door slid open and Cade wondered whether his fate had just improved or worsened.

The long rectangular room with dull gray walls had bunk beds lining both sides, most of them occupied.

As the *woosh* of the door sounded, all the chatter and shuffling stopped for a second. Then, making Cade flinch, all the men in the room quickly hopped out of their beds, away from the corners, dropping everything that they were doing, and stood in front of each bed in pairs, facing each other along the aisle.

With that, Hewn resumed walking with Cade while the other enforcers stayed back, guns up. He followed Hewn until they reached an unoccupied bed where he removed Cade's chains and simply turned around without a word. As he left, the other enforcers retreated from the room, still on guard, walking backward.

As soon as the door shut, the men broke formation and everyone in the room looked at Cade in unison.

Some looked at him warily, while some looked downright predatory. He didn't know whether to ignore them or introduce himself but he'd never been much of a speaker, so he went with the former.

Assuming he was going to be here for a while, he turned around and scanned the unoccupied bed behind him before inspecting the folded uniform at the foot of the bed.

Just before he removed the sheets, he heard a voice call from behind him. "Hey." He might not have been addressing him in particular, so Cade didn't bother to turn around. "You're one of the outsiders." Cade half-turned and flicked his eyes over to him but didn't respond. Apparently, word traveled fast in here.

"You were on the big screen in the cafeteria. In the city center." Cade had no idea what he was talking about so resumed his task, removing the blankets from the bed before preparing to take a seat. The one who had spoken stepped up beside him. He was tall and built, with an ugly snarl on his face.

"Hey! I was talking to you, you know."

Murmurs began to rise around the room when Cade still remained silent. He didn't know what the guy wanted from him. It was obvious that he knew who Cade was and he didn't exactly ask him a question. He was just stating the obvious.

That only seemed to aggravate the man more as he took two steps forward causing Cade to stand up straighter, instantly on defense. "Where are your friends? Why are *you* here, outsider?" He spat the last word like it was an insult, his face inches from Cade's.

What was his problem?

Cade didn't bite. Just held his gaze. He was tired of people asking him questions he didn't even know the answers to.

"What, are you deaf or something? Can't talk?"

Cade held his ground and ignored the fact that his questions didn't even make sense. It was nothing he hadn't heard before.

"You know what?" The man leaned down and grasped the bedsheets, stripping them from Cade's bed, then proceeded to pick up his pillow, and then his thin mattress. With a cruel smirk he turned and walked leisurely back to his bunk, Cade's belongings held lazily in his arms.

Cade stared at the back of his head for a moment, his anger rising. He wondered if he should do something but thought better of it and opted to take a seat next to his bunk with only a metal frame left on it.

Cade was no stranger to men like him. He'd lived with one.

A bully.

Escalating was more Lia's thing, not his. Besides, he still didn't know where he was or why he was here so he didn't think it would be smart to let this guy get a rise out of him.

He took the time to observe the room as the others gradually went about their business.

Through the small arch at the back of the room, Cade could see tiled floors and what looked like shower heads attached to the walls. That was a relief. He'd grown up in a home with running water but the small house that he shared with Lia didn't have such a luxury.

He spent the better part of an hour taking note of where the showers were, the toilets, and the times in which they were empty and most busy.

Midway through his observation, a small "Hey," from somewhere near him had his head whipping around.

No one was there. Shaking his head, he went back to his observation.

"Hey, new guy."

Okay, he definitely heard that.

Looking in all directions, he was sure he had gone mad until something soft hit his head.

"Up here."

Cade looked up, and in the bed directly above his was a grinning man, or boy because he couldn't have been more than eighteen, sitting cross-legged with a pillow dangling from his hand and an amused smile on his face.

"I'm Devin." He awkwardly held his hand out.

Cade stood from the ground and stared at him, eyebrows furrowed. He wasn't sure what to make of him.

The kid took his hand back. "You could at least tell me your name." He tried to offer an encouraging smile.

Cade debated in his mind whether it was wise to give his name to him when Devin gasped, hands coming up to his mouth.

"Oh my Gods! You actually can't speak. I am so sorry. I just thought-"

"Cade," he said, cutting him off.

Relief flooded his features. "Oh. Cade. Cool, well I'm Devin and..." He shook his head. "Anyway," His words became hushed as he leaned in to speak to Cade out of anybody else's earshot. "Um, you need to go get your stuff back."

Cade huffed, pushing down the annoyance that had reared its head earlier. "It's not that big of a deal."

Devin's face scrunched sympathetically. "No, it kinda is. It's your first night and that guy over there, Crew, basically just called you a bitch. Trust me, *you do not* want to start your sentence like that."

The hairs rose on the back of his neck. "Sentence?"

Devin frowned. "Uh, yeah. This is a disciplinary program. Did they not tell you how long you'd be here?"

Cade shook his head.

So he wasn't going to be executed?

"Ah, that sucks." He shrugged. "But my point still stands. You're just asking for trouble if you let that slide." Cade could feel Devin's concern for him, but also a hint of trepidation. He wondered if Devin was speaking from experience.

Cade looked over at Crew and saw him standing with his back turned, talking to another inmate.

Devin cleared his throat. "Listen, it's probably not gonna be pretty but trust me when I tell you that it's worse if you don't. It's almost lights out so if you're gonna go, now's your chance."

He pondered on that for a moment.

The kid seemed genuine and he had nothing to gain from him confronting Crew. If anything, he was looking out for Cade so his advice didn't go unheard.

Safe for now or safe later?

Mind made up, Cade gave Devin an appreciative nod and started walking toward Crew's bunk. His footsteps must have caught Crew's attention because he was soon turning around to face Cade. Instantly, his face lit up like a dog given a new toy. "What can I do for you, outsider?" he smirked, eyes flicking to his company for validation.

Cade didn't speak as he bent down and began to gather his things, but he was stopped by a firm push to his shoulder.

"Whoa. I don't think so, new guy. If you wanna sleep with your blankie tonight, you can always share my bed. You're pretty enough." His laugh echoed around the room as others joined him in mocking Cade.

Cade turned and gave Devin an irritated look. Devin rolled his eyes and gestured for him to continue.

He sighed. If he was going to make a statement, now was as good a time as any.

Still watching Devin, he took a deep breath and discreetly made a fist with his right hand.

Quick as lightning, Cade spun around and sent his fist into the Crew's nose. He instantly fell to the hard floor, unmoving.

It took a few seconds for Crew's friends in the surrounding area to catch up with what just happened, but as soon as they had recovered, they were on Cade like bees to honey.

Cade could take a hit. He'd taken many in his time, so as fists started coming, he didn't stop swinging and kicking. There were a lot of them, but he did his best to keep up until the blows seemed to slow down.

Taking a breath, he took a quick look around him and saw that there were three still standing. He may have been on a roll but even Cade had his limits. He was growing tired and didn't have much left in him.

The first one came at him with a punch to the gut causing Cade to double over. Using his low position, he tackled him to the ground before throwing fists at his head repeatedly until he stopped fighting back. Cade didn't have time to stand and turn around before the second guy was dragging him off and sending a hard blow to Cade's eye. He fell to the ground, dizzy, but he could just about make out the figure approaching him and rolled before his attacker could get on top of him, tripping him up in the process. They fought and rolled on the ground, throwing punches until Cade managed to hold him down.

Though Cade had taken a fair amount of beatings, he'd never been one to fight back. He often preferred to contain his anger, to take the hits. In a weird way, it made him feel more in control, but letting the anger take over was exhilarating. The pain and the adrenaline mixed together felt surprisingly... cathartic. It was as if he was finally free of some imaginary restraints, finally able to let go. He wasn't falling, he was flying.

Feeling slightly unhinged, his knuckles bruised, Cade dropped onto his attacker and wrapped his hands around his throat. He squeezed and squeezed and when he felt his muscles about to give out, he pulled up and forced the man's head down into the ground. The man looked somewhat dazed but he was still moving. So Cade did it again, and again. Three more times, Cade bashed his head into the floor and the man went still.

Cade rolled off of him and laid back on the floor exhausted, still riding the high. Even knowing that the last guy was probably going to descend on him at any second, he couldn't find the strength in himself to move.

Lying there, bloodied, bruised, shirt torn and half hanging off his body, Cade watched a blurry figure approach.

At least I tried... he thought.

"Cade. Hey, you good?"

Devin?

Cade let out a sigh of relief at the voice as his vision started to clear. Head lolling to the side, he managed to make out the third guy lying on the floor with a bloody book next to his head. He looked back up at Devin with questioning eyes.

Devin gave him a toothy grin, holding a hand out to help him up. "Yeah, that was me. You're welcome, by the way."

Cade didn't know whether to laugh or enlighten him to the fact that one guy wasn't that much work considering what he'd just had to do, but he was grateful all the same. So taking the hand that Devin offered him and wincing as every muscle in his body burned, he got up.

Crossing the short distance back to Crew's bed, he slowly bent down and retrieved his things. Devin came up beside him and offered him an arm as he limped over back to their bunk.

After Devin helped him remake his bed, Cade carefully settled in and looked around to see many others doing the same thing just before the lights went out.

So this was his future.

Despite what had just happened, Cade thought it was merciful. His mind was struggling to catch up with the recent events but a disciplinary program was very low on the list of his worries, so thankful for the peaceful silence, he rested his head back.

Approximately two seconds after Cade closed his eyes, Devin's voice whispered out into the air. "Hey, Cade?"

Cade sighed and mentally kicked himself for not ignoring him. "What?"

"Not to fangirl or anything, but you were kind of badass back there."

"Thanks," he smirked. He always thought of himself as a pacifist but a strange sense of pride at his actions settled over him. He'd fought back, and quite well.

After a few seconds, Cade closed his eyes again, ready for some much-needed sleep. But of course, Devin spoke up again making Cade wish he'd been given a different bunk. "So, are you like a cage fighter or something?"

"No."

"Ninja?"

"No," he whined.

"What ab-"

"Devin?"

"Yeah?" Devin responded gleefully.

"Go to sleep," Cade said dryly.

"Oh, of course. Yeah, cool… night."

The kid was beyond annoying, but Cade still found himself responding quietly into the darkness. "Night."

Chapter Eight

Deianira had already prepared herself for what would greet her when re-entering the building, so she didn't even flinch when Jude rounded the corner. "What the hell was that?"
I can't read him.
Deianira replayed Finch's words in her head, searching her mind for some sort of explanation.
"I don't know," she responded dismissively, not bothering to stop.
"What do you mean you 'don't know'?" He followed her. He wasn't letting her get away with that.
"I mean, Finch couldn't get a reading," she hissed.
Jude's eyes narrowed. "So he's just going to walk away, no punishment?"
"Of course, not. You know me better than that. I had Hewn take him to the enforcer program."
Jude reared back, disbelief written all over his face. "You know that it does not work that way. That unit is strictly for criminals *inside* The Dome. Not just any stray you pick up and decide to take mercy on because you couldn't get a reading."

Deianira stopped walking and whirled on Jude. "You think I don't know that? You think I wanted to spare him? The arrogant fucker didn't even look at me until I demanded it. I wanted nothing more than to rip his eyes out of his skull."

It was a lie but Jude didn't know that. Deianira wasn't sure what had struck her about the man but killing him was the last thing on her mind.

Jude's rage mellowed at Deianira's convincing tone and he took a calming breath. "Of course, not. I'm just trying to understand why it makes a difference whether you could read him or not when there's proof."

"Because it does," she stressed, glaring at him. "You know as well as anyone that I am no slave to compassion but I refuse to take another life because of a mistake. My people fear me enough as it is and I don't need them questioning my ability to uphold the law too. There was no judgment, so there was no execution. That's it." She left no room for argument.

Deianira appreciated Jude's concern, but Salem's earlier words were true.

She was the Evil Queen, the wicked bitch, the girl who overthrew her own parents for the crown. Her people's concerns about her ability to reign weren't necessarily misplaced, but she didn't need to give them any more reasons to doubt her. The Prima Act was clear, no exceptions.

Jude just watched her for a moment. "I understand. We'll keep an eye on him."

Nodding at him and resuming her journey deeper into the palace, Deianira's thoughts trailed back to the third man in the city center.

There was something about his eyes. Not just their appearance, but the look in them. Kind, but pained. She didn't like the way he made her feel. It was as if she was forgetting something.
She definitely needed to keep an eye on him.

Chapter Nine

As Cassian signaled to the bartender for another drink, his mind drifted back to his father's words, spoken only a few hours ago at the last council meeting.

"My guy says that their Prima Ball is coming up in a month." Drake pointed his finger to the side of The Dome on the plans laid out on the table. "Barely anyone will be in the streets and there'll be a witch waiting for us right here to make an opening."
At that, Young cringed. "But are you sure we can trust a witch? Those demons don't owe us any loyalty. What if it's a trap?"
"At the moment, it's all we've got, and my guy hasn't failed us yet. For months, he's given us the trading routes and the times the officials would be there. He hates that bitch just as much as we do. Trust me, he wouldn't go this far just to trap us."
Something didn't feel right. Cassian couldn't put his finger on it but escalating these plans only days after his brother's death felt wrong. Of course, he was angry. He wanted to burn The Dome to the ground for taking his older brother but did he have much standing? After all, he had

watched those enforcers take Cade right in front of him while he stayed silent. He'd let his brother die for his own mistake. He'd been scared of the consequences of his own actions. But in the end, thanks to Cade, he didn't have to worry about that.

"Cassian!" Drake's shrill exclamation drew him out of his thoughts.

"Yes, dad," he responded, shaking his head.

"Are you even listening? You'll do well to remember that those were your friends that they dragged out from their homes like dogs. Do you want to avenge them? Or will you let their deaths go unanswered?" Drake fixed him with a disapproving stare.

Cassian took particular notice of the fact that his father only spoke of avenging Theo and Bron. Not his brother, not his father's own son.

He couldn't even begin to process the twisted nature of that thought but still found himself nodding. "Of course," he muttered, under his breath, placating his father.

"That's my boy."

If he was honest, Theo and Bron's deaths didn't bother him as much as he thought they would. His only association with them was a result of their shared interest in bringing down The Dome. But now, as he thought of his brother's reluctance to support their father before his untimely death, he didn't know if he was really interested after all.

What Cassian did know though was that he was quickly losing interest in blindly supporting his father.

Lia burst into the Tavern, fuming.

She'd been in the middle of cleaning out her traps when the owner's son came knocking at her and Cade's door.

Well, just hers now.

The young boy had looked at her as if she was a monster. He knocked and retreated several steps from the door before he gave her the message, but she was used to reactions like that. Her kind were not common in the outer sectors and the fear and close-mindedness of the western sector in particular was nothing new.

Why me? she thought as she scanned the room for the one responsible for interrupting her night.

Walking up beside his barstool, she woke Cassian with a fist slamming down onto the bar next to his head. He jumped half out of his seat and whipped his head from left to right before his eyes landed on her.

She had never hated him more than she did in this moment.

The owner had the wrong idea calling her to pick him up.

"What are you doing here?" he slurred, narrowing his eyes as he wiped the drool from the side of his mouth.

Lia didn't bother responding, she just grabbed him by his collar and began dragging him out of the tavern and into the night's rain.

"What are you doing? Let go of me!" Cassian yelled, stumbling and slipping behind her.

Only once they were outside and several feet away did she release him.

She whirled on him, her drenched curls whipping water across his face. "You selfish bastard!" she seethed. "For the past two days, I have consistently been *this close* to beating your ass and then you go and pull this shit!"

Cassian didn't say anything and Lia watched as his eyes left her face to look at the ground, some of his anger fading into guilt.

"No! Don't you dare start with the self-pity!"

"I don't pity myself," he said through clenched teeth, anger resurfacing.

"Then what the fuck do you call this?!" she screamed. She was so angry but she was so tired. Cassian didn't respond so she took the opportunity to tell him about himself. "You stood there, and said nothing! You *did* nothing, and now he's gone. And then you come out here," she threw her arms out. "sulking? Getting blackout drunk as if you even have a reason to be upset. You didn't seem to care before, so why now?" She took a breath, blinking away the tears that sprung in her eyes. "He was all I had," she whispered. "You may already know this but I don't have many fans around here and I have never cared because I always had him and *you* took that from me! Not the queen, or the enforcers, or The Dome. YOU!" Lia couldn't help it as she started shaking. Not because of the cold, but from sheer rage. "And after everything, his last words to me were a request for me to take care of you. Not a 'goodbye' or an 'I love you'. He just wanted me to look after your sorry ass." She shook her head with disbelief.

"I don't need you to take care of me," Cassian said, stumbling over his words, still not meeting her eyes.

She quickly advanced on him and shoved at his chest, momentarily knocking him off balance. "Shut up! Shut your damn mouth! He is the only reason you are still alive right now and I'm not talking about him sacrificing himself for you." Her voice became scarily hoarse. "I mean that if he didn't ask that of me... I would've killed you myself." She meant every word. "You need to grow the fuck up, Cassian."

They stood still and stared at each other for several moments. Drained, both physically and emotionally, Lia shook her head and mumbled, "Come on. You can't go home like that."

She could have taken him back to the council lodge but she knew that the head councilman wouldn't take kindly to Cassian's state. Though she hadn't responded when he asked, she couldn't live with herself if she didn't grant Cade his final wish.

Having nothing left to say and not even looking back to see if Cassian had followed her, she turned and started in the direction of home.

Not that it even felt like home anymore.

Cassian walked through the door behind Eulalia, scanning the room through blurry eyes.

He only then realized that he had never been there before. He'd never visited his brother's own home, nor had he held a casual conversation with him since he moved out. And his exit wasn't really an excuse either. They hadn't been close even when Cade did live at the lodge.

"You can sleep on the couch," Eulalia said over her shoulder as she left the room.

He nodded even though she couldn't see him.

Looking around, Cassian noticed a wooden trap on display in the corner of the room. He assumed it was Eulalia's and taking a step closer to it, he was awed by the detail. It was odd that something only meant for practicality was so beautifully crafted.

Running his hand along it, he took note of the smoothness of the oak under his fingertips. Picking it up for a closer look, he spotted a small E engraved into the base.

He would recognize an engraving like that anywhere. Cade had made it for her.

A whole new wave of guilt washed over him but he reminded himself that no matter how much he was hurting, Eulalia had it worse.

That thought almost knocked him off balance. She'd been closer to Cade than his own brother.

On his seventh birthday, Cade had given him a hand-crafted truck replica made from the same oak with a C carved into the bottom. The only trucks he'd seen at that age were those that belonged to the trading officials who occasionally passed through the western sector. He'd always been so fascinated by them. He loved it and remembered the heartbreak he felt when his father had broken it right in front of him. That same night, Drake had even beaten Cade for giving him something that even remotely represented The Dome. Cassian was well aware of his father's dislike towards Cade but before, he'd always been blissfully ignorant and kept quiet in an effort to stay out of trouble. Even at the price of his relationship with his brother.

"Put that down." Eulalia's voice was cold as ice.

Cassian sheepishly returned the trap to its place and turned around.

She had changed out of her wet clothes and her hair was in two messy braids as she stood at the edge of the living room, a blanket in her arms.

As Cassian opened his mouth to apologize, her eyes went white. Her head snapped in the direction of the ceiling and she began shaking stiffly, dropping the blankets.

Cassian jumped back, horrified. "What the..."

He must've been seeing things.

She looked possessed.

Was he really that drunk? As he rubbed his eyes and looked again, he was sure that she was still there.

"Eulalia..." he called out. "Eulalia!" he called louder.

But she didn't stop nor did she respond. In fact, she seemed to become even more distressed.

Cassian watched, feeling helpless as she shook, sweating and gasping for breath.

In the next second, she dropped to the ground startling him.

Very slowly, he ambled towards her.

"Eulalia?" he whispered.

Eulalia was breathing heavily, on hands and knees as she slowly lifted her head and met Cassian's eyes. Thinking that tonight had been about as much as he could take, her next words threw that theory out of the window.

"Cade," she whispered.

His heart twisted mercilessly. "No, it's Cassian."

She frowned at him before rolling her eyes. "No, it's Cade. He's alive..."

And just like that, he was sober.

"Cassian, he's alive!" She stood on shaky legs.

"Eulalia, no..." Cassian shook his head slowly. He wasn't sure what had just happened but he was dreading the thought of having to tell her that Cade was gone and watching her lose him all over again. He was still sporting the shiner she had given him the first time.

"No Cassian, he's alive. But he's in danger." As she spoke, she began speed walking out of the room.

Huh? "I-, Eulalia?"

She exited what must've been her bedroom with a bag slung over her shoulder. "Listen to me, Cassian! He's alive, I know it. I saw him..." Her voice grew quiet. "But someone was... hurting him. I'm not sure who it was but I know what I saw."

Visions.

He'd heard about them before. He knew that Eulalia was a seer but in the moment, he didn't know what to make of it. His knowledge on gifted people were the stigmas that he'd absent-mindedly adopted from his father and the people in his sector.

They were enemies, not to be trusted. Eulalia's conviction, however, had him second-guessing his beliefs.

She went to pick up a sheathed knife that had been sitting on the mantle. "Why are you just standing there like an idiot? Are you coming or not?"

Cassian reared back. "Coming where?"

"The Dome, obviously," she said as she unsheathed the knife and took off her boot.

This was going too far.

"Eulalia, listen to yourself. We saw him get taken," he said, starting to feel grim. "You know what they do to outsiders in there. And even if he is alive, how the hell do you plan on getting inside The Dome?"

At first, she ignored him. He watched her as she placed the knife onto the sole inside the boot before securing it back on her foot. Then, Eulalia moved slowly, making him want to retreat into a corner with the way that she stalked toward him like a predator. She spoke very quietly. "I do not know, and I do not care but if there is even a chance that he is still alive and I can help him stay that way, I'd be damned if I let a group of pretentious fuckers in a glorified tent stop me. I *will not* lose him again. Now, are you coming or not?"

Cassian didn't know why, but he believed her. He believed her and given the chance to do right by his brother for once, he would take it.

It was the least he could do.

Lia must've seen his decision on his face.

"We're going to the lodge. You need to pack."

Chapter Ten

Cade.

After speaking with Hewn, trying to appear casual about the matter, she found out that his name was Cade. She hadn't cared to learn his name before. Seeing as he was to be executed, she preferred not to know, but now it was the only thing occupying her mind.

As Deianira made her way out of the palace and into the gardens with her sentinel, she reminded herself that her growing curiosity for the blonde enigma was only to keep an eye on him. Nothing else. It was nothing out of the ordinary for her to visit the arena's training fields. She often observed their drills, keeping an eye out for promising candidates. After all, it was Deianira who implemented the disciplinary program some years ago. Out of the tens of thousands of civilians in The Dome, there were currently only a few hundred criminals, and hence, not much need for prisons. Crimes on the more sinister end of the spectrum were punishable by death but petty crimes would land you in her enforcer program. It was her own version of reform and the results had been exceptional. After training was complete, they were allowed back into the general population but were still required to serve their sentence, however long it was, in the queen's force.

Exiting the palace gardens and walking into the arena, she allowed herself a small smile as she recognized the drill that they were doing today. It was one of her favorites. A grueling obstacle course that required speed, strength, and teamwork. It was virtually impossible to complete the course by oneself and the key was to move along with your group, separating as little as possible.

Upon arriving at the center of the field, she spotted Crew Bennet dragging himself up a steep inclined wall by a rope. Crew was one of the best. He was very strong and relatively fast considering his size. But he was cocky and impulsive. Being a good enforcer required both physical and mental attributes.

Eyes seeking out the man who had been infiltrating her thoughts since she'd laid eyes on him, Deianira scanned the field and came up empty.

A squeal to the left of the field drew her attention.

Passing her gaze over the man crumpled in a pile of limbs on the floor, she snorted and rolled her eyes.

Devin Jacobs.

The boy was smart as a whip but may the Gods help anyone in his vicinity if he had to do anything physically tasking. Devin was her youngest trainee and his performance in the program showed that, but he still had a good head on his shoulders. She was sure he would catch up with a little training.

Searching each inmate's face, she hunted again for the green-eyed man. Just as she was about to turn to Hewn to inquire about his whereabouts, she spotted a tottering man getting to his feet and leaving the mud crawl.

Cade?

Even with all the dirt obscuring his face, she could still make out his features.

And the bruises.

Deianira was taken aback by the ice-cold anger that slowly crawled up her spine.

He'd been beaten. Badly.

Altercations in the dorms were far from uncommon and occurred for a range of reasons. But this felt different. Was different. One man couldn't have inflicted this much damage. Either he was targeted or he pissed *a lot* of people off.

As his injuries became clearer, a busted lip, a black eye, an almost broken nose, those green eyes landed on her and narrowed. Deianira quickly realized that she had been walking towards him the whole time. That she was standing right in front of him and all the activity in the arena had paused.

Breathing heavily, muscles aching, Cade pushed up off his mud-covered knee to stand.

This course would be difficult for anyone but in his condition, it was nearly impossible. Cade wasn't going to draw any more attention to himself by complaining though. Pain was nothing new to him.

"Uh, Cade?"

Cade turned to Devin who had just managed to untangle himself from his comrades. They spat insults at him for slowing them down, but he didn't seem to be paying attention to them. Devin's eyes were focused on something over Cade's shoulder.

He inclined his head to Cade. "Incoming."

At the same time that Devin spoke, Cade noticed that, slowly, everyone on the field had stopped what they were doing to look at him. A cool sense of dread came over him as he started to turn around.

Pivoting slowly, Cade wasn't surprised to see Queen Deianira hastily walking towards him. He certainly hadn't been expecting her, but it was as if he could sense her presence. Like he already knew who was behind him.

He also wasn't surprised by the anger he could already feel seeping from her pores either, but what did have him shocked was the look in her eye. She wasn't angry at him. Her rage was zoned in on his cheek, his eye. His bruises.

What shocked Cade, even more, was his own rising anger.

Of course, he was grateful to her to an extent. She'd spared his life. But she was also the reason that he'd been in the dorms in the first place. He was an outsider. Was she expecting the other inmates to give him a warm welcome? In his mind, it was as much her doing as it was Crew's.

He searched her eyes deeply, looking for that same cold-blooded woman who brutally killed two young men, right in front of him. But he couldn't find her, he only found anger and concern and even ... distress.

For him.

Cade didn't want her sympathy.

Coming to a stop in front of him, she let her gaze travel up and down his body. Cade's uniform covered most of the damage but his haggard stance alone was telling.

"What happened?" she said in a neutral tone. She didn't quite whisper but Cade knew that she was only speaking to him.

The lack of inflection in her voice suggested that it wasn't even a question. She wasn't requesting information. She was demanding it. Still feeling the whiplash from her change in character, Cade cast his eyes down at her and spoke his next words without thinking, out of both annoyance and curiosity.

"What do you care?"

All the concern, the worry, and the sympathy bled from her leaving only chilling rage behind.

Shit.

One second, Cade was looking into her eyes, chest heaving, and the next, he was in the air. In the same second, he felt hands around his neck, but not the queen's hands. They were shadows.

Hands coming to his neck, gasping for breath, eyes wide, Cade looked down to see that he was at least five feet off of the ground and Queen Deianira standing where he left her with her hand in the air.

She inclined her head, speaking calmly, coldly. "What do *I* care? The only reason I spared you was so that I could make you suffer." Even with the air rapidly leaving his lungs, Cade could smell the lie. "You *murder* four of my men, you *steal* from me, I let you live and you have the audacity to question me?" She tilted her head. "You think a beating is the worst of it? You think this is bad?" The shadowy hands around his neck got tighter and black spots started to fill his vision. " It *can* and it *will* get worse. By the time I am finished with you, you will wish that I ripped your heart out, just like your cowardly friend."

Just when Cade thought that he would certainly pass out, the shadows disappeared and he fell through the air and onto the ground in a gasping mess. Queen Deianira wasted no time in advancing on him and dropping a knee onto his sternum. Cade's hands flew up to hold her leg as he squirmed in pain from the pressure on his bruised chest.

She brought her face close enough for him to feel her breath on his lips and whispered harshly, "Cade Alden, I wish you would give me a reason to make an example out of you."

Despite her words and his current position, he couldn't help but be drawn in by her eyes.

The day before, he was too distracted to differentiate the deep gray from the black. Even as she threatened his life, he found himself spellbound by the way her pupils expanded and contracted as she hissed at him. They doubled in size as she said his name and narrowed as she delivered her lethal words. It was mesmerizing. After a few seconds, his eyes fell to her lips, which promptly stopped moving. As Cade met her gaze again, the queen stared back at him for a few seconds before she quickly stood and stumbled back a few steps.

Devin rushed up beside Cade to aid him, drawing his attention away from the queen. Standing shakily, he let his eyes wander in her direction one last time, but he only saw her retreating figure.

Chapter Eleven

Deianira quickly retired to her bedroom, ignoring the looks from servants, bystanders, and even her sentinel.

Slamming her door shut behind her, she walked over to her desk and placed both hands on the surface, taking several steadying breaths.

What the hell was that?

Why did he look at her like that?

Why did she look at him like that?

He wasn't even scared. Usually, the absence of fear might have sparked anger in her but he didn't look arrogant. There was something else behind those eyes. And she didn't like it one bit.

Her door opening interrupted her effort to ease her mind, but she didn't bother turning around.

"What was that?"

"There's something off about him, Salem," she replied.

"I agree, but if you keep this behavior up, people are going to talk. Your interest in him is far from discreet."

Deianira turned abruptly. "Interest?"

Salem didn't even need to find her words. She just spoke from her mind. "Deianira, I supported your decision to spare him. You don't just execute people without grounds, even outsiders, but I remember standing next to you in the city center while you watched him. That was even before Finch tried to get a read on him. If there is something more going on, I advise you to tell me. I can't help you if you don't let me."

Deianira watched Salem for a while. It was true, there *was* something more. But Deianira didn't know what it was either. If she knew, perhaps she wouldn't be so twisted up over it.

Nodding, she said to Salem "I have no *interest* in him. Something about him just rubs me the wrong way." That was partially a lie. "Tell Hewn to find out what he can about him. I will review the data personally." At her sentinel's unsatisfied breath, she amended. "We will review it."

<hr />

"Hey."

Cade jumped and quickly turned to look behind him. There stood Devin, naked as the day he was born.

"You okay?"

Cade narrowed his eyes. "Seriously? You couldn't wait until I was done?" He gestured to himself, just as bare.

"Ah. Sorry about that. But for real, are you good? That cut looks real nasty." He reached out a finger to poke the gash above Cade's eyebrow.

Cade stepped back, his lips parted in disbelief at Devin's lack of social awareness. Shaking his head, he turned off the shower and reached for his towel, wrapping it around his waist.

"I'm fine."

He wasn't fine. He didn't know what he was, but it certainly wasn't fine.

After that display in the arena, he should have been furious. Honestly, a small part of him was, but above all, he was confused. He didn't understand the queen's actions towards him. One second livid, the next concerned. But even more than that, he couldn't understand his need to figure her out rather than despise her. She had attacked him but instead of sulking or being embarrassed, he felt the strangest inclination to get closer to her.

Those eyes.

There was so much behind them. Looking into her eyes earlier, he had felt more at ease than he had since his arrival, which was odd because she looked at him like she wanted him dead.

He needed to get inside her head. His abilities as an empath only allowed him to know what she was feeling in the moment, but her thoughts and motives were still a mystery to him.

That line of thought struck a question in Cade's head.

Flicking his head back to Devin while dressing, Cade looked around before speaking. "What are you, anyway?"

Devin cocked his head at him, confusion written all over his face. Lowering his voice, as if telling him a secret, Cade adjusted his question. "Your gift, I mean. What are you?"

"Oh. I'm a warlock. But don't ask me to do any tricks, I didn't grow up very rich and I have like a hundred siblings so my parents didn't have enough money to send me to a school that catered to my specific ability."

He wondered whether he should tell Devin about his gift but he hadn't known him for long and the fewer people that knew he was gifted, the better. It was his only advantage. "Oh, cool."

Both dressed, Cade gathered his commissary and started towards his bunk. Of course, Devin followed.

"I mean, I learned a few spells here and there so I'm not completely useless, but I'm not that good. If I was, I wouldn't be here."

That made Cade pause. He knew that everyone in the program was here for a reason, but Devin's childlike nature made him overlook the fact that he was a criminal too.

"Why *are* you here?" Cade asked carefully.

Devin burst into a fit of laughter, clumsily swinging his body up onto his bunk. "You know when people say 'love makes you crazy'?" he asked, raising an eyebrow. "Well, my girlfriend's a baker and her old boss was a premium asshole. One day she told me that he'd made some remarks about her food." Devin's eyes darkened momentarily before shining with amusement once again. "So I told her to get a new job and when she did, I set his house on fire." His humor only seemed to increase. "I tried to use a cloaking spell to conceal myself when I was leaving. Emphasis on the word 'tried'," he smirked. "He wasn't in the house though." He sighed regretfully as if that was a hiccup in his plan.

Cade looked at him. Blinked.

Before, he would never have thought that Devin could commit such a crime but he was beginning to see a slight edge to him. It was the way he laughed while recounting the story casually as if it was a funny, nostalgic anecdote concerned Cade.

Not knowing what to say, he simply nodded and slowly continued tucking his things under his bunk.

The sound of the door sliding had everyone turning toward the entrance. As Hewn stood in the doorway, Cade remembered the way that everyone had reacted when he was first brought into the dorms and made quick work of dropping his things and moving to stand next to Devin in front of his bunk.

Hewn's boots were the only sound heard in the room as he walked down the aisle and stopped directly in front of Cade.

What did I do now?

"Hands," was the only thing Hewn said.

Instinctively, Cade put his hands out in front of him before a thick pair of handcuffs were slapped onto his wrists.

Hewn said nothing as he gripped Cade's upper arm and began walking him toward the entrance.

He looked back at Devin who stared at him along with the rest of the inmates, just as confused.

Considering that he had been in a constant state of confusion since his arrival at The Dome, Cade just went with it and hoped for the best. That didn't do much to ease his anxiety though as the queen's words replayed in his mind.

It can and will get worse.

As Cade lets his eyes drift around the sterile, white room that he had been escorted to only minutes ago, he began to wonder if the whole thing was some sort of test. On arrival, he was instructed to sit on the low table, one of the only pieces of furniture in the room, and he had been sitting there ever since. Looking up into the corner of the room, he noticed a small white box with a black circle in it and a little red light, blinking at him. He'd seen all types of weird things since arriving at The Dome so he let his eyes pass over it without much interest. No one had come in or out and his anxiety rose by the second. Was he supposed to do something, say something, escape? Just as Cade went to rise from where he had been sitting, the door slid open revealing a beautiful blonde woman with a beaming smile. "Hi, I'm Octavia." She gave him a small wave as she entered the room.

After a few seconds of her looking at him expectantly, he responded "Cade."

Her smile seemed to get even bigger. "Oh, I know," she said, eyeing him. Refocusing herself she went on. "Well, Cade, I'm here to check injuries. I'm a witch. Healer in training." She giggled. "Usually I would assist my father but he's not available at the moment." She moved to the other side of the room and opened a drawer, seemingly trying to keep herself busy. Turning to look over her shoulder at Cade, she said, "If you could just take off your shirt, I'll have a look and see what I can do."

He was reluctant.

"Don't worry, I've done this before."

That wasn't his concern but still, Cade obeyed slowly, warily.

Lifting his right arm to get his shirt over his head, he winced as he felt that familiar throbbing pain in his rib prompting Octavia to rush over to help him.

"Thank you," he mumbled.

She looked into his eyes, their faces only inches apart. "No problem. Just doing my job."

Cade looked away first.

Stepping back to survey the damage, Octavia grimaced.

"Okay, so I don't think that your nose is broken and most of your facial wounds are superficial but I can still offer some pain relief for that." She stepped closer again and gently placed her hand on Cade's side. "You definitely have a broken rib or two so I'll speed up the healing process and you should be back to normal in no time."

Cade only nodded.

She took a deep breath and began muttering words under her breath while moving her hands over his skin.

While she worked, Cade couldn't help but notice the way her eyes kept finding his as the tension slowly began to build in the room. He didn't need to look too deep to get a read off of her. Her lust was palpable.

Cade knew lust.

A number of women in his sector had made advances toward him but he almost always found himself uninterested. Not that there was anything wrong with them, he just didn't like new people, they made him feel uncomfortable.

Emotions were often relative and the intensity of them varied from person to person, so he preferred to stick to those whom he had already acclimated to. Besides, as the Head Councilman's son, he knew that a great deal of them were only interested in his name, in rolling around with 'the rebellious son of the head councilman', so he found himself going back to the same particular few who were genuine enough.

Octavia, however, seemed genuine. The type of girl he might have gone for in his back sector, but he'd only been in The Dome for a few days and that was ignoring the fact that he was essentially in prison. Now wasn't the time.

"All done!"

Cade took note of how her hands lingered on his chest for a few seconds longer than necessary before she removed them.

Giving her a quick 'thank you', Cade rotated and picked up his shirt when quickly noticed that the pain in his side was gone. He began moving his arms and twisting from side to side in awe of how his aches had instantly subsided.

Octavia giggled when she saw his face. "Pretty cool, huh?"

For the first time since he'd been brought to The Dome, Cade felt a genuine smile touch his lips. "Yeah, it is." He didn't expect it to work that quickly.

"Don't go getting yourself hurt again," she said conversationally. "I doubt Her Majesty would feel so generous next time."

That had Cade looking up. "What do you mean?" he asked, on edge all of a sudden.

Octavia blanched. "Oh. I'm sorry, I didn't mean to worry you. I just meant that she put in a request for you to be seen by my father. I'm sure that if you got hurt again she'd allow you to be treated." She nodded reassuringly. "Besides, even if my father couldn't, I'd be more than happy to see you." She emphasized the last sentence with a smirk.

Cade absently smiled back at her while trying to order his thoughts.

So the queen had been concerned about how he got his injuries, then strangled him, and now she was requesting for him to be seen by a healer.

Now more than ever, he wanted to know what was going through her mind.

Cade resolved in himself that he would thank her when he next got the chance, and hopefully get close enough to get a better reading.

Chapter Twelve

Devin let out a satisfied hum as he took his place in line behind Cade.

"What?" Cade asked.

Devin was sporting a wide grin. "Look over there." He indicated to the two servers carting in a wide barrel. "It's watered down as shit, but after two months in here? I'd drink it out of a dirty sock."

Cade snorted, shuffling forward as the line moved. "They give you guys alcohol?"

"You're one of us too," he said with a head tilt. "And yes, they give *us* beer, occasionally. But it's only the winning team from yesterday's drill. I guess it's just an incentive to push ourselves, but I'm not complaining."

With his food and drink in hand, he and Devin moved to take a seat at a small table in the corner of the cafeteria.

What Devin had said nudged something inside of him. He *was* one of them now and he didn't know if he'd ever be allowed to return home. Surprisingly though, even with the events of the past three days, he didn't hate the thought of staying here for a while. He missed his best friend dearly, even his brother, but all other thoughts of home had Cade mentally rejecting the idea of returning. Not that he had a choice in the matter, but the appeal of staying might have had something to do with a certain woman who hadn't left his mind since his first interaction with her.

Cade knew that it was silly and most likely just his curiosity getting the better of him so he pushed all thoughts of her away as he dug into his food.

"You good?" Devin asked after a while.

"Yeah, just thinking." Cade brushed him off.

But of course, he didn't take the hint. "About what?"

Cade looked down at his plate and thought that it couldn't do any harm. "Yesterday in the infirmary, the witch told me that it was the queen that requested for me to be seen," he whispered.

Devin spoke with a full mouth. "Oh yeah, I could've told you that for free."

"What do you mean?" Cade asked, brows furrowed.

"I mean, we don't get medical care until we've completed our training. If you're friends with a witch or a warlock and they're nice enough to help you out, then good for you. But if not, then you count your losses and heal up."

"Then why did she do that for me?" Cade began to feel uneasy.

Devin snorted. "I don't even want to know. All due respect, she is next-level nutty."

Based on her actions in the past few days, Cade didn't argue with that but there seemed to be something more.

Once he'd swallowed his food, Devin continued.

"For starters, she offed her whole family at thirteen. Mom, dad, sister, the whole gang. That's how she became queen. And you probably already know this, but she has a real boner for violence. I mean, the only people she seems to not want to kill are her sentinel, Officer Hewn, and Sir Ivar."

She killed her own family?

After processing Devin's words and locking them away in the back of his mind, Cade asked, "Who's Sir Ivar?"

"Jude Ivar? You haven't seen him around here?" When Cade shook his head, Devin waved a hand dismissively. "Anyway, he's her uncle but kinda like her dad now. He helped her run The Dome until she was old enough. But that's just what I've heard, I wasn't even around back then."

Cade knew he was young, but not that young. "Gods, how old *are* you?"

"Eighteen." Devin sighed like it was a question he'd been asked many times before.

That didn't add up. "Then, how old is she?"

Devin chewed on the end of his fork, thinking for a second. "One hundred and thirty-two." After looking up and seeing Cade's confused expression, he added, "Oh, outsider. Gifted people age a lot slower."

Cade knew this. He'd read up on gifted people when he was younger but it was now dawning on him that he might live that long too.

Devin smiled proudly. "You can live even longer than that with a trusty warlock and an anti-aging spell. So basically, you stick with me and you're all set."

Cade stifled a laugh. "I thought you said you weren't good at spells."

The smile slipped off Devin's face. "Okay, wow. No need to shame me, I can still learn."

He sputtered, suddenly aware of the fact that he just insulted a potential pyromaniac. "No, that- sorry, I didn't mean-"

Devin burst out laughing. "Don't worry, I was just playing with you." Cade let out a discreet sigh of relief.

Out of the corner of his eye, he spotted the queen and her sentinel walking past the entrance of the cafeteria. He wasn't sure if he was allowed to leave the room unattended but none of the enforcers were looking his way. Thankful for the out, he told Devin to hang on and got up from his seat to catch her.

"Wait, Cade!" Devin called out from behind him.

He turned back expecting him to ask where he was going.

"You gonna drink that?" he asked with a lazy smile, pointing to Cade's beer.

"Go ahead." Cade waved, resuming his brisk walk towards the entrance.

As he exited the cafeteria and saw her walking a few feet ahead, he realized that he didn't know much about the customs in The Dome. His past interactions with the queen had been far from formal but he still didn't want to accidentally offend her, so he went with what he remembered Octavia saying the night before.

"Your Majesty," he called awkwardly. He hadn't spoken very loudly and was about to call out again when she turned around and met his eyes.

By the way she was looking at him, Cade assumed that he must have said the wrong thing, or that maybe it wasn't customary to speak to the queen directly.

Instantly, her sentinel stepped out in front of her and advanced on Cade as if he could be a threat to the queen.

Hands coming up, he backed up several steps. "Woah, easy. I just wanted to talk."

In the same second that the words left his mouth, the sentinel stopped and returned her hands to her sides, her face a show of calmness and tranquility.

Cade blinked. That went a lot smoother than he thought it would. He looked behind her to see the queen, her eyes flicking between him and her sentinel, the same look of surprise on her face. Shaking her head, she met his eyes and nodded her head to her sentinel, silently telling her to leave them.

Once they were alone, she stared at him, waiting for him to speak. Suddenly uncomfortable, Cade wiped his sweaty hands on his pants and sought out her eyes again. "I uh, I just wanted to say thank you. For the healer. Last night. I appreciate it." He cringed at his obvious lack of composure.

He waited for her to say something, but she didn't. Just stared at him.

Understanding that he had been dismissed, Cade jerkily nodded and started to turn to make his way back into the cafeteria when she spoke from behind him.

"Don't thank me," she said evenly. "After all, it's no fun torturing a dead man." As he heard her slow steps towards him, he turned to find her much, much closer. "A little word of advice," Each cold word was laced with simmering rage. "You will find that it is in your best interest not to flirt with my staff. It'll do you no favors and I promise, you *will not* like the result."

Cade cocked his head back, both shocked at her insinuation and curious as to why the possibility agitated her so much. "I wasn't-"

She cut him off with a hand in the air and Cade was grateful for it. He didn't know what he would've said, didn't know why he felt the need to explain himself.

"That was a warning, and make no mistake, you won't get another one."

Addled and unable to speak, Cade simply nodded.

Apparently satisfied, the queen turned and left in the direction of her sentinel, leaving Cade beyond puzzled.

Stupid. Stupid. Stupid.

Deianira flipped to the next page in the file that she had spent hours looking at. Salem had left ages ago but she still couldn't take her eyes off it. She didn't know what she was looking for, but she knew that she hadn't found it yet.

You will find that it is in your best interest not to flirt with my staff.

Why did she say that?

She knew exactly why she said it.

As much as Deianira hated it, she didn't like to lie to herself. She knew that it was jealousy brewing in her stomach. But why?

What she also couldn't figure out was why Octavia had been in that room with him. When she put in the request, it was for Octavia's father, Mikhael, a warlock who specialized in healing.

She had only spoken to Octavia on a few occasions and as far as she could tell, she was a nice girl. Pretty, intelligent, and she had a passion for helping others. But when Deianira reviewed the footage from the infirmary to study his behavior and see what she could learn, definitely for no other reason, she found herself fantasizing about all the ways she could inflict pain on Octavia. Wondering what her eyes would look like as the life in them fled.

Watching her hands move all over him, the way she giggled and perused him, left Deianira with a bad taste in her mouth. Then, he went and smiled at her.

A real smile.

She had thought that he was beautiful before, but when she zoomed into his face and saw the way that his lips stretched, the way his eyes crinkled in the corners, she was taken aback. Then she remembered that he wasn't smiling at her and her mood soured.

Did she want him to smile at her? No, definitely not. He was a murderer, a thief. Maybe, it was that she just didn't want him to be happy in general.

Yes, that was it.

When he approached her outside of the cafeteria, all that cold rage came back in full force and was redirected at him. He was only trying to show his appreciation but she wanted to punish him for some reason.

She needed to get a hold of herself before she did something she would regret.

As her eyes roamed over the pages in front of her, she thought of something that she hadn't paid much attention to before.

Alden. His last name was Alden.

Why did that name ring a bell?

Standing, she walked over to her library and pulled out a few of her old journal entries. She knew she was onto something but just couldn't quite put her finger on it.

It was those eyes.

Finding the right year, she quickly opened the journal and spread the loose papers on the floor, desperate to make a connection.

On the edge of abandoning the task out of frustration, her eyes snagged an entry, almost four decades old.

Her heart dropped to her stomach as the last piece of the puzzle clicked into place.

Hadrick.

It couldn't be.

Could it?

Abruptly, she closed the book and left her room to find Jude and tell him what she had discovered.

Chapter Thirteen

As Cade got back in line to be escorted back to their dorms, he had even more questions than before.

Had I been flirting?

How did she know?

Why did she care?

He also remembered Devin's words about Deianira's family. He'd never been this curious about anyone before and if he was going to understand her motives, he needed more information.

Filing into the dorms, the inmates moved to stand in front of their bunks and stayed there until all the enforcers had exited.

Not wanting to waste any time, as soon as the door closed, Cade turned to Devin. "Hey, Devin?"

Devin turned to look at him but didn't respond.

Okay?

Not too talkative.

"Devin?" Cade called again.

Again, Devin didn't respond, just stared into his eyes. A bad feeling brewed in Cade's stomach.

Opening his mouth to call him again, Cade noticed Devin's skin. His smooth chestnut brown skin was a sickly pale color. His short dark curls were drenched in sweat too.

Something was definitely wrong.

"Hey, are you feeling okay?" Cade asked, concerned.

Eyes glossy and locked onto Cade's, Devin slowly shook his head, his normally amused face contorted into a pained expression.

Before Cade could ask anything else, Devin slowly sank to his knees, clutching his throat, heaving. Cade immediately dropped to his knees beside him, placing a hand on his back.

"Devin!"

"I can't breathe," Devin rasped.

Panic. Pure panic set in. The fear coming off of Devin must have been making its way through Cade too.

Cade pulled Devin onto his back and laid a hand on his shoulder.

"I-... I can't..." Devin's mouth kept opening and closing, his words beginning to blend into one another.

He needs help.

Thinking quickly, Cade told Devin to hold on and rushed over to the dorm entrance. Looking for some sort of handle or button, Cade noticed a red switch next to the door.

Behind him, he could hear the others start to catch onto what was happening, but he kept his mind focused on the task at hand.

To get help.

Not knowing what else to do, he tensed and flipped the switch. Then he waited for something to happen. He waited, and waited, and waited some more until it felt like he had been standing at the door for an eternity. Just as he was about to return to Devin's side, the door slid open and enforcers were spilling through the entrance, guns up, shouting commands.

"Stand back!"

"Hands up!"

"He needs help! Something's wrong with Devin! He needs help!" Cade shouted over them, trying to draw their attention.

Hewn, he recognized, stepped out from the group of enforcers and lowered his gun. "Where?" he asked, eyeing Cade.

Letting out a sigh of relief, Cade started to jog back to his bunk, waving for Hewn to follow.

They had to push their way past where the inmates had been gathering and as they broke the circle, there lay Devin, on the floor, lips pale.

He wasn't gasping for breath anymore. In fact, he wasn't moving at all.

Cade felt like all the oxygen had left his lungs. Devin was fine just an hour ago.

He already knew what Hewn was going to say as he locked eyes with him, a dark expression on his face. He also knew what he would feel if he reached out, but he tried anyway. He searched far and wide as he let his eyes fall on Devin's still figure.

And he felt nothing. Not even the fear that he had been emanating only minutes ago. Absolutely nothing.

Hewn put a hand on his shoulder, bringing him out of his daze. "Sorry, son."

What?

That's it?

Cade was still reeling as the other enforcers slowly lowered their guns and walked to either side of Hewn to help lift Devin.

At that moment, a thought occurred to Cade.

As soon as his gift presented itself when he was a young boy, he began researching. There weren't many books outside of The Dome and those that were available were not very detailed. But Cade read, and read. He knew he couldn't tell anyone what he could do, so he taught himself the full extent of his abilities, and that knowledge only grew when Lia presented. They set out to learn all they could about their gifts and gifted people as a whole.

It might have been a long shot, but if there was a chance he could do something, he would run for it.

So he did.

He ran.

Cade broke into a sprint towards the dorm's entrance, not looking back, even as he heard the enforcers shouting and starting up to chase him.

He passed room after room and still didn't find what he was looking for but undeterred, he kept his pace. Darting through the corridors and hallways, he realized that he didn't even know where he was going, but he kept running, looking for a sign, for anything.

The shouts grew louder and Cade pumped his arms harder.

He was glad that he did too because as rounded a corner and smacked into a small figure, he looked up to meet a face of pure fury and he knew that he had found it.

Chapter Fourteen

Hand raised to knock on the door of Jude's study, Deianira's advanced hearing caught the sound of commotion on the other side of the palace. It wasn't the usual bustle of the servants milling around after lunch. Something was happening.

Though she had a sentinel, Deianira was more than capable of protecting herself and had no quarrel with handling trouble alone, so task forgotten, she took off in the direction of the noise.

The closer she got to the source of the noise, the more uneasy she felt. She saw that she was nearing the enforcer's wing. A familiar feeling of dread churned in her gut, but ignoring it, she picked up into a run.

Rounding the corner, she readied her hands to summon shadows to quicken her pace when she was mowed down by a large body. Halfway to anger at whichever servant that had just run into her, Deianira righted herself only to see the same face that had been haunting her these past few days.

Was he really trying to escape?

Not even bothering to draw a shadow, she pushed at his shoulder, turning him before jumping up and sweeping an arm around his neck. Successfully pulling him into a chokehold, she realized that his size made it much harder for her to keep him in place, so she kicked at the back of his knee and tugged. His legs slipped from beneath him and she held him up as she landed on her feet.

"Are you delusional or just that stupid?" she seethed into his ear.

"Please!" he gasped out, tapping her arm.

Her brows furrowed.

Please?

Please what?

Before she could question him further, Hewn and several other enforcers barreled into the hallway.

Deianira stared down her third in command.

How could he be so careless?

Coming up to her side, Hewn looked down at Cade, who was still in her hold. "I'm sorry, Your Majesty." He glared at Cade.

"What is the meaning of this?" she asked, enraged.

Hewn looked nervous and he had every reason to be. Incompetence was not dealt with lightly. "I don't know. We received a riot alert, but when we arrived, we found Devin Jacobs deceased and then he just ran."

Horrified, Deianira pulled back her arms, stepping back as if she had been burned, and Cade fell to the ground on his back.

She knew he was a murderer but some delusional part of her mind told her that he wasn't what she thought. It was the way he looked at her sometimes. Like he was just misunderstood.

But this? To kill another inmate as a distraction to escape justice? And a young boy too? Devin might not have been the most capable but he had a good heart. It was despicable.

That familiar, comfortable, icy feeling settled inside of her and while looking into Cade's eyes she said to Hewn, "Leave us."

"Your Majesty-"

"Leave us!" she lashed out.

Hewn only nodded and began retreating, followed by the remaining enforces.

"Get up," she whispered to Cade.

She would kill him just like she should have days ago. Slowly, painfully.

As he rolled over to stand, Deianira caught Cade's glum expression.

"Please, I need your help," he panted quietly, getting to his feet.

Deianira had heard many last words, but this was a first. Not bothering to disguise her disbelief, she stared at him, open-mouthed.

"I know you don't owe me anything and if you want to kill me for the trouble I've caused, then go ahead but please, help him."

Help who?

Devin?

Deianira was beyond confused now. "You killed that boy, and now you want me to help him?" She spoke each word slowly, wanting him to hear how they sounded.

His expression morphed into one of shock and offense. "What? You think I killed him? He's my friend."

Deianira took particular note of the fact that he referred to Devin in the present tense and instantly, her hackles rose. Something about the way that he spoke told her that there was another explanation. But until she figured out what it was, she wouldn't clear him.

"Are you saying you didn't? You had no problem killing four innocent men before you even arrived here. Am I supposed to assume that you've miraculously converted to pacifism?"

His chest rose, eyes narrowing menacingly. "You want to talk about killing innocent people? Your own fam-" he abruptly cut himself off, looking just as surprised by his own words.

But the damage was already done. She knew what he was going to say and once the shock of his words wore off, she was left with a pit in her stomach. He was right.

It had been years since anyone had even spoken words of that incident in her presence, but that didn't stop her from reliving those moments every night before she slept.

If she thought she couldn't be any more surprised today, she was quickly humbled by his next words.

"You're an azrael, right? I-I read a book that said that you can restore people." Cade whispered as if he was scared of what she might say.

Deianira's eyes widened.

"If you want to punish me, punish me but I'm begging you." His voice became thick with emotion. "He's just a kid."

The pain in his voice told her that his concern for Devin ran a lot deeper than a bond that could have been formed in only a few days, but he still seemed genuine. Pocketing the thought she re-focused her attention on Cade.

It appeared that her brain and body were not in accordance with each other because as she opened her mouth to tell him that there was nothing she could do, the words that left it suggested otherwise.

"Where is he?"
What am I doing?

What am I doing?
Cade couldn't believe his luck when Deianira conceded, but waiting in the infirmary for Devin to be brought in, he began to second-guess himself. He hadn't even spoken a word on the way over for fear that she might change her mind. She was already so unpredictable and he wouldn't have been surprised if she did, so taking the win, he sat silently and just hoped that she wouldn't. Just being in the room with her made him anxious.
He briefly thought back to the last time he was here, with Octavia. For someone who could read people, and quite well too, he still found himself perplexed when it came to Deianira's reaction earlier today. Deciding to push his luck after all, he broke the silence.
Cade cleared his throat. "Octavia said that her father was sent to see me." Looking down at his slightly worn boots, he continued. "How did you know I was in here with her?"
She took a while to respond, making Cade think that she might ignore him.
"I watched you," she said, staring at the blank wall in front of them. After a beat of silence, she looked up to see questions written in Cade's eyes. Sighing, she pointed to the corner of the room. At the

same box on the ceiling that he had been looking at last night. "It's a camera."

She was spying on me?

Any more of Cade's questions were cut short by the familiar *woosh* of the door sliding open and he quickly got his feet.

Hewn wheeled Devin into the room, followed by his deputy. As he caught Hewn's gaze, Cade wanted to apologize. He knew that if he had asked to see the queen, he would've been denied and while he didn't regret his decision, he still felt bad for the commotion he had caused. Getting Hewn in trouble was the last thing he wanted to do, especially because he was the first to step in when he had called for help.

As the enforcers left the room, Cade's eyes fell on Devin's still figure. His heart ached at the sight and it was only then that he figured out why.

Cassian. He reminded him of Cassian.

They were nothing alike in personality, but it was his age and the absence of the relationship between him and his brother that made him feel so despondent when he looked at Devin. The light bond he had formed with Devin in only a few days was more stable than the bond he had with his own brother. Cade regretted not making more of an effort with Cassian and now he wouldn't get the chance to.

Deianira walked up to Devin's side. "How did he die?" Her voice was shaky.

"I don't know," Cade responded, still watching Devin.

She looked up at him, puzzled. "What do you mean, you don't know?"

He met her gaze. "He couldn't breathe and he started choking, but he was fine before, and then... he wasn't. I don't know what happened," Cade said under his breath.

As her eyes left his, she took a shaky breath looking at Devin, regret flowing from her.

Apprehension filled Cade's veins.

She was changing her mind.

"I can't do it," she whispered, and as if sensing his own disappointment, she took a step back from the table. From Cade. "Physically, I can," she leveled. "but I shouldn't. You should just let him go peacefully."

Even Cade was surprised by his tone of voice when he said, "Do it."

Deianira shook her head jerkily. "You're not listening to me. It will only make it worse." Her eyes became glossy, on the verge of brimming.

Cade *was* listening. But he didn't care. Maybe it was selfish but strangely, he felt like he was losing his brother again.

"Do it. Please." There was nothing more he could do than beg.

Staring straight into his eyes, her tone was daring, holding threat. "You will speak to no one about this."

Cade nodded. He didn't need her to tell him what she would do if he failed to keep his word to know that it wouldn't end well for him.

Wiping her hands on her long black dress, her eyes flitted to Cade momentarily before she stepped back up to the table. As she began to secure Devin's hands in the restraints beside the bed, she spoke to Cade, working simultaneously.

"I've only done this once before. There is a reason that you don't hear of azraels restoring people anymore, and it's not just because we're rare." She picked up a pair of scissors from the tray and started cutting open his shirt. "It's not natural, and therefore there are consequences." Setting down the scissors and picking up a scalpel, she carefully made a deep incision across his left pectoral. "Nature has a very cruel way of retaliating when you toy with the balance." And then his right. "When they come back, they're never quite the same." Placing the scalpel down, she closed her eyes and slowly rubbed her hands together. "There were tales of people going mad. Some became violent, some hysterical. Some were just absent of all emotion. There are many unpredictable outcomes." Her voice was unsteady now but Cade couldn't focus for long enough to work out if it was fear or distress because, to his horror, she placed both hands on Devin's chest and began to wedge her fingers into the cuts. "There are a lot of factors though. It can depend on when and how they died. But the process is unstable nonetheless."

Shadows slowly began to seep out from her hands and surround Devin. Cade took his eyes off him to look at Deianira, wondering if this was supposed to be happening, but the second his eyes shifted, Devin began to convulse on the bed.

Watching Devin's body thrash, Cade started to think that this might have been a grave mistake. Of course, he wanted Devin alive, but not at the cost of his soul.

He went to touch Deianira's shoulder to tell her to stop but thought better of it. She'd said that the process was unstable so disrupting her didn't seem like the wisest course of action.

The seizing only became more violent before all the shadows disappeared and Devin's body lay still.

Deianira removed her fingers from the incisions and stepped back, her hands lifted and trembling.

Cade watched her and waited for something to happen or for her to speak, but she didn't.

It didn't work.

He'd done all of this for nothing.

A choked breath stole his attention away from Deianira as he threw his gaze to Devin who was trying to sit up, gasping for air.

Not knowing what to expect, Deianira slowly stepped away from the table until her back hit a wall, her bloody hands shaking at her sides. She had sworn to herself that she would never use her ability in this way again. Not after what happened the last time. It was a promise she had kept for over thirty years so why did she let this man convince her to break it?

It didn't take much either. Looking into those desperate eyes, she just couldn't find it in herself to say no.

After his gaze skipped around the whole room, Devin finally noticed Cade.

"What the fuck is going on?" he asked, jarring his hands in the restraints. Quickly seeing Deianira standing behind Cade, Devin straightened up. "Oh shit. Your majesty." He nodded his head awkwardly in his horizontal position.

She wanted to roll his eyes at his formality considering her hands had just been inside his chest.

Neither Deianira nor Cade responded.

"Cade? You're kinda starting to freak me out. What's going on? Why am I strapped to a bed?"

He looked scared, confused.

Deianira stepped forward and spoke so that Cade wouldn't have to. She didn't filter her words. Just spoke plainly and got straight to the point. "You died this evening and Cade asked me to restore you. I did. What is the last thing you remember?" she asked.

Devin widened his eyes at Deianira as if she had asked had been speaking a different language.

"What the fuck do you mean, I died? I'm right here. And why am I still strapped to this thing?"

All formalities apparently forgotten, he began aggressively spewing more questions, hyperventilating. As she went to calm him, Cade finally found his voice, interrupting Devin's spiraling.

"Devin," he said firmly, trying to get his attention, but Devin wouldn't settle.

Midway through his breakdown, Devin finally noticed the incisions in his chest and his panic doubled. "What the fuck?!" He was manically tugging at his restraints now.

Deianira understood his reaction. To him, he'd blacked out and woken up again only to be told that he'd died. It was a lot to take in. What was unexpected though was what she saw when she looked closer at his hands in the restraints. Squinting her eyes and focusing, she watched the threads on the leather straps begin to snap and fray. They were designed to hold people much stronger and much more powerful than Devin Jacobs, and they were on the verge of breaking. If he didn't calm down soon, he'd tear them apart.

"Devin!" Cade called again, bringing Deianira's attention back to him. "You're okay. You're fine," he said in a low voice.

And like a switch had been flipped, the rise and fall of Devin's chest began to slow and he nodded, looking to Deianira.

Eyes flicking back to Cade with suspicion, she studied him. She'd seen him do something similar with her sentinel but he'd seemed just as surprised as her. He obviously wasn't aware of whatever he'd done.

She shoved her thoughts away and resumed her conversation with Devin. "What is the last thing you remember?"

"All I remember is going back to the dorm and not feeling too good. Then I was here," he recounted.

Deianira watched his face. He was telling the truth but at the same time, it didn't make any sense. That couldn't have been it. She had read every file on each inmate before they were entered into the program and Devin didn't have any pre-existing medical conditions. As a precaution, the dorms were designed to dampen abilities, so it couldn't have been someone in the room either. But this didn't seem like an accident, people didn't just choke and die. Especially not the gifted.

Why Devin though? He certainly hadn't made any friends with his little arson act, but the homeowner was heavily compensated. He was a seer too, not usually the vengeful type.

Who would want him dead? And why?

Deianira pushed her mind for an explanation.

No one in the dorms could've used their gifts on him.

This was more discreet.

Something happened between the lunch hall and the dorms.

As a possible explanation came to mind, she asked, "Devin, what was the last thing you ate?"

He pondered over the question. "I can't remember. Whatever was for lunch today. I ate in the cafeteria just like everyone else."

Cade nodded, eyes constantly flicking between Deianira and Devin. "Yeah, I sat right next to him and we ate the exact same thing."

"And you don't have any allergies?" she asked just in case his file wasn't up to date.

He shook his head. "No, not that I know of."

Hands on her hips, Deianira bit her lip becoming agitated at her cluelessness.

What am I not seeing?

"Hey, erm, while you're thinking over there, can one of you get these off?" Devin asked, shaking his hands.

"No!" Deianira exclaimed at the same time that Cade stepped forward to remove them.

"Why not?" Devin whined.

"Because restoration isn't an exact science. There's no way to know if you're still you."

She was already concerned by what she'd seen with the restraints but she refrained from mentioning it, she didn't want to scare him any more.

He jolted his hands in the cuffs, annoyance rising again. "Well, I'm feeling perfectly normal."

"Good for you but that's not a risk I'm willing to take." she retorted, matching his tone.

"Can you at least loosen-"

"Wait! Just wait one second." Cade put his hands out as if to shush them.

On a normal day, Deianira would've scoffed at his nerve, but the past ten minutes had her shaken.

"The beer... I gave you my drink. I didn't touch it." Cade declared with his hands up.

Devin rolled his eyes. "So did at least twenty other people, genius." That had Deianira shushing *them* now.

Think!

They ate the same thing.

Multiple people drank the beer.

Cade gave his to Devin.

Deianira began to slowly pace from wall to wall. She had already erased the idea that Cade had tried to harm Devin so she knew that he hadn't tampered with the drink. But still, the only thing that set Devin apart from the others was that he drank from Cade's c-

"The cup," she whispered as she froze, eyes flicking around the room.

Cade's look of confusion reminded her that the others in the room weren't privy to her thoughts.

She attempted to steady her heart and explained. "Poison. If the cup was poisoned, it wouldn't matter what either of you had. Whoever drank from that cup would've been hit." She tilted her head to the side as she muttered under her breath. "It's quite smart actually." Despite the nature of the situation, she was still able to appreciate the thought that was put in. "You guys are lined up alphabetically, correct? It wouldn't have been hard to tamper with a specific cup if you knew where the person was positioned on the register."

When she briefly looked to Cade to see if he was catching on, she witnessed his confusion wash away as understanding lit up behind his eyes.

Now, it was only Devin who was confused. "Poison? Wait, why would someone try to kill me?" He looked genuinely offended. Just as he asked the question, he frowned with another one. "And how would anyone know that I would drink from Cade's cup?"

Cade, now caught up on Deianira's line of thought, met her eyes as he answered Devin's question.

"They didn't. It was meant for me," he said quietly, releasing a shuddery breath.

Chapter Fifteen

The door slid closed behind them, leaving Devin with Mikhael for a full examination.

Cade started to feel the gravity of the decisions he'd made tonight as his adrenaline plummeted.

Guilt over the fact that Devin had gotten hurt in the process of an attack on him warred with shock at the thought that someone wanted him dead.

He was glad that Devin was alive, especially because he wasn't the target of the attack, but he couldn't help but wonder if he'd only made matters worse. He thought back to the words Deianira had said before she restored Devin.

When they come back, they are never quite the same.

Had he made a mistake?

What would happen to Devin now?

What would happen to him now?

Whatever his punishment was, he'd take it. He meant what he'd said to Deianira now more than ever. If Devin hadn't come back and he found out about his connection to his death, Cade wouldn't have been able to forgive himself. If he had to die now because he chose to save Devin, he wouldn't object.

Remembering that he wasn't alone, he turned his head to look at Deianira, and what he found made his heart clench.

It was as if she wasn't there. Back still facing the door, she stared at the wall in front of her, breathing lightly. All remnants of the fierce woman he'd met only days ago were gone and replaced with a scared girl. The amount of guilt, fear, and regret coming off her was almost enough to choke Cade.

He knew that she didn't want to restore Devin. He knew but he asked her anyway and in the end, it might have been for nothing. He'd pressed her, uncaring of her warning or personal objections. Cade didn't know enough about azraels to know if the restoration process could have been costly for her. He'd seen how Lia's visions took a toll on her and the same might have been the case for Deianira, but he didn't think about that in the moment. He'd just pushed.

Cade had never felt worse than he did right now.

As he moved to stand in front of her, her eyes didn't stray from their position. She just stared at his chest as if she was looking right through him.

In an effort to bring her out of her daze, he brought his hand to her upper arm. At his touch, she flinched, eyes snapping to his, but Cade didn't startle. He wasn't afraid of her. He was afraid of what he might have done to her.

"I'm sorry," he said softly. "I'm sorry I asked you to do that."

"No, you're not," she whispered. "You have your friend now." She extricated her arm from Cade's hand and turned her face to discreetly wipe a tear from her eye, but he saw. "I'll be on my way." She didn't even look angry, just empty.

What have I done?

Cade obstructed her path when she tried to leave. "No. You said no, and I didn't listen. I'm sorry."

"Well it's done now," she said, narrowing her eyes. "Just keep an eye on him. Report to Hewn if he exhibits any strange behavior and I'll figure out the rest." Her words were hurried as she looked at everything in the hall but Cade.

He knew that she didn't want him to see her right now, but he couldn't quite let her go. Not like this.

Taking a risk, he gently gripped her chin and tilted her head up so that her eyes met his. He needed her to *hear* him.

"Earlier... Earlier I said some things. I wasn't in a good frame of mind, but I had no business judging you for your past because I'm here for a good reason too," he told her earnestly. "Even after that, you did this for him, so thank you. And I *am* sorry."

Cade was mildly aware that while he'd been speaking, his hand had moved from her chin to the side of her face in a gentle caress.

Deianira closed her eyes as a single tear traveled down her cheek. Leaning into his touch, she opened her mouth as if she was about to say something when the door slid back open.

Both of them quickly separated, breaking the moment as the warlock stepped out of the infirmary, hands clasped.

Mikhael looked between them suspiciously before speaking.

"Everything looks normal physically so I think it's best to release

him for now and schedule a follow-up. He healed rather quickly so that's a good sign, but please let me know if anything changes."
Cade let out a huge sigh of relief.
Devin was going to be okay.
But like a tide coming back to shore, he felt Deianira's icy exterior slip back into place.
Sighing, he looked down at his shoes. He knew that he wouldn't be seeing that side of Deianira again anytime soon or ever for that matter. The thought had him both relieved and disappointed. Cade never wanted to see her so defeated again, but it was the first time that she'd strayed from her usual cold demeanor.
"Thank you, Mikhael." She dismissed him in a neutral voice.
Once Mikhael was far enough down the hall, Cade stepped to go back into the room, suddenly desperate to be out of Deianira's presence, but just like he had done earlier, she blocked his path.
Out of nowhere, there was a blade at his throat. He hadn't even seen her grab it.
Cade almost shivered at her chilling tone when she spoke.
"Touch me again, and you will quickly learn how much harder life can be for a man with no hands." Deianira emphasized her threat by pressing the blade harder against his throat pulling a small groan from him.
Knowing he wouldn't achieve anything by arguing, Cade nodded like a child scolded.
"Get out of my sight," she hissed, lowering the blade.
As he brought a hand to his throat, pressing against the small cut, Cade wondered if he should inform her that he didn't know which way he was supposed to go.
A throat cleared to his right.

Hewn stood at the end of the hall, waiting with a pair of cuffs in his hand.

Walking down to Hewn, he spared a hopeful glance over his shoulder but Deianira was already gone.

Chapter Sixteen

Why did he have to come here?
Deianira felt as if she was being punished. As if the Gods were laughing at her. It had been decades since she'd even shed a tear but there she lay, staring up at her ceiling, crying. It had to be some sort of twisted joke sent from above that he of all people would be the one to break the dam.

She couldn't silence the battle in her mind as to whether she regretted what she'd just done or not. Devin was alive and she was glad for that but she might have introduced something way more sinister into Terra.

The past and present were blending into one. It started just like this the last time. Everything seemed fine, and then...

Deianira knew that she was spiraling but she couldn't do anything to stop it.

For some reason though, Cade saw that. The way he looked at her was past surface level. He saw her pain. Tried to assuage it. Not even

her own people, who she had killed for, could see past the cruel exterior, but Cade did. And then he went and touched her.
Why did he have to touch me?
Didn't he know that bad things happened when people got close? Innocent people.

Blood.
So much blood.
Eyes wide, blinking back into reality, Deianira stared at her red-stained hands, shaking from head to toe.
What have I done?
"What have you done?"
She whipped her head behind her to see her uncle, Jude, standing in the doorway, horrified.
The tears came instantaneously.
"I- I don't know. I- It was an-n accident."
"Oh, sweetie..." *He walked briskly to her and swept her up in his arms, cradling her head.*
"I'm sorry, I'm sorry, I'm sorry..."
"I know, it's not your fault."
But it was her fault.
Her eyes caught little Calliope's still body on the floor of their parents' bedroom. She was only six. Next to her lay their parents, their faces unrecognizable.
So much blood.
Deianira cried even harder into Jude's shoulder.
She didn't mean to do it. She just lost control.
"Settle, settle. It's okay." *Jude swayed with her in his arms.*

Walking her out of the room and into his office, he set her down on his desk. Reluctantly she removed her hands from around his neck so that he could take a step back.

"Sweetheart, it wasn't your fault. You didn't do it on purpose."

Deianira nodded emphatically, wishing that it was true, as her legs dangled above the floor.

"I know this is the last thing you want to hear, but things are going to change now and there are going to be a lot of people depending on you. If you are going to do right by them, you have to be strong, okay? I'll be there with you every step of the way, but this is on you now," he told her sternly.

"The Dome is yours."

Aggressively wiping her eyes, she hiccupped. "Ok."

And then began her reign.

A sharp pain in the back of her head brought her from her distressing memory.

Just thinking about it gave her a headache.

Was she really fit to rule if she couldn't even control her own emotions?

Hadrick.

That name played on her mind in an endless loop.

Those faces. Those lives destroyed.

It was all too much.

Deianira brought a hand to her cheek, remembering Cade's touch.

He touched me.

It shouldn't have been, but it was comforting, soothing even. Something that she hadn't felt in a very long time. The kind of comfort that she couldn't even get from fighting or killing. It was strange. But it didn't feel wrong.

She had been seconds away from crumbling when Mikhael interrupted them.

What would've happened if he didn't?

Chapter Seventeen

Lia set down the last log.

"Here." She waited for Cassian to look up and tossed him the lighter. "Set up camp. I'm gonna go see if I can scrounge up something to go with dinner."

Cassian flicked the lighter on and off and rolled it in his palm. "How long will you be?" he asked quietly.

"Scared?" Lia asked dryly.

He rolled his eyes. "Actually, I need to take a piss and didn't want to leave the fire unattended, but go ahead, make fun," he retorted, giving her a sarcastic, tight-lipped smile.

Lia huffed at his grumbling. "I'll be back in twenty if I don't find anything." She pointed at the stack of wood. "Nothing too big, okay? Don't wanna draw attention."

At Cassian's affirmative grunt, she was on her way through the trees.

Over the few days that they had been traveling, their dynamic had shifted slightly. Lia was still far from willing to see him in a positive light, but he had been surprisingly useful.

Despite growing up in the same home, he was so different from Cade. On the rare occasions that she managed to drag him out to hunt with her, their trips mostly consisted of walking, watching, and waiting. But they liked it that way. They didn't need words.

That was a huge contrast from Cassian. She didn't know if he was trying to reach out to her or if he was just genuinely curious, but it seemed like he was asking a question every two seconds. What kind of animals you could find at what time of day and where, how to prepare the meat, how to know if a fruit was safe for foraging.

Though it was mildly irritating, she answered his questions each time. It reminded her of his age. He seemed so much older when working with his father, but out in the wild, his youthfulness came out in small bursts.

A twig snapping in the distance had Lia freezing.

Behind.

By the sound of it, it wasn't a small animal. She needed to be gone as soon as possible. Carefully though.

Lia didn't even breathe as she waited for another noise or some indication that she still wasn't alone.

"What do we have here?"

She closed her eyes for a second, dread filling her.

Not an animal.

Lia turned quickly to see a large man a few trees away, donned in animal furs, hair hanging over his shoulder in a long braid.

A deep chuckle to her left revealed two more of similar stature with the same braid.

Shit.

Inbetweeners.

She had never had a run-in with an inbetweener before but everyone who'd grown up on the outside knew of them. They were common in each sector but usually stuck to the outer borders. Inbetween.

Lia quickly scanned her surroundings, searching for a way out. She was normally prepared for any situation she might encounter in the forest but she'd been caught off guard. She was usually smarter than this.

Absently, she remembered that she left her bow and arrow in her bag back where Cassian was setting up camp. She'd only planned to pick some fruit, she didn't think she'd need it.

Big mistake.

Her only other weapon was a small blade in her boot, but she couldn't reach for it without them seeing. She didn't think she could outrun them either.

"What are you doing out here all alone?" The second man grinned widely revealing a missing tooth.

She stifled a shiver. Everyone knew the kind of barbaric acts the inbetweeners practiced. They were primitive and didn't listen to reason so if Lia was going to make it out unharmed, she needed to be smart about this.

Getting an idea, she plastered a sugary sweet smile on her face. "Oh, hi." She waved at him, angling her body to keep them all in her sight.

"Hey, sweetheart," he smiled back ravenously. "Where are you off to?"

She tucked a loose curl behind her ear, shrugging. "My husband and I are on our way to the northern sector."

Much to her annoyance, an inbetweener was more likely to leave her alone if they thought that she was with another man than if she was holding a blade to his throat. She wanted to curse at the stupidity of that logic, but at the moment, she was more concerned about getting far, far away.

"I don't see no husband," the first man grunted, taking a step forward.

Lia took a step back to mirror him.

Ugh. She just needed to grab her knife.

Her smile stayed in place despite her rising anxiety. "He's just off grabbing something for dinner. I would have gone with him but dead animals just make me squeamish." She didn't need to fake her giggle. The thought that she would be put off by something she did every day was laughable. That was the whole reason she was out here alone.

"Is that so?" The third man piped up.

They were advancing on her slowly and she was running out of time.

My knife.

If she was quick enough, maybe she could-

"Babe, I told you to stay put."

Lia could have cried from relief as Cassian stepped out from the brush, a dark expression on his face.

The men all paused their advance and eyed him warily. "She yours?" The first man gestured at Lia, watching Cassian closely.

"Yeah, she is, so fuck off," he barked, stepping up close to Lia, subtly keeping his back to hers so that all sides were covered.

"Of course, brother," One of them said, cocking his head to the side. "You might want to keep her on a tighter leash. The forest can be a dangerous place."

Lia was stuck between rolling her eyes and launching her dagger at the idiot who'd spoken. They were the ones that accosted her.

Cassian, however, looked like a kettle about to boil over.

He wrapped his hand around her upper arm. "I'll keep that in mind," he bit out with finality.

"Not so fast," The man started and the hair on Lia's neck instantly rose.

The second man grunted his assent.

"What do you want?" Cassian asked, irritated.

Lia stifled a glare in his direction. He shouldn't have asked that.

The man stepped a little closer. "Well, we kept an eye on her for you while you were gone. You could at least pay us back. You know, for the trouble." The smirk he gave them made Lia's stomach churn.

Cassian sighed beside her. "We don't have any money."

He didn't understand.

"We don't want your money, brother," The first said with a subtle smile. He looked Lia up and down. "I must say, your wife is quite beautiful."

Lia's gut was sinking. She'd overestimated the protection that Cassian's presence gave her. He was a man, but he was young, and these men could see that. Besides, they were outnumbered.

It seemed that Cassian had finally caught up as his grip on Lia's arm tightened.

"No!" he said loudly, eyes flicking from one man to the next. "We're leaving."

The one behind her cackled. "What, your mother never taught you to share?" he laughed as he stepped closer.

Lia chose that moment to yank her arm out of Cassian's grip.

Bending her right leg back to snag her knife from her boot, she spun and brandished the blade in his direction.

"Step. Back." she said through clenched teeth.

The man's smile only grew as he raised his hands in mock surrender. "Not so timid after all. Not a problem, I like that."

As the men grew closer, Lia was running out of ideas when she heard a clear click.

Cassian's voice was calm and cold. "I said. We're leaving." he repeated as he pointed a gun at the man in front while keeping his eye on the second.

Lia had no idea where he had gotten it from but she wasn't about to look a gift horse in the mouth.

"Woah…" The man on the other side of the gun retreated several steps. "We're not looking for any trouble."

"Yeah, sure as hell looks like it," Cassian snapped. "Go."

Apparently, they weren't moving fast enough for him as they slowly shuffled back because he raised his arm and sent a bullet into the tree behind the first man. At that, they all startled and took off in different directions.

When they had put enough distance between them, Lia felt like she could finally breathe again.

As soon as they were out of sight, she turned to Cassian. "Thanks," she mumbled. She didn't have to like him but she wasn't too prideful to recognize that he'd done her a solid.

Cassian's eyes flitted to hers before he looked back out to the trees. "Don't thank me," he muttered. "Sorry I took so long."

"It's fine," she said quietly. Looking down at his hand, she asked "Where did you get that?"

He looked down at his gun. "I snuck into my dad's study and took it when I was packing. Figured it might come in handy." He met her eyes again. "It did."

After walking for another hour, Lia and Cassian managed to find a new spot to set up camp. As she sat opposite him in front of the fire, she thought about how much worse tonight could've gone. If it hadn't been for him, she would've-

No. She wasn't going to think about it. She was just grateful that she wouldn't find out.

Pushing those dark thoughts away, she ripped into the pigeon that she had managed to catch. It was skinny and dry but after half a day of trekking, a hot meal was a hot meal.

"I'm sorry."

At the quiet voice, Lia looked up to see Cassian staring into the fire.

"For what?" she asked, though she had an idea.

"Everything."

He paused for a second before continuing.

"I didn't know he would do that for me. At the lodge," he said, releasing a pained breath. "I was scared and I didn't want to step forward but I didn't know that he would." Cassian let his head fall. "I know it makes me a really shitty brother to admit this but I'm not sure if I would've been able to do the same thing if he was in my position."

Lia let his words sink in for a moment. It didn't make him a shitty brother. It made him a child. He was a child in a sense. Not many people could have done what Cade had but that's what made him Cade.

"He talks about you a lot, you know."

Cassian met her eyes as he blinked rapidly.

"He never hated you even though he had every reason to." She thought her words might be cruel, but he needed to hear them. "Most of the time, he was scared shitless that your father would get bored because he left and start on you. "

He averted his eyes and sniffed. "I think I hated him a little bit for that. For leaving. I can't honestly say that I was a good brother to him when he was at home but I was so angry that he left. That he could get up and leave when I couldn't even tell my father 'no'. He was a lot stronger than me."

"*Is*." Lia corrected him.

"Hmm?"

"You said 'was'. He's still alive, Cassian, and you still have time to make things right. He deserves the apology, not me."

"Yeah," he whispered.

To Lia's surprise, she found herself wanting to comfort him, to offer him some peace. She wanted to stay mad at him but it was so obvious that he was hurting.

"You're not weak."

She paused trying to order her words. "Your father's a bastard, but he's smart. He pitted you two against each other your whole lives and it only worked on you because of your age." Cassian was looking at her now but she could tell that he still didn't understand. She sighed and continued. "What he did to Cade physically, he did to you emotionally. You were both in pain, just in a different way, so you thought the other had it easier when you were hurting just as much." Lia looked up and watched the sky for several moments. "I'm not going to sit here and tell you that none of what happened to Cade is your fault because you are responsible. But you deserved better. Both of you."

After a few moments of silence, she figured he might want some space so she tossed her scraps onto the ground and dusted her hands, coming to a stand. "Get some sleep. I'll take first watch," she said softly.

Chapter Eighteen

Cade and Devin circled each other as the inmates cheered and clapped.

Over the last few days, Cade had made sure to stay close to Devin, watching out for any sign of abnormal behavior, but as far as he could tell, he was his regular self. To be sure though, he hadn't left his side much and even found himself lying awake some nights, staring up at the bunk above him, wondering if Devin might switch. Deep down, he felt guilty to admit that he didn't hate the idea of Devin acting out of character if it meant that he might have a chance to report back to Deianira. To just talk to her. He didn't like how things were left the last time they spoke and he feared that even if he could speak to her, there wouldn't be much he could do to earn her favor.

Cade considered the current dilemma a good distraction from what he'd recently learned too. He hadn't been in The Dome for long and didn't think that he'd made any serious enemies so when he wasn't keeping an eye on Devin, he was racking his mind, trying to work out who would want him dead. He briefly thought that Crew might have had something to do with it but quickly erased the thought. Crew was showy and arrogant. Poison didn't seem like his touch.

It also had to have been someone with the credentials to have access to the kitchen. A warlock perhaps? Their range of abilities was the widest and alchemy wasn't uncommon in their skillset. They could not only create various elixirs, but they could turn something seemingly harmless into something dangerous.

There were too many possibilities and Cade knew that there was no way he could figure it out on his own, so he focused his attention on current matters.

"Can't we just sit this one out? We all know you're just gonna drop my ass," Devin whined, fists up.

This morning, the inmates were escorted to the training gym for an indoor drill. The first lesson was disarming.

Cade found the activity quite difficult. Due to his size, he wasn't as fast as Devin so his moves were easier to predict and more conspicuous. Devin, on the other hand, breezed through the exercise. He was quick, fast thinking, and surprisingly agile.

Sparring, however, was Cade's forte. In the short time that he had been in the training program, he had excelled in that area. He wasn't necessarily timid when he lived on the outside, but since his training began, he had changed. After years and years of taking hits, he was finally able to give it back in an environment where he was encouraged to. And he loved it. The adrenaline high, the calculation, even the pain.

Given how well he was doing in the program, Cade was advised to pick a partner on his own skill level but he insisted on sparring with Devin. It wasn't just because he needed to keep him close for the time being, Devin was his friend and he enjoyed training with him.

"Nope. Practice makes perfect, kid." Cade shifted his weight to and from his front leg.

Devin rolled his eyes. "You only picked me to boost your ego. You should be ashamed of yourself," Devin quipped as he feigned annoyance. "And don't call me kid. It makes you sound old."

Cade smiled, shaking his head.

Hewn stood off to the side of the square with his hand up. Silence fell upon the room. Raising his hand slightly before slicing it down through the air, he yelled, "Go!"

Hoping to catch Devin off guard, Cade quickly advanced on him, aiming to disable his left leg. To his surprise, Devin pivoted and sidestepped his advance, simultaneously elbowing him in the side.

Nice one, Cade thought proudly. He'd taught him that.

Instincts kicking in, Cade dove for the ground into a roll to save his fall. Quickly getting to his feet, he attempted to right his stance but by the time he looked up, Devin was already there.

Cade swerved the arm he threw out, grabbing it and twisting himself around so that his back was to Devin's front. Cade lowered his hips and bent forward in an attempt to flip him.

But then, Devin was gone. The arm Cade was holding disappeared. After grabbing at the air behind him, utterly dumbfounded, he quickly spun in a circle looking at the other inmates with the same expression of shock on his face. But no Devin.

In the next second, Devin reappeared out of the air and Cade didn't even have time to startle as Devin's arms locked onto his shoulders and pulled down, bringing his knee to Cade's gut.

Doubled over and trying to comprehend what was happening, Cade's face was quickly met with Devin's fist.

Fuck, that hurt.

Devin wasn't pulling his punches. So, Cade didn't either.

Taking advantage of Devin's position, he got up on one knee and used his hand to drag Devin's right leg from beneath him, sending him flat on his back. Before he could advance on him again though, Devin rolled out from beneath him.

Damn, he's quick.

Kicking up while pushing off of his hands, Devin sprung up and landed on Cade's right. Cade only had time to get to his feet before Devin was on him again.

Still reeling from the speed of Devin's recovery, all Cade could do was deflect as Devin sent a spinning kick to the side of his head. That one caught his arm pulling a grunt out of Cade, but he pushed the pain down as Devin sent another. Then a fist.

Cade knew that he was fast, but not this fast. His moves were all in quick succession to one another, barely giving Cade time to take a breath.

Contrary to his actions, Devin's face was a show of serenity. His moves were effortless, his face was impassive, calm as if he was exerting no energy while Cade was heaving, struggling to keep up. Arms up to cover his face, Cade kept shuffling back in defense of the onslaught.

The aim of the activity was to get your opponent to tap out or step outside of the square. They were a long way out of the lines but Devin kept on. If Cade kept backing up, he'd soon run into the wall. That was enough. "Devin!" he called as he brought an arm up to block Devin's left hook.

But Devin didn't stop. He sped up.

He jumped several feet in the air to kick Cade but ended up kneeing his shoulder. Cade had to drop a hand to clutch his shoulder as he felt his muscle pulse.

"Devin, enough!" Cade panted before Devin sent a fist into his cheek. He wasn't given even a moment of reprieve but Devin didn't even seem to break a sweat. Cade noticed then that all the shouts and cheers around them had stopped. He didn't know whether they were impressed or as scared as him.

As Devin threw his hand out again, a stinging sensation brushed the side of Cade's face. Taking his eyes off Devin for only a second to investigate, he was greeted by a burst of flames shooting past his head. His wide eyes whipped back to Devin and noticed something different about him. His eyes. They were orange.

Glowing orange.

What the -

"JACOBS!" Cade heard from the other side of the room just as his back hit the wall.

There stood Officer Hewn, gun pointed at Devin.

Finally, the attack stopped.

Thank the Gods.

Devin blinked a few times, shook his head, and blinked again. Looking around the room, he only then appeared to notice that all eyes were on him. Some with horror, some with awe.

Looking at Cade, his face fell. "Shit. I'm so sorry. I got carried away." If he were anyone else, Cade would have thought he was lying but he didn't need to read Devin to know that it wasn't on purpose.

The restoration.

Hewn held his gun steady. "You are out of line. This was supposed to be a clean fight. No abilities! Take the bench!"

Devin cast his eyes to the ground, embarrassed, as he made his way to the bench and activity gradually started to resume.

Flicking his eyes to Hewn, Cade gave him a subtle nod, indicating that he was okay.

After catching his breath, he went over to the bench and sat next to Devin, taking a swig of water.

Touching the left side of his face, he winced at the sting. At Devin's apologetic look, he tried to assuage his guilt.

"I'm okay. Don't worry about it," he said. And he meant it.

"I don't know what happened. I swear I didn't mean to go at you like that," Devin sputtered.

Cade shook his head. "I know. Seriously, it's fine. Only a scratch," Devin nodded, his eyes returning to the ground.

"Last week he couldn't throw a punch without sending himself spinning to the ground. The moves he used, he'd merely seen and he replicated them flawlessly. And that was before the fire show. His file says he wasn't schooled in magic but if I hadn't stopped him, he would've grilled Alden," Hewn explained but something about his tone suggested that he was more impressed than anything.

Deianira didn't look at anyone in the room. She knew that if she lifted her head, she would be met with Jude's look of disapproval. She already knew this was her fault and didn't need him reminding her.

"Is he exhibiting any behavioral abnormalities or was it just the combat training?" she asked, head down.

"Just the combat training? You speak as if that isn't reason enough to-"

Deianira's sharp glare had Jude shutting up. She turned back to Hewn for his response.

"Not that I've seen," Hewn told her.

Salem chose that moment to speak up. "Perhaps it's not a change in his personality. It could've just been a response to overstimulation." She looked over to Hewn. "You said he doesn't usually perform well in combat training. Maybe it was an instinctive response? Self-preservation?"

Hewn nodded his agreement.

"And what of the other one?"

Deianira finally looked at Jude. She knew who he was talking about. Without thinking to dial back her defensiveness, she spoke up before Hewn could. "This has nothing to do with him."

"Oh, I think it has everything to do with him. There is a reason restoration isn't practiced anymore. It is dangerous and reckless-"

A biting pain on the side of her head had Deianira clasping her temples. It was just like the one she'd felt the other day. She tried to breathe through it but the pain only increased, and apparently no one else in the room had noticed because Jude continued his rant.

"-you have no idea what he could do. Disturbing the balance is-"

"I know, fuck!" she yelled, her hands running through her hair. "I know," she repeated under her breath, blinking rapidly as her vision began to blur. She could feel her heartbeat in her head.

After a beat of silence, Jude met Deianira's eyes. "Hewn, can you give us a second, please?"

Hewn nodded and left the room.

As the bite gradually faded to a sting, Deianira took a deep breath, thankful for the ease. She was the overstimulated one.

Salem spoke quietly to Deianira. It was her way of being gentle when she feared her words may be blunt. "Whether it was the right thing to do or not, there's nothing we can do about it except damage control. We will limit his training to less tasking activities and take him out of the dorms. That way, we can observe him in a controlled environment and simultaneously hone his more intellectual abilities. I'll arrange for him to have a tutor and upon release, he'll be given a less daunting position. He's smart, perhaps in defense administration."

See? Pragmatic.

"You don't think that isolating him would only make matters worse? Given the wrong circumstances, anything can happen," Jude argued.

"And what would you suggest I do?" Deianira retorted.

"What you have to do. What you have always done. Cut the problem at the root-"

"No," she responded before he could finish his sentence.

"Deianira," Jude's tone was slightly less aggressive now, more reasoning. "He's a bomb waiting to go off. Whether he's in the dorms or miles away, he's still a threat." He shot Salem a disapproving look when he said, "Tutoring him would only mean that when he does flip, which he will, he'll be harder to contain. Smarter. We'd be aiding our own downfall."

Deianira thought for a moment. What Jude had said held some truth. If her actions created a problem for The Dome, she wouldn't be able to live with herself. But at the same time, a small part of her felt that this might be a good thing. Devin's shift could make him a major asset.

Her sentinel took the seat beside her, eyeing her. "Deianira, plenty of people have lived and died in your lifetime and you've never toyed with the balance of nature. What is the real reason you restored Jacobs?"

She had a feeling Salem already knew the answer, but she wasn't going to validate her suspicions, so she pulled rank.

"Taboo as it may be, I acted within the law," she said as evenly as she could, rising from her seat. "I am your Queen before I am your friend and I don't need to explain my motives to either of you." She took a step back from the table. "You shouldn't make a habit of questioning me. It hasn't worked out well for others."

Deianira felt a slight tug of guilt for the last thing she said. She may have been angry, but threatening her council wasn't something she usually did or thought to be acceptable. She just needed space. A second to breathe.

Sparing them a final glance, Deianira stepped around the table and left the room.

Chapter Nineteen

"If you are here, you have already taken the gun safety course, but I will go over the rules one more time. Rule number one: Do *not* aim at anything that you do not wish to shoot at! Rubber bullets can be just as dangerous as real ones and relying on the safety is not good enough." Finch explained as he walked behind the line of inmates. "Rule number two: One shot at a time! These are not automatic weapons so don't treat them like they are. You shoot, you step back, and wait to check your target. Rule number three: Do *not* rest your finger on the trigger! You'd be surprised at how easy it is for your hand to slip. Rule number four: Keep your hands away from the barrel if you want to keep your fingers! That sounds like common sense, but considering you're all here, it's evidently not that common."

Cade wasn't Finch's biggest fan. He hadn't done anything to him specifically but his attitude often rubbed Cade the wrong way. It wasn't as if Hewn was a ray of sunshine but Cade would've preferred for him to supervise the drill.

Devin's absence didn't help much either. By now, he would've made a funny comment or crack about Finch, lightening the air, but he had to sit this one out.

"Last but not least, rule number five: This is not a game, this is a drill. You will be assessed on this course so if you like, don't take it seriously, but I can assure you that there will be a desk job calling your name at the end of your training."

Cade had never shot a gun before, never even held one. Despite growing up in a house full of them, he'd never understood the appeal. He could understand that they were useful at times but they weren't a commodity to him like they were to his father.

He stood, feet shoulder-width apart, and eyed his target. Even though the figure was made out of cardboard, shooting at something that represented a person didn't sit right with him but he reminded himself that it was just a drill.

"These are already loaded so the rules apply the second it touches your hand," Finch projected as three enforcers moved along the line, handing a pistol to each inmate.

Cade weighed the gun in his hand as the others fiddled with theirs, laughing and messing around quietly. It was heavier than he expected.

"Okay, shut up! Team A! Take your position!"

Cade moved his right foot back and his left a little forward.

"Aim!"

He narrowed his eyes on the target and lifted his gun with both hands, arms extended.

They hadn't been told what to aim for, but they were supposed to try and make it a kill shot.

"Fire!"

Four shots went off relatively close to each other. Not Cade's though. He waited an extra second. He needed to be precise.
BANG!
Cade flinched at the pushback of the small weapon.
Lowering the pistol, he stepped back and assessed his shot.
Headshot.
Despite his feeling towards guns in general, he allowed himself a small bit of pride over his accuracy. Sure, the target was ten meters away, at most, but it was his first attempt.
"Interesting choice, Alden." Cade didn't know what Finch meant until he looked at the others' targets.
Everyone else had aimed for the chest, some slightly off.
Cade nodded his thanks to him.
Finch's thoughtful expression changed to a more threatening one.
"But when I say fire, you fire, outsider!" he hissed quietly.
Okay, then.
"Sir, yes, sir," Cade blurted sarcastically before he could stop himself. He didn't know where that came from but Finch was really starting to aggravate him.
Finch's eyes narrowed and his head tilted up at Cade. He looked like was about to say something before he stopped himself, offering Cade a smirk instead.
"Team B!" Finch yelled in his face.
Cade thought it might have been an attempt to startle him, to make him flinch. He did neither.
He made his way back to the sidelines.
As he waited for his group's next turn, he let his mind drift back to home. Being around all these weapons reminded him of how he'd landed himself in The Dome in the first place. He briefly thought of

how Cassian might have fared in the program. Cassian was smart. Not necessarily in the conventional sense but he was calculated. Cade thought that he would've excelled in an environment like this. That didn't mean that Cade would've changed anything if he could go back in time.

Cassian was actually guilty, he wouldn't have made it into the program like Cade did-

BANG!

Despite the bullet having already embedded itself in the wooden wall behind him, Cade still ducked.

What the hell?

He brought his arms down and looked back toward the line-up. Crew stood at his post, facing him, a cruel smirk dancing across his lips.

'Oops,' he mouthed.

Cade's lips were parted in shock.

Any lower and Crew would've shot him right in the face. Cade whipped his head toward Finch hoping to see the same look of outrage that he'd given him. He shouldn't have been surprised by what he saw.

Finch stood, his side facing Cade with the same smirk on his face as he looked out into the distance. He wasn't looking at Cade but he wasn't trying to hide his amusement either. He didn't even call Crew out.

Regardless of the rage brewing in Cade, he knew that he would achieve nothing by making his disapproval known. So he did what he'd always done when something irked him.

Nothing.

That didn't stop his gaze from assessing Finch with new eyes though.

What is his problem?

Chapter Twenty

As footsteps sounded behind her in the training room, Deianira steadied the punching bag without looking back. "I don't want to fight right now, Jude."

"That's good," he said. "Because I didn't come here to fight."

Deianira was thankful for that. She wasn't sure how much longer she could keep her head if she had to get into it with him again.

He continued as she started unwrapping her hands.

"You know that I only want what's best for you, right?"

Despite her annoyance, she nodded.

"I wasn't trying to condemn you. I only want you to be prepared for what people might say if this got out. You've led these people successfully for over a century and I would hate for anything to make them question you."

Deianira turned to her uncle then caved. "I know. There's just a lot going on right now and I can't change the past."

She felt like her mind was constantly on overdrive. They were still no closer to working out who had made an attempt on Cade. Devin's condition was becoming more obvious, a problem she wasn't sure would remain a secret for much longer. On top of that, the Prima Ball was only weeks away and while she was usually able to plan it around her duties, the load was growing heavier. It was becoming physically tasking.

Jude looked at her affectionately. "You just need to learn to delegate. You don't have to do everything yourself. Salem can take point on the issue with Devin and I'll handle the ball. It'll all be fine."

That was exactly what she needed. A break.

Deianira also silently reminded herself to visit Mikhael. The headaches had been getting more intense. Being gifted meant that she had almost perfect health. In her long life, she'd never even had so much as a cold so whatever was causing the headaches had to be serious.

"Thank you," she sighed appreciatively.

"I love you too, sweetheart."

Chapter Twenty-One

Cassian's legs were growing tired, but he didn't complain. Eulalia was powering on in front of him and he didn't want to give her an excuse to chide him. They'd been walking for over a week now and while they hadn't had any more run-ins, the journey was beginning to take a toll.

"You sound like an overused engine," Eulalia called behind her.

So maybe he wasn't being as discreet as he thought he was.

"Excuse me for being human," he said under his breath. "Not everyone is gifted and has unlimited strength." The journey was making him tired and irritable.

"Not unlimited. Enhanced," she replied as she kept walking.

Of course, she heard.

"And it's not like we're running, you shouldn't be this-" She abruptly cut herself off and stopped in her tracks.

He looked around for the source of her distraction before nervously asking, "What?"

"I just thought of something," she said distantly. "How are we gonna get in? It's not like we can just knock on a door. We can't even get past the exterior border without being ambushed."

Cassian sighed and rolled his eyes. "You're only thinking about that now?"

Eulalia turned to him. "Well... yeah. I'm still going, we just need a plan."

Cassian shook his head and walked ahead of her. "So if I wasn't with you that night, you would've just waltzed up to The Dome with no idea how you were going to get in."

Eulalia started again to catch up with him. "I would've thought of something. I'm not just some impulsive idiot."

Cassian threw a look over his shoulder. "I already have a plan. You're welcome."

Purposely not expanding, he allowed himself a small smirk when he heard her grumble behind him. "Care to share?"

He wanted to gloat but decided to put her out of her misery. "We're not knocking on any doors. I've been memorizing their trading routes for months." His thoughts momentarily darkened as he remembered why he had learned those routes but pushing them down, he continued. "In twenty hours, there will be a trading stop a mile west of the northern border. We're hitchhiking."

Eulalia snorted. "Okay, Cassian. We're gonna walk up to the nice officials and ask them for a ride into The Dome."

"I never said they would know we're catching a ride."

She huffed. "Alright, but where are we gonna hide? They're traders, it would only take them opening the trunk to find us."

"We're getting on after the stop. Blockade." He'd done it a hundred times but he left that part out. He wasn't so proud of it anymore.

"They'll get out to remove it and we can hop on. Hide behind the merchandise. It's their last stop too so it'd only take a day to get into The Dome."

Eulalia thought about it. "Okay, I'll admit, that's a good plan. But, what do we do once we're in? They'll arrest us the second they unload."

At that Cassian turned to her. "I can't do everything. I got us a way in. You figure out the rest."

He expected a comment dripping with sarcasm but she only watched him for a while, then nodded.

Chapter Twenty-Two

He wanted to see her. He really wanted to see her.

Cade wasn't vain enough to think that she was avoiding him in particular, but it had been days since he'd seen her face and he didn't like it. Their interactions so far had been far from pleasant but there was this pull. This urge to be around her. He didn't know why but her absence left him feeling edgy so when she walked into the training room this morning, he thought that the Gods had decided to let up on him for the first time in forever.

Gods, she's beautiful.

She didn't walk in gracefully. No, her strides exuded power and confidence.

Cade wasn't expecting her to search for his eyes, but that didn't stop the stab of disappointment he was hit with when she moved to stand next to Hewn without so much as a glance in his direction.

Hands on her hips, Deianira surveyed the inmates on the dead hang. Occasionally she whispered to Hewn, who corresponded with her and noted down the time when each inmate dropped from the bar.

She was in her usual practical outfit, her hair gathered in a tight ponytail. It swished and swayed each time she nodded or turned to Hewn and Cade was caught off guard by an image of himself running his fingers through it. Wrapping his hand around it and giving it a firm tug at the root. Deianira, mouth open, gazing up at him with those eyes. His-

Cade's perusal was interrupted by Hewn's booming voice.

"Okay! Whitlock, Bennet, Dalton, and Alden. You're up!"

Cade flinched and stood up from the bench, quickly walking to the bars.

Picking the bar on the end, he stepped up onto his box and wiped his hands on his pants before gripping the cool metal. He looked at Deianira again but it seemed like she was looking everywhere but him.

Maybe she *was* avoiding him.

At Hewn's whistle, the enforcers behind each bar stand removed the boxes leaving the four of them hanging from the bars and Finch started his stopwatch.

The aim was endurance. Though it wasn't a competition, there would often be a shout or 'whoop' at the sidelines from inmates cheering on their friends, but with Devin being excluded from this session, there was nobody cheering for Cade.

He stifled a snort. He knew, without a doubt, that Devin would've been there making a fool of himself, screaming at the top of his lungs for him.

He hadn't realized how much time he spent with Devin until they were separated when he would be restricted from certain training exercises. The solitude made him miserable.

Cade was still sore from his altercation with Devin so that didn't help his endurance on the bar. He didn't let that deter him though. He'd learned a long time ago that no one would make excuses for him, so he didn't either.

First, Ty Dalton, a friend of Crew's, dropped from his bar.

Thank the Gods.

Cade really didn't want to be the first to drop and his arms were beginning to ache.

Chancing a look at Deianira, he was surprised to find her finally staring back at him. In that same second, the ache disappeared. So did everyone in the room. It was just him and her. His chest warmed at the small crumb of attention she had given him and the burst of energy only spurred him on.

Grip tightening on the bar, he let her eyes hold his captive as Whitlock dropped.

It was like she was speaking to him without words. Telling him to stay on just a little longer. So he did.

That ache reared its head again but Cade held steady. It was only him and Crew left and though he wasn't the egotistical type, he didn't want to drop before Crew of all people. Especially with Deianira watching him.

Cade's grip on the bar began to loosen as his wrists screamed for reprieve. He began wondering if the pain was worth the win and considered dropping when he caught Deianira's almost imperceptible head shake.

Not yet, her eyes said. *Hold on.*

He might have been seeing things but apparently, it was motivation enough because Cade held on even as he felt his muscles burning strenuously.

Seconds later, Crew dropped.

Cade held on for one moment more for good measure, then dropped. Panting, hands on his knees, he looked up to see Hewn give him a respectful nod as he noted his time and was instantly filled with pride.

No one cheered. No one said anything. But he didn't care. It wasn't *their* validation he was seeking.

Looking at Deianira, he could've sworn he saw a hint of a smile on her lips. His face lit up with a genuine grin and he set his mind to walk over to her. He didn't get the chance though because as a high-pitched voice came from behind him, Deianira's expression straightened and Cade felt as if a bucket of ice had been poured over him.

"Cade!"

Octavia.

Evidently, the Gods weren't that generous.

Though everything in his body told him to ignore her, Cade turned around out of politeness, but didn't bother to give her a pleasant smile.

She motioned for him to come over but before moving, he looked back at Deianira to find her talking to Hewn again, no longer paying attention to him. Despite the ugly feeling that washed over him, he followed Octavia out into the hallway.

Once outside the door, she turned to him with a sultry smile.

"Hey, how's everything going?"

"Good," he responded, but his eyes were straying back into the training room, trying to catch Deianira's.

"Great. Well, I heard what happened with Devin and I was going to be passing through here anyway, so I saved my dad the trip. Do you want to head to the infirm-"

"I'm good."

Deianira still wasn't looking at him.

Look at me.

"Oh." She seemed surprised. "Are you sure? Because I have time."

"I'm sure. All good." He gave her a fake smile and a nod before moving his gaze back into the room.

She nodded, eyes downcast. "Okay well if you change your mind, you know where to find m-"

"Sure." He was already walking back into the training room.

At the entrance, he took a quick scan of the room.

Deianira was gone.

Cade wasn't sure why, but he felt like he'd done something wrong. He briefly remembered the way she had reacted after his first meeting with Octavia and if she felt anything close to that right now, he was in trouble.

Stepping back into the hallway, he looked left, then right, and saw a familiar shadow turning around the corner. Quickly looking back into the room to see if Hewn was paying attention, Cade saw that he was watching the next group.

Taking the opportunity, he jogged down the hall in the direction of her retreating figure.

Deianira had been avoiding him. She'd skipped her observations and even stayed in her room during the program's transition periods. It wasn't his presence that caused trouble, it was the way she felt when she was near him. There was too much on her mind right now and she didn't need Cade Alden adding to it.

During her visit with Mikhael, he'd told her that her headaches were due to stress and she was offered some pain relief. That alone should've told her to stay away from Cade, but she soon found herself seeking him out despite all the reasons not to.

In her many years, she'd never been drawn to someone like she was to him. She'd never found it so hard to keep someone at a distance. Deianira had done her best to avert her eyes, but watching him on the bar in the gym set her on fire. The way the muscles in his arms bulged under the strain, the way his veins popped from under his skin, the way a few sweaty locks of hair fell from his tie. She couldn't look away.

She had been quietly rooting for him and couldn't help the wave of pride she felt when he held out.

He'd been in the program for the shortest amount of time but he was already outperforming his peers. She'd been paying particular attention to his stats during Hewn's weekly updates on the trainees and was beyond impressed. But seeing him in person was a whole other type of high.

Then Octavia walked in. Despite her annoyance at what might have been happening in the hallway, she was glad for the interruption. It put things into perspective. These weren't feelings she should have been having toward him. It was inappropriate. She was the queen, not some civilian who could afford to be lusting after a man, a criminal at that. Not like Octavia.

Having seen enough, Deianira nodded her goodbye to Hewn and quickly left the room, not looking in Cade's direction.

She had just turned the corner when she heard a baritone rumble behind her.

"Deianira."

She knew that she shouldn't have stopped, but hearing her name from his mouth did something to her. There were only two people who had called her that name in over a hundred years. It was just a name, a word. But on his lips, they were like a siren's call when they should have been cause for punishment.

So like the fool she was, she waited.

Once he caught up to her, she stood and stared at him expectantly, trying to feign boredom, to pretend that his very presence didn't set her alight.

But he just stood there, opening and closing his mouth.

Annoyed at herself, she spoke first. "If you have nothing of substance to say, you ca-"

"I didn't do it," he blurted, and by the look on his face, that was the last thing he meant to say. It was like he'd just been grasping at words and that was the first thing to come out.

Didn't do what?

Blinking at him, she silently urged him to explain.

Taking a deep breath, Cade shook his head, eyes flicking around the hall. "I didn't rob that truck and I didn't kill those officials."

Huh?

Deianira didn't know what to say.

She'd based her entire opinion of him on the fact that he was a criminal. It was how she managed to shut him out, to deny her interest in him, but now?

Deep down, a small part of herself didn't think that he was capable of the crimes he was accused of. Nothing about his behavior since he'd arrived at The Dome suggested that he was a cold-blooded killer. Not his demeanor either. Deianira had met murderers, many of them, she was one, and either Cade was a master manipulator or he was telling the truth. But why now?

Why did he admit to the crimes?

"Why are you telling me this? Did you expect me to absolve you?" She had meant to sound bitter, but it came out as more of a breathy whisper.

He took a step closer, shaking his head slowly. "No. I-... I just wanted you to know."

She took a step back, feeling overwhelmed. "Why now? You didn't have a problem with me thinking you were a killer last week."

Cade sputtered before settling on a non-answer. "I don't know," he whispered.

His gaze was bouncing off the walls. He seemed to be having some sort of internal battle but when his eyes locked onto hers, she knew that it wasn't the Cade she knew that won. The man standing before her was not the same soft soul she'd met weeks ago.

He advanced another confident step, but she didn't step back this time.

"I have no fucking idea," he told her with an amused grin before his hand came up and gripped the back of her neck and his lips collided with hers.

He didn't know what came over him.

Why did I tell her that?

In that moment, Cade would have said anything just to get her to stay another second.

It was true though, he did want her to know. After all her harsh words towards him, he just wanted her to see that he wasn't who she thought he was.

Cade knew that kissing her was a huge risk. But it was as if something had switched in him.

His whole life, he'd never had much control over what happened to him. He just wanted to do something for himself, regardless of the consequences.

Cade had expected that taking matters into his own hands would give him a rush, but nothing could have prepared him for the tide that almost knocked him over as his lips met Deianira's.

Ascension. That was the only word he could think of that described the feeling. He felt like he was flying, a high better than any feeling he could get from throwing a punch or a kick.

Cade could tell she knew it was coming, but she still stiffened when his lips touched hers. Attempting to ease her, he slid his free hand to the small of her back and pulled her body in, tight against his. Instantly, she melted into his touch and brought a hand to his chest. As her fingers grasped at his shirt, Cade felt himself harden. That sensation only intensified when her nails dug into his chest.

She opened her mouth to speak between kisses.

"I know…" he murmured against her lips.

He knew what she wanted to say.

We shouldn't be doing this.

But Cade wasn't in the mood for reason.

Threading his fingers through her hair, Cade pushed his luck, nudging the tip of his tongue at her lips. As she opened her mouth, Cade's groan of approval echoed in the hall. Their mouths danced with one another harmoniously but before long, Deianira was grabbing at him and tugging his lips harder onto hers. She wanted more.

Taking the hint, Cade backed her up against the wall, lips never separating, and positioned a leg in between hers, sliding the hand on her back lower to grind her against his thigh. Deianira moaned her assent, arching into his hold, but Cade didn't let up as her breaths quickened.

Pulling her up with one hand, he brought her center to his and she immediately wrapped her legs around his waist, grinding harder. Deianira broke from the kiss with a deep moan as she lifted her head. Cade practically growled and attacked the soft skin on her neck with demanding kisses. Her hands left his chest to grasp his hair at the scalp when he ran his tongue up her throat and nipped the area just below her jaw, only pausing to groan as she ground herself down against his length with more urgency.

With the hall that they were in and the sounds that they were making, it wouldn't have been hard for someone to walk in on them, but Cade didn't care. He pushed his hips into her center again and again, living for the little gasps and moans that fell from her lips.

A small beeping noise from Deianira's bracelet had them both freezing.

As Cade removed his lips from her throat, she sighed and buried her head in the crook of his neck, still holding his head.

Gutted and already prepared for her rejection, Cade slowly released her, letting her slip down his body and onto her feet.

He knew that the small interruption was like a reset button that allowed her to go right back to hating him.

Cade averted his eyes. He knew what was coming but he didn't have to see the cold look in her eye when she said it.

"You need to come with me."

That wasn't what he expected her to say. He chanced a look at her and found her eyes on the hologram coming from her bracelet, brows tense. He'd seen Hewn with the same one but by the look on her face, this wasn't a standard alert.

That wasn't necessarily a rejection, so grateful for any extra time with her, Cade agreed quickly. "Where?"

Deianira looked at him suspiciously. "Sub-level. There's been a breach."

It seemed as if she was watching his face for some sort of reaction but he didn't give her one.

What does a breach have to do with me?

Chapter Twenty-Three

Cade had been on edge the whole way to the sub-level. It had little to do with the breach and a whole lot to do with the fact that Deianira was still yet to acknowledge what had just happened between them. She walked briskly through the halls and down the stairs with Cade as if she had nothing but the breach on her mind.

He could just about handle her indecisiveness, her anger, her coldness. But her silence? Cade wished she'd just yell at him or choke him out again.

In front of a door at the end of the hall was Finch. Cade knew from the first day in the city center that he was an empath so he did his best to mask his emotions, to hide any hint of what he and Deianira had just been doing, but by the way that Finch eyed the pair, he hadn't done a good job.

Finch spoke to Deianira as they approached, flicking his eyes to Cade suspiciously. "One male, one female. Found them sneaking around on the loading dock, probably off the back of one of the trucks. They won't give us names or any other information. Just kept asking for him." He gave his head a curt jerk in Cade's direction.

Me?

Cade's brows rose as Deianira's lowered.

After using his bracelet to unlock the door, Finch stepped aside to usher Deianira into the room but nudged his shoulder into Cade when he tried to follow. Cade shoved away his annoyance and shook it off as he entered behind Finch.

As his foot stepped over the threshold, Cade halted.

He must have lost his mind because there was no other explanation for what he was seeing.

There was no way his brother and best friend were sitting at a table, only feet away from him.

"Lia? Cassian?"

Their heads popped up simultaneously.

There was a moment of stillness before a squeal filled the air.

"Cade!" Lia shouted, uncaring of their company.

Standing so abruptly that her chair fell back, Lia ran to Cade and launched herself into his open arms. He wrapped his arms around her, still not understanding how this was happening.

She was shaking so much that he thought she might have been crying, but when she lifted her head from his shoulder and he saw that familiar twinkle in her eye, he couldn't help but laugh along with her. They hadn't spent a full day apart in sixteen years and he just couldn't believe she was here.

Setting her down, Cade looked over at Cassian. He could feel his brother's trepidation from the other side of the room. Wondering what he could be scared of, Cade took a slow step toward his little brother. He didn't need to step any further because Cassian met him in the middle, firmly wrapping his arms around him.

Cade stood still, shocked for a few seconds, before returning the gesture.

Looking over Cassian's shoulder, Cade lowered his brows at Lia. She gently shook her head and waved a hand. She'd tell him later.

Then it dawned on him. Cassian couldn't be here. Cade had only survived his first day by the grace of the Gods and he was innocent. What would Deianira do to his brother if she knew that she was in the same room as the real killer?

Stepping back, Cade patted his brother on the back, suddenly all too aware of the fact that they weren't alone.

Clearing his throat he turned to the other two people in the room. "Dei-" He quickly amended his address. "Your Majesty, this is my brother, Cassian, and my friend, Lia."

Deianira didn't speak, but just motioned for them to sit. And she didn't look impressed.

By the time they had all seated, Salem, Jude, and Hewn were at the door, per her request.

Waiting for them to get settled, Deianira surveyed the two strangers. Cassian, as Cade called him, didn't bear much resemblance to him. If it wasn't for the shade of his hair, she wouldn't have been able to guess that they were related. He was tall like Cade but he was leaner, his features were slightly sharper too. Younger, yet sharper. From his hard blue eyes to his diamond-cut jawline, they were almost opposites.

Moving on to the next, Deianira struggled to contain her anger as she examined Lia. She was beautiful. With her almond skin and thick dark curls, she and Cade complimented each other perfectly. They made sense. What they had wasn't some delusional fantasy. Their embrace had been nothing short of loving. The thought only had her anger rising.

For two seconds outside the gym, she'd allowed herself to breathe for the first time. To live for herself. As much as it pained her to admit after seeing him embrace his 'friend' like a lover, she'd never felt more alive than she did in that moment.

But it was over. The bubble had burst.

Despite her desire to rip his tongue out and feed it to him, Deianira couldn't blame Cade. He obviously didn't think he'd see her again so he made the best of a bad situation. He took the consolation prize. Her.

Once silence descended upon the room, Deianira got straight to the point.

"Start talking."

Lia looked to Cade and at his nod, she turned to Deianira.

"So, I'm a seer and-"

"Excuse me?" Deianira interrupted, all her other comrades just as taken aback.

"I'm a seer?"

"How?" Jude asked this time.

"I don't know." Her voice quieted. "I was born on the outside but I'm an orphan."

That had Deianira's hackles rising. "What is your name?" she asked bluntly.

The girl looked confused. "Uh, Lia."

Deianira wanted to roll her eyes. "Your full name." Seeing the others watching her suspiciously, Deianira quickly came up with an excuse. "I'm assuming Cade and Cassian share the same last name. I don't have yours," she said, flicking her eyes to Cade briefly.

"Oh, Eulalia Sambor."

No.

She'd heard Cade introduce her as Lia, but Eulalia Sambor? There was no way that was a coincidence.

How hadn't the thought occurred to her in the first place?

Memories attacked Deianira from all sides.

That familiar ache began to throb in the back of her head.

Not again.

A hand on her shoulder brought her out of her trance. She looked up to see Salem staring at her, brows furrowed in question.

Deianira gave her a small nod and focused back on Eulalia as she continued.

"A few nights after Cade was arrested, I had a vision of him. Up until then, I thought he was dead so when I saw him, I knew I had to come here. But in the vision, he was… hurt. I can't explain it but someone was hurting him." She shook her head. "I couldn't make out a face either but whoever it was really wanted something from him. I don't know what, but they weren't taking no for an answer. We came to warn him. To help him."

"Finch?" Deianira called, eyes still on Eulalia.

She couldn't get past the resemblance. How didn't she realize the second she saw her?

Deianira had been so distracted by her own emotions that she didn't even think about her name or look past her face.

After a few seconds, Finch responded, "Truth."

Deianira closely observed their reactions. The girl didn't seem phased in the slightest. The brother, however, went ashen.

Interesting.

"There's something else."

Everyone turned to look at Cassian. Those were the first words he had spoken since he'd arrived.

"What is it?" Deianira asked. She couldn't take much more tonight.

"I'm the one who killed the officials. Cade took the fall for me."

Chapter Twenty-Four

Cade spun to look at his brother. He appreciated the cyclical nature of the situation, but this was not how it was supposed to happen. He was supposed to protect his brother, just like his mother told him to. Cassian should've been back in the western sector, living his life. Not here in The Dome, handing it over.

"Truth," Finch declared, cutting through the shocked silence, unprompted.

Cade barely held back his glare but that only seemed to put a satisfied smirk on Finch's face.

"It was an accident. I didn't mean for any of it to happen and I'm sorry. But it did happen and I'm turning myself in. Cade shouldn't be punished for my crimes."

By the look on Lia's face, this wasn't part of the plan. Cassian had blindsided her too. But along with the shock, there was a hint of pride coming off her.

Cade started to regret the impulsive words that he'd spoken only minutes ago. He had already told Deianira that he wasn't the killer. Now, there would be no doubt in her mind that Cassian was responsible and he would lose his brother all over again. For real this time.

Deianira nodded to Hewn and he stood, cuffs already coming off his belt.

"No, wait!" Lia interjected.

Hewn didn't stop. Cade's heart clenched as Cassian stood from his seat and brought his hands together.

He was really going through with this.

Lia stood and physically put herself between Hewn and Cassian.

Cade was shocked, yet again.

What changed?

"Back up!" Cade discreetly cringed at her tone. He knew that Hewn wouldn't respond well to her order. "We have information that you're gonna want to hear." Lia looked at Deianira while she spoke. Cade stared at her, amazed to see that the same girl who would never have stood up for his brother a few weeks ago was not only defending him, but protecting him.

Deianira's cold eyes stared Lia down. "I'm going to need a little more than that."

Lia turned her head to Cassian and motioned for him to go ahead. At Cassian's hesitant look, Lia delivered a hard smack to his shoulder.

That got him talking.

Ah, that's the Lia I remember.

"My father's leading a resistance on the outside. He's planning an invasion."

Deianira looked bored. "We've had resistances before."

"But this one might work," Cassian responded, eyes flicking to Lia for approval. She gave him an encouraging nod.

Cade's head was spinning. Not only at Cassian's words but at his and Lia's behavior.

"What makes you think that?" Deianira asked as she shifted her elbows onto her knees, legs parted, and looked at Cassian intently. At her change in posture, Cade couldn't help the bolt of lust that shot through him, but he quickly shook it off as Finch's eyes flitted to his with a look of confusion.

Get it together.

"He has allies outside of the western sector," Cassian said nervously before adding, "And on the inside. In here."

Deianira's face momentarily tightened before she schooled her expression in a flash. Cade's best friend, however, didn't miss anything.

Lia held her hand up to Cassian. "That's enough. If she wants more, she can grant your freedom." Seemingly satisfied, Lia retook her seat. "So?"

Cade didn't have to look at Deianira to know that she was furious. If he knew one thing about her, it was that she didn't like not being in control and Lia had just put her in a really bad position. On one hand, he hated that she had been cornered like this but on the other, he couldn't be mad at Lia for putting his brother first. It's what he asked her to do and Cade wasn't sure if he could've thought as quickly as Lia just had.

"We'll let you know."

That was all Deianira said before she left the room without a glance in Cade's direction.

He was protecting his brother.

The fact only had Deianira more conflicted. Cade had risked his head so that his little brother might live. While she didn't want to take that from him, she had a job to do. She was Queen and her emotions were not supposed to interfere with her duty. Her conflicted feelings were enough to tell her that she should take a step back and get her priorities straight.

One thing Deianira wasn't conflicted about though was Eulalia. Deianira had to admit, it was a good move. But at that moment, she wanted nothing more than to throttle her. She came to *her* palace making demands. If it weren't for the potential threat, she would have dragged her over the table.

Leaving Cade and his companions in the room, Deianira and her council stepped outside of the room to deliberate.

She stayed silent, waiting for someone else to speak. She didn't know what to think and hoped that someone else could set the tone. Jude did.

"We know he's telling the truth but how do we know his information is any good?"

"If he was just trying to save his ass, I would've seen through it," Finch interjected, offended.

"No, I'm not saying he's lying." Jude corrected Finch. "But what if he's just delusional or has bad info? We would've caught word of a resistance that big."

"Not if they have an insider. We would have intercepted," Hewn considered.

Who would conspire against me with outsiders?

"I think we should listen to them. It's more logical to overshoot than to come up short." Salem responded.

Deianira looked at her sentinel with a cold, sarcastic smile. "Didn't you hear the girl? If he isn't absolved, we're not getting anything else. We release the murderer or we risk our lives. All we have is their word."

She scolded herself for the bitterness that laced her tone as she referred to Eulalia when Salem's eyes honed in on her, seeing something on her face that everyone else was yet to pick up.

"I think it would be a mistake," Jude argued. "Since when did we negotiate with criminals?"

Hewn nodded. "I agree. I believe them but the Prima Act is clear as day. He committed a crime and there is a punishment."

Salem cocked her head at Hewn. "So you're suggesting that we ignore potentially vital information that could save thousands of lives for a law that was put in place centuries before any of us were born?" She wasn't trying to have an attitude with him, she was genuinely trying to understand his thought process.

"Well, It's protected our people this far and as Her Majesty said, we've had resistances before."

"But this one might work." Salem reiterated Cassian's words almost robotically. "It is highly unlikely that they would make such a bold statement if it weren't true. Sooner or later, we'd find out if there truly is a resistance and if it were untrue, they'd be punished anyway. They can't afford to not be sure."

"Have you no faith in our defense systems and security?" Jude defended Hewn.

"I did before two outsiders walked in here like it was nothing," she responded calmly.

While they had been arguing, Deianira had already made up her mind. It was a huge risk, but she was willing to do what had to be done, as Jude loved to remind her.

Blocking out the startled objections, she opened the door, slipped back into the room, and locked it behind her. As Jude reopened the door, she summoned two shadows to hold it in place while she retook her seat and ignored the confused faces in front of her.

As the pounding on the door grew louder, Deianira spoke over the noise from her council. "How do I know your information is good?" she asked, parroting Jude's earlier concern.

Deianira didn't pay any mind to Cade's sigh of relief and kept her focus on his brother.

"The informant gave us the officials' trading schedule. That's how I knew the route that the truck would be taking for us to sneak on and get in through the loading dock." Cassian rushed out.

Deianira considered for a moment. They'd already established that he was being truthful and his explanation made sense. What were the chances of him stumbling across the truck at the right place and the right time?

This could be a huge mistake. If her people heard that she had violated the act, they would lose faith in her. But if they were alive at the end of it, it would be worth it.

Taking a deep breath, she met Cade's eyes for the first time since he'd been seated.

"Cade Alden and Cassian Alden, you are hereby absolved of your crimes in the eyes of the Gods and under the ruling of Her Majesty the Queen, Deianira Rikar. For the rest of your time here, however long it may be, you will remain in the guest wing of the palace, under guard. You are not to leave your rooms unattended for any reason." She flicked her eyes to Eulalia. "You too." Deianira leveled them all with a blank stare, masking the crippling anxiety she felt over the words she'd just said. "Talk."

After taking down as much information as she could from Cassian and Eulalia, Deianira requested for some enforcers to escort them upstairs and left the room.

Releasing the door, Deianira walked out into the hall paying no mind to the shocked, angry, and confused faces of her council.

"We need to talk," she called over her shoulder, heading to Jude's study. "Now!"

Chapter Twenty-Five

Deianira relayed all the information she had been given to her council feeling oddly numb.

They had a detailed plan of The Dome, the palace, and the entrances. It seemed the only thing she couldn't verify was the name of the informant. The depth of Cassian's knowledge of The Dome was scary. It made her feel vulnerable.

Could it be the same person who made an attempt on Cade?

The Prima Ball.

It would've been perfect. The city would be quiet as most of the residents would be in the palace. Along with her anger at the fact that she had a traitor on her hands, there was a small shot of fear over what could've happened had she not made the deal with Cade's brother.

Deianira briefly thought about canceling the ball but now that Jude knew of their plans, he could increase security and make changes with Hewn where he saw fit.

Regarding her realizations about Eulalia, she needed to see Grace. Even thinking that name made her anxious.

As her friends filtered out of the room to complete their new tasks, despite their earlier protests, Salem stayed behind.

Her eyes found Deianira when the door closed.

"I'll come with you."

Salem was too observant.

"No," Deianira responded.

"You're not in a good frame of mind and it would take little for you to set her off in her condition. You shouldn't go alone," she said with finality.

Deianira sat silently, staring at the desk.

"It might not even be her," Salem said. "She said she was born outside The Dome. I'll admit, the facts line up but it's still unlikely that-"

"It's her."

Salem blinked thoughtfully. "Then we go."

Approaching The Haven, Deianira's hands shook at her sides as her sentinel held the door open for her. She hesitated before heading to the reception desk.

The lady behind the desk did a double take before her eyes widened at Deianira.

"Your Majesty," she breathed. "How may I help you?"

Deianira couldn't even speak so Salem did.

"We're here to see Grace Sambor."

"Oh. She hasn't had a visitor in quite some time."

"Her room?" Salem urged.

"Yes. Just through that door, take the stairs on your left and she's in B-06."

"Thank you."

With that, Salem led Deianira through the facility and stopped outside of the door labeled B-06.

"You don't have to do this. We can turn around and go back to the palace. What she doesn't know can't hurt her." Salem reasoned.

"No," Deianira whispered. "She deserves to know."

Salem nodded. "Okay."

Pushing open the door, Deianira wanted to cry at the sight.

One of her oldest friends sat in the corner, braiding the fringes of the curtain, unbeknownst to her presence. She was in her own world, so distant.

"Grace," she choked out.

Grace didn't startle but turned her head slowly to the door.

"Your Majesty," Grace smiled.

Deianira giggled despite herself. "Don't start with that bullshit."

At that, Grace let out a full laugh, standing up to greet Deianira. She looked tired, wrinkles marred her bronze skin, but as always, she found it in herself to smile.

Wrapping her arms around Deianira, she whispered, "It's been some time, my friend."

"It has," Deianira replied.

She felt guilty enough for what she had done to Grace and though she felt bad for not visiting her anymore, seeing her face was a reminder of her mistakes.

"Salem," Grace untangled herself from Deianira to give Salem a grateful nod.

Salem nodded back, face straight.

"Grace, I've actually come to tell you something," Deianira said, losing her smile.

"Is it about the boy? He's quite the looker if I say so myself." Grace smirked.

Of course, she'd seen him. Deianira knew who she was talking about but she still subtly glanced at Salem, hoping she hadn't understood Grace's comment. Deianira flushed as she hoped even more that Grace hadn't seen what happened between her and Cade outside of the training room.

"No, Grace. Maybe we could sit?" she offered nervously.

"Of course,"

As they settled, each taking a corner of the bed, Deianira couldn't stop fiddling with her hands.

"It's okay, child. Speak." Grace placed her hands over Deianira's.

After trying to calm herself, Deianira met Grace's eyes.

"She's here."

Grace had always been an intelligent woman. Deianira constantly told her that she should've gone back to school rather than remain as her servant. She even offered to cover her expenses multiple times, but Grace was content. Deianira suspected that Grace's choice to remain working for her had less to do with loving her job and more to do with wanting to stay close to her and she was eternally grateful for it. To Deianira, Grace was a friend, a mother, an advisor, and so much more.

By the way Grace's beautiful face lost its pleasant smile, Deianira knew she didn't have to elucidate.

"No," Grace whispered.

"Grace…" Deianira tried to console her, knowing what was about to happen.

"No, no, no,"

"Grace, please."

"NO! She can't be here!" Grace stood and backed away from Deianira, sitting back in the corner.

"Grace, she's your daughter… You don't want to meet her?" Tears sprung in Deianira's eyes as her voice wobbled.

"Of course, I do!" She was screaming now. "But Deianira, she can't be here!"

"Why?" Deianira asked.

Grace's hands covered her eyes as she began weeping.

"My sweet Eulalia. Oh, my baby…" she whispered.

Salem got up from the bed and crouched down beside Grace.

"Grace, why can't she be here?" she demanded, causing Deianira to wince. Salem wasn't the most gentle person.

Eyes red, she looked up at Salem. "You have to get her out of here. Please, get her out of here."

Frustrated Deianira stood. "Grace, why?"

"He'll kill her if he finds out who she is…" she hiccupped.

Deianira's tears flowed freely. This was her fault.

I ruined her life.

Deianira had taken everything from her and she'd descended into madness because of it. This wasn't the same bubbly woman who'd danced with her when she had a bad day or kept her in check when she had to make difficult decisions.

When Deianira discovered that Grace's child went missing twenty-three years ago, her stomach had flipped. Grace had done something to her own daughter for fear that someone was after her. Deianira remembered all the times that Grace would cry to her, telling her that someone would try to hurt her baby. The paranoia was killing her.

She was suffering.

And it's my fault. I did this to her.

Feeling helpless, Deianira met Salem's eyes.

'Make her forget.' Deianira mouthed to her sentinel.

At Salem's head tilt, Deianira sobbed. *'Please,'*

The only thing she could do was ease Grace's pain. Salem was right, what she didn't know couldn't hurt her.

Salem turned back to Grace.

"Grace,"

Grace lifted her head, tears streaming down her face.

Salem's eyes narrowed intently. "Deianira and I didn't come here today. Eulalia isn't in The Dome. She's living happily in the western sector. There's nothing for you to worry about. You're going to go to bed now, you're tired and you've had a long day."

Instantaneously, Grace's face relaxed. She stood up from the corner and walked over to the bed, completely ignoring Deianira and Salem's presence. As she folded back the bedsheet and climbed in, they swiftly made for the door.

Once the door closed, Deianira stood, back against the wall, head tilted to the ceiling.

"For what it's worth, I think you did the right thing. She would've been in distress-"

"Don't try to make me feel better!" Deianira hissed.

"I'm not. There's no reason for her to suffer. Her mind is at rest now."

Though she didn't say them, Deianira could hear Salem's silent words.

There's no reason for her to suffer *anymore.*

"I'll visit her to undo the compulsion when Eulalia leaves," Salem said, turning to the stairs.

Deianira gave Salem a questioning look "Why?"

She turned back to Deianira. "Why what?"

"Why would you undo it?"

"Balance of nature," Salem said plainly. "I've just taken something from her and her mind will eventually try to get it back but it won't be easy. It'll be a lot better for her if I give it back."

Huh. "So what would happen if you left her alone?" Deianira asked cautiously.

Salem's eyes moved up and to the left as if she was retrieving information from her archives. "She'd get flashbacks of our conversation in little snippets that would gradually lengthen until she got the full picture, but it can be quite painful. Headaches, paranoia, delusions, hysteria. It would be cruel."

Deianira didn't know why that information evoked something in her, but it did. There was something in the back of her mind trying to speak to her but she couldn't quite hear it.

Salem observed Deianira. " Jude's almost finished planning. Why don't we go to see the seamstress and check on your dress?"

Deianira stared at her sentinel blankly. She couldn't have been more obvious.

Salem inclined her head. "Ok, that time I was trying to make you feel better."

Deianira snorted and rolled her eyes.

Chapter Twenty-Six

A loud snore woke Cade.

Blinking his eyes sleepily, he tried to get up but quickly noticed the foot laying over his chest. Leaning up on his elbows, he looked down at the owner of the leg.

They had each been given a room but chose to stay in Cade's last night. After the time spent apart, they didn't want to leave each other's sight.

Lia lay with her head on the opposite end of the bed, her thick hair draped over her face, mouth open, snoring loud enough to wake the palace. Cade couldn't contain his smile.

Lia had walked for almost two weeks through the forest with his little brother to get to him. Then on arrival, she managed to convince Deianira, Queen of The Dome, to let his brother walk free. She was truly amazing.

A noise from the bathroom drew Cade's attention from Lia.

Cassian.

He hadn't managed to talk to his brother much since his arrival and felt like there was so much more to be said.

Removing her leg as carefully as possible, so as not to wake her, Cade rolled off the bed and headed to the bathroom.

As he opened the door, Cassian's head turned to him from where he'd been standing at the sink. He wore the same plain black shirt and trousers that they were all given when assigned their rooms. Cade held his fingers to his lips until he closed the door behind himself.

"Are you okay?" Cade started.

"Yeah," was all Cassian said.

Cade watched his brother. He wasn't doing anything. Just standing in front of the mirror. He looked pained.

"Thank you," Cade whispered. "For keeping her safe."

Cassian snorted.

"It was the other way around." As soon as the words left his lips, the smile slowly slid off his face. "The word 'sorry' doesn't seem to cover it," he said quietly.

Cade's brows lowered in confusion.

"For what?"

Cassian seemed just as confused now. "Are you serious, Cade?" When Cade only cocked his head at him, he carried on. "You're here because of me. You were minding your business and I dragged you into this shit-"

"You didn't ask me to do that." Cade cut him off. "And I'm here because I didn't mind my business." He laughed quietly before sobering. "I spoke up. That was my decision, and I'd do it again," he said earnestly.

"But I didn't say anything either." Cassian shook his head. "I should've."

"So we could both get locked up? 'Cause that would've been real smart."

Lowering his voice, Cade started again. "My point is, you don't need to ask me to protect you. I would do it anyway. And as you can see, I'm very much alive so you don't need to be sorry either."

Cassian's eyes glistened as he met Cade's.

A knock at the door had them both turning.

"Once you guys are done kissing and making up, we need to talk!" Lia called through the door.

Cade huffed a laugh and shook his head.

"I didn't see his face, I only know that it's a guy. You were in so much pain, I could practically feel it."

Cade nodded, taking it in.

He'd already assumed that whoever poisoned Devin would try again since he failed the first time. He just couldn't work out what they stood to gain from his death. Lia said that they were trying to get information out of him, but the attempt was aiming to kill him. It didn't add up.

"Okay, I know you're emotionally constipated but you are taking this a lot better than you should be. What's going on?"

Cassian hid a laugh behind his fist.

"Emotionally constipated?" Cade looked at his best friend, offended.

Lia rolled her eyes. "Let's be honest, you don't have a very wide range, but don't try to distract me. What aren't you telling me?"

Under his breath, Cade rushed his next words out.

"They already tried to kill me."

Cassian's humor faded and Lia stopped fiddling with the bedsheet.

"Excuse you?" she said, her head cocked back.

Sighing, Cade went on.

"Last week, someone tried to poison me. I don't know who and I don't know why, but they tampered with my drink. I didn't get hurt though, a friend did." Lowering his voice, he continued carefully, eyes down to the bed. "He died actually. Deianira had to restore him."

Both of them paled before speaking at the same time.

"What?"

"He died?"

"Poison?!"

"What do you mean *'restore'*?"

"What the fuck is wrong with you, Cade?!"

The last question was Lia's.

Brows drawn together, he tilted his head at his friend. "I tell you that someone tried to *kill* me and you ask what's wrong with *me*?"

"Yes, what is wrong with you?" She stood. "Someone is actively trying to *murder* you and you're sitting around like it's an everyday occurrence!" she snapped, arms thrown out. "Your friend actually died! That could've been you, you should be ten sectors away right now!"

Cade held his hand up defensively. "First of all, he's completely fine now." He corrected himself. "Okay, not completely fine but that's beside the point. We're both alive. And, why would I run? As you said earlier, whoever it was is really determined, so running would only delay it and put me in more danger because I'd be alone. Right now, the safest place for me is right here."

Lia watched him for a few moments before rolling her eyes and flopping back onto the bed.

"Whatever, you're right. I miss the old Cade that didn't argue with me."

"Too bad." He grinned.

Cassian held a hand up. "So no one's gonna answer my question? What the hell does restore mean?"

Oh yeah. He should probably fill him in.

Walking into the cafeteria, Cade found himself watching the entrances for any sign of Deianira. It felt like he was seeing her less and less. The last time he'd gone this long without seeing her, he wasn't so sure, but she had to be avoiding him now. He'd even taken different routes around the palace to get everywhere, hoping to run into her, but she was nowhere to be found. She didn't want to be found. Their interrupted kiss left things unclear and he just wanted a second alone with her.

Refocusing his attention on the people with him, Cade could just tell that Cassian was dying to ask him more questions.

"Just ask," Cade told his brother as they joined the line.

"So you can like, read my mind?" Cassian whispered.

"Nope, just emotions. But they can give you a good idea of what someone's thinking."

"That's kinda cool," he muttered as they moved up the line.

"Not always," Cade replied evenly. "You don't just know what someone's feeling, you feel it too, so negative emotions can be pretty suffocating. Plus, everyone feels things differently and has different thresholds for them. Sometimes, I have to be around someone for a while before I can gauge their feelings accurately."

"I think I take the cake when it comes to shitty gifts," Lia piped up behind them. "It comes in handy sometimes but I can't even control mine."

True, Cade thought.

"Where the fuck have you been?!"

Cade whipped his head in the direction of the voice from across the cafeteria as the room went silent.

Devin, face furious, left his table and came marching up to Cade and his companions, uncaring of the looks being thrown his way.

Cade couldn't help but smile.

So dramatic.

"Devin, meet my friend, Lia, and brother, Cassian."

"Hey." Devin barely spared them a glance. "Again, where have you been?"

"Sit. I'll catch you up."

"So you're the one who died?" Lia asked conversationally.

Cade kicked her under the table for her blunt question, but he should've known that Devin wouldn't be offended.

"Yep, and back from the dead." He smirked proudly, digging into his food.

"Huh. What was it like?"

"I'd love to tell you some bullshit about seeing the Gods and walking into the light but I don't remember a thing." Devin sighed.

"Speaking of," he turned to Cade. "This whole deal isn't so bad. I've got my own room now, huge bed." He smiled. "I get to train alone with Hewn too and I've actually learned a few new spells."

"Spells?" Cassian asked.

"Warlock," Cade, Lia, and Devin said simultaneously.

Cassian nodded and gestured for them to continue.

Devin picked up his napkin and placed it in the center of the table. "Watch this."

He focused on the napkin and began mumbling under his breath.

And nothing happened.

Cassian looked at Cade, his expression half-bored, half-amused.

"Give it a second…" Devin assured them and resumed his mumblings.

Then, very slowly, the napkin began to rise from the table. At Devin's wide grin and continued mumblings, it began to float in the air, making its way around the table.

Cade quietly laughed at Cassian's awe-struck expression.

Lia looked just as amazed as the napkin floated over her head. That was before it promptly burst into flames.

She screamed and started aggressively slapping her head.

"Shit!" Devin screeched.

"What is it with you and fire?" Cade hissed, fanning the remnants away from Lia's hair.

"Sorry. I'm still getting a handle on the control part."

"Yeah, I can tell," Lia spat, pulling her curls apart, looking for cinders.

As they returned to their meals, Cade noticed a strange look in Cassian's eye across the table.

"You okay?" he asked.

"Yeah, I just thought of something," Cassian replied, shaking his head.

"What?" he inquired. He was surprised at how easy it felt to speak to his brother now. They never had this before.

Cassian frowned. "How come you guys have gifts when you were born in the western sector?"

Cade opened his mouth to give him a vague idea but Devin, the history buff himself, answered for him. "Well, way back before The Dome was put up, gifted and non-gifted people lived together. They'll tell you that we were constantly at war and it was built to maintain peace, but that's a load of crap." He waved a dismissive hand. "The king at the time wanted a superior nation, to rule the most powerful people there were, but unfortunately, the non-gifted 'weakened the gene pool'," Devin said with air quotes. "So he cast The Dome to separate us. Problem was, some people didn't want to separate from their friends, husbands, wives, and loved ones. So they didn't. Some chose one side, some chose the other, but you won't find a human here. No, after the divide went up, the non-gifted in The Dome were either killed or bred out. On the outside, however, there are a few but their abilities aren't usually that strong."

Cade stared at him, taken aback. He was kind of glad that Devin had interrupted him because he couldn't have given Cassian an explanation half as detailed as that.

"So, if it's genetic, then why don't I have a gift but Cade does?" Cassian asked Devin.

"That, brother, I cannot tell you."

Good question.

Cade had never actually thought about that.

Lia leaned in. "Not to get your hopes up, but I read that some people present later. It's not likely but it's possible."

Chapter Twenty-Seven

Deianira had the training room to herself.
She often trained in the early hours of the morning because it was one of the only times the room was free and she really needed to clear her head. In the last couple of days, her headaches had become worse, more frequent. She kept replaying Salem's words at The Haven, but all she wanted right now was to push everything away for a few hours.
Stepping back into the middle of the room and securing her blindfold, Deianira pressed the remote to turn on the electric arrow launcher. Salem had had it made for her for Prima day a few years ago and she was over the moon with the gift.
It was equipped with over two hundred steel arrows and she set it to delayed release, her favorite. Deianira blocked everything out as she waited for the first one to fly.
Sensing the first coming at her head-on, she didn't move, but instead used a shadow to deflect the projectile. As the next two aimed for her left, she sidestepped but landed right in the path of two more. Ducking them, she summoned another shadow to send away the

three she heard coming for her legs. Arrow by arrow, she ducked, dived, and deflected.

This was one of her favorite pastimes. It allowed her to hone her skills and sharpen her senses all while having fun. She was yet to be hit or nicked by an arrow in her years of using it and to up the difficulty, she often sped up the release to quicken the assault. Deianira could tell that it was coming down to the last few as their volume began to decrease so she allowed herself to slow down and take some breaths as she continued dodging.

"Are you crazy?!"

As she whipped her head in the direction of the voice, even though she couldn't see, sharp steel sliced the side of her cheek as she heard the last arrow hit the wall behind her.

There goes my streak.

Ripping off her blindfold, Deianira blinked, eyes adjusting to the light, to see Cade standing in the doorway staring at her, horrified.

He is everywhere!

"Where is your detail?" she demanded.

"Outside of my room," he responded absently before circling right back. "What the hell are you doing?"

She should've been angered by his tone of voice with her, but she wasn't.

"Training," she said evenly.

"By shooting yourself, blindfolded? Are you trying to kill yourself?" he asked with disbelief.

Deianira was slightly offended that he thought that mere arrows could end her.

"It helps w-" She shook her head. He was the one doing something he shouldn't be. "No, I'm asking the questions. Why are you here?"

At that, Cade quieted. "I wanted to see you." Noticing her cheek, he strode right up to her, eyes focused on the blood beginning to seep from the cut on her cheek, hand already coming to touch her. "Hey, are you okay?"

Deianira stepped back, rolling her eyes, and walked over to reload the machine. "Go back to your room, Cade."

There was a beat of silence.

"No."

She turned to face him. "Excuse me?"

"I said no." Cade crossed his arms, testing her.

"You're not very smart, are you?"

He shrugged. "Probably not, but you can't keep avoiding me because of what happened."

Right. The kiss.

"Nothing happened, Cade," she tried to say evenly.

"That's not how I remember it." Cade moved closer.

"Well, whatever it was, it can't happen again."

"Why not?"

"Because it can't," she said firmly. "You already know why."

His features tightened before he sighed. "If that's what you really want, then fine, but I actually came to ask you something too."

"Will you leave after?" she asked, exasperated.

"Probably not," he smirked.

She turned away from him to hide her smile as she reset the arrow launcher. "Hurry up."

"I want to resume my training."

Deianira gave him a confused look. "You're no longer in the program. You don't have to do that anymore."

"I know, but I *want* to."

It wasn't an unreasonable request. There was someone after him and they were facing a high-level threat. "Okay. I'll speak to Hewn."

"I don't want to train with Hewn." His voice was much lower now. His eyes told her exactly who he wanted to train with.

"No."

"Come on."

"No."

"Please."

She cocked her head at him. "Cade, I'd lay you out."

His lips tipped up as he stepped closer. "Go ahead, I quite liked it the first time."

She stared at him, open-mouthed, as her heart rate doubled.

Who is this?

"You're not gonna drop this," she said, mostly to herself.

"Nope." He stifled a smile.

Doing her best to keep her face bored, she responded. "Fine. It's your funeral. I want you here at three, every morning. Take off your shoes and move that mat to the center." She pointed to the stack of mats without meeting his eyes.

"Now?" Cade asked, seemingly shocked that she'd accepted his request.

"Do I need to repeat myself?" She looked up at him, impatient.

"No." His eyes gleamed. "Never."

Chapter Twenty-Eight

Lia was content. Besides the fact that she was no closer to figuring out who had tried to kill Cade, she was just glad to have her friend back.

She'd never seen him more alive. Back home, Lia could tell that he wasn't happy and it broke her to see someone who deserved the world be so broken down. Life on the outside wasn't meant for him. She didn't know what it was back then but she'd always known that he didn't belong there.

This new Cade though? He was vibrant, energetic even. She didn't want to ruin that by constantly reminding him that he was in danger.

She'd also picked up on his behavior toward the queen. Lia didn't say anything at the time but earlier in the room, he'd called her 'Deianira'. Lia was by no means an expert on the customs in The Dome but she knew that calling the queen by her first name wasn't normal. And it was the way his face changed when he spoke about her.

Cade liked her. Really liked her.

Though he had been in a few short 'relationships' outside of The Dome, Lia had never seen him act this way. Her feelings towards the queen aside, Lia couldn't have been happier for him. Cade was an empath and quiet as he may be, he was strong-willed. If he wanted to get close to the queen then she trusted his judgment.

Per her request, her guards arrived at noon to escort her through The Dome's woodlands.

Lia loved the outdoors and being cooped up in a room with two guys was quickly losing its appeal.

She didn't like that she couldn't be alone to explore, but she understood the queen's conditions all the same. She was a stranger, an outsider. It was reasonable.

Running her hands along low branches, a familiar high-pitched noise began to ring in her ears. Knowing what was coming, she stopped by the next tree stump and took a seat. Resting her head against it, she paid no mind to her guards.

Here we go again.

"Please, hurry."

"Are you sure, Miss?"

"Yes. Here." *A cloaked woman held her hand out holding a small pouch. Turning her back, the lady picked something up from behind her and returned with a small bundle of blankets, something moving inside.*

A baby.

"Take her to the school in the western sector," *she whispered urgently.* "There's a woman there. A teacher. She'll be safe there."

She gave the child a small kiss on the forehead, then handed over the small bundle reluctantly.

"Okay, but keep the coin. It's on our trading route anyway."

"No," she insisted, her voice becoming thick. "Take it. Thank you for this. I can't protect her here."

The cloaked woman stood still, but her cloudy figure retreated into the distance.

"Ma'am, are you ok?"

Lia blinked back into reality, wiping the sheen from her face.

"Yeah, I'm fine. Just feeling a little nauseous."

She let the guard help her up from the ground.

As they began walking again, she tried to decipher what that vision meant.

It didn't feel like one of her usual ones. They usually came with a sense of foreboding, but this one didn't. It was like her mind was trying to show her something. Something that had already taken place.

That thought gave her pause.

Lia had only ever seen into the future. Why would her mind show her this? What did it mean?

She ran it through her head again and again, trying to pinpoint something of significance. Then, it clicked.

The school.

The sector.

The teacher.

Lia was only weeks old when she was found behind the school in the western sector. Found by Eliza Alden. By Cade's mother.

The beautiful Eliza Alden had schooled her and raised her. Little Lia wanted Eliza to take her home more than anything, but as she grew older and became aware of Cade and his mother's home situation, she knew that it wouldn't have been possible. So the school was her home. She lived there until Cade opened his new home to her when she was only fifteen. Lia didn't want to leave the school at first, it was the only way she could connect with Eliza since her passing, but she found that being with Cade was just as good. He looked so much like her after all. Eliza wasn't just his mother. She was their mother. Lia's breathing became light as she began to put the pieces together. Whoever that woman was, she'd purposely sent her to Eliza. The teacher.

Who would do that? And why?

Chapter Twenty-Nine

Cade dragged himself out of bed, sleepy-eyed.

Deianira had not been going easy on him during their sessions. He didn't mind though if it meant he got to spend more time with her. Sometimes, he felt like her intensity was meant to be a deterrent. To make him quit.

That wasn't going to happen.

"Where are you going?"

Lia was curled up on the sofa, squinting her eyes in the darkness.

"Training. Go back to sleep," he whispered.

"Okay... But, Cade?"

"Mhm?"

"I'm happy for you." She smiled softly. "The predicament isn't great but I'm glad you're here."

He knew what and who she was referring to. Lia was perceptive.

"I'm glad you're here too."

At that, even in the dark, he saw her face dim slightly.

"Yeah..."

Lia had been quieter over the past week, but Cade put it up to the change in circumstances. She didn't like change very much. He was sure that she would be back to normal in no time.

Waiting in the doorway of the training room, Cade couldn't stop the smile that settled over his face as he watched Deianira repeatedly throw knives at a moving dummy. In rapid succession, she threw five knives, pinning it in the head, heart, neck, and both legs.

She was incredible.

"You've just waited five minutes being a creep," she called, stepping forward to remove the knives.

That only made Cade's smile grow.

Of course, she knew he was there.

"Just observing," Cade quipped, walking into the room.

She finally turned to face him. "Well, that observation just earned you an extra thirty minutes of conditioning."

Great.

"Where do you want me, boss?" he asked, removing his shoes.

She cut him a dry look. "On the 'X'. And don't call me that."

So it was going to be an icy day. Cade didn't mind.

After moving the dummy and replacing it with a wide plank of wood, Deianira strode up to him with two knives, one in each hand. Holding up one, she said, "This is a Kunai thrower and this," she held up the other, "Is a twin peak. What's the difference?"

Cade studied them before answering. "That one's double-edged," he said, pointing to the second.

She gave him a curt nod. "Good. We'll start with the twin peaks. It won't help with aim but it'll give you a bigger window for errors, which I'm sure you'll make, so you don't have to worry about catching the handle."

Ignoring her encouraging faith in him, Cade allowed her to adjust his stance before she placed the first blade into his right hand, moving to stand on his left.

"You're going to set your aim before you pull back. Throw with your arm, not your wrist. Try not to flick your hand too much, it'll send the knife spinning only to bounce off the board. Just pull back and follow through. Go."

Nerves started to crawl up Cade's spine. His faith in himself was wavering now.

"Breathe, Cade," Deianira whispered on his left, standing closer. "Breathe and follow through."

Warmth bloomed in his chest at the way his name rolled off her tongue.

He brought the blade up in front of his face and set his aim. Taking a deep breath, he pulled his right arm back and sent the knife flying toward the board.

With a dull thud, it lodged itself into the plank.

Cade didn't even try to hide his smile as he turned to Deianira.

"What were you saying about making mistakes?"

She rolled her eyes but Cade noticed her stifled grin.

"Congrats. You threw a training knife into a piece of wood thirteen feet away."

He rolled his head to the side. "Would it kill you to give me a 'well done'?"

Sighing she said, "It was okay. Take this and go again." She handed him the next blade. "Aim above the first one."

Deianira was impressed.

Cade had missed a few times but he was picking it up fairly quickly. Deianira took particular notice of the fact that each time she would give him a pointer, he'd follow her advice perfectly. He listened to her.

As Queen, it wasn't out of the ordinary for people to listen to her, but that was out of blind obedience. However, in every look that Cade gave her, she could see that he listened because he trusted her. Trusted her to guide him.

In the training room, she didn't have to be Queen.

It was becoming increasingly hard for Deianira to push Cade away, especially when he did everything right. Up until his brother's arrival, she had an excuse to keep him at arm's length. Now, keeping those walls up with every smile he gave her and each comment he made felt like swimming with a cement block attached to her ankle.

"That was good," she told him quietly after his last throw.

His entire face beamed at her approval.

Looking away to keep herself in check, she walked to the board to retrieve the blades. "We'll try the Kunai tomorrow. Go get ready for breakfast."

Cade frowned. "What about the conditioning?"

"Forget about it," she said over her shoulder. "You did well today."

"Oh. Okay."

He almost sounded disappointed.

After placing the box of knives back on its shelf, Deianira went to let her hair down when a blinding bolt of pain shot through her temple.
Blood.

"Ahh!" Deianira fell to her knees gripping the sides of her head.
So much blood.

"Deianira!" a voice called, but it sounded so far away.

"What have you d-... You will kill them."

Deianira cried out, tugging at her scalp.

"What's wrong?!"

"Start with your father-"

"Deianira, look at me!"

"Deianira, look at me! Then your mother-"

"Hey, talk to me! What's wrong?!"

", then Calliope."

Deianira vaguely felt herself being lifted.

So much blood.

"Help! She needs help!"

"What have you done?"

"I'm sorry-"

"I don't know, just do something!"

"It's not your fa-... This is all your fault."

A blood-curdling scream tore out of Deianira's throat as her mind tried to cave in on itself.

"Why are you just standing there?! HELP HER!"

"We never had this conversation. This is all your fault. You lost control and you did this."

Deianira gasped and choked, jerkily sitting up.

Mikhael, whom she had almost just headbutted, jumped back. To his left, she saw Cade staring at her helplessly before he rushed past Mikhael.

"Deianira..." he breathed, eyes wide.

Why is he looking at me like that?

"What?" she asked, suddenly uncomfortable.

Mikhael glared at Cade and pushed past him to stand in front of Deianira.

"Your Majesty, are you okay?"

"She's obviously not fucking okay." Cade glared right back at him.

Feeling something warm on her lips, she touched the skin below her nose and when she drew her hand back, blood coated her fingers. Her heart sped up as her eyes darted around the room trying to understand what was happening.

"Wait- what, why am I-"

She felt fingers wrap around her other hand. "Hey, hey, it's alright. Breathe..."

Cade was at her side again and instantaneously, she was able to breathe easier as their eyes met.

"That's good. Just breathe."

In, out.

She'd never felt so calm.

Mikhael, obviously tired of Cade's presence, moved back into his spot. "Do you remember what happened, Your Majesty?"

Deianira refreshed her memory of what happened in the last ten minutes. As it all came back to her, her heart began thumping again.

That night.

The blood.

Wait...

Someone else was there.

They told her to...

No.

No.

Deianira had hoped she was wrong as the facts started to align earlier but this had just proved her right.

She needed to find Salem. Now.

As she hopped up off the bed, Cade blocked her.

"Woah, where do you think you're going?"

"I need to go." She tried to move around him.

"No, you need to get checked out." He stepped into her path again.

"I'm fine," she hissed, growing annoyed with his stubbornness. "It was a little headache, now get out of my way."

"A little headache?" His eyes narrowed at her.

"Yes," she gritted out. "It happens all the time."

"You black out for *three hours* all the time?! Gods, Deianira, you had a seizure, your nose is bleedi-"

What?

"Three hours?" she asked in a terrified whisper.

His eyes softened at her change in tone. "You don't remember?"

"Of course, I remember but it's been like ten minutes."

"No, it hasn't." He shook his head "You went down in the gym and you wouldn't stop screaming, so I brought you here. You've been out ever since."

Heart pounding, Deianira glanced at her bracelet.

09:37

How?

With newfound determination, she looked up at Cade.

Her voice was ice cold when she said, "I do not care if I've been here three minutes, three hours, or three days. I need to speak with Salem, right now. Move or I will move you."

Mikhael looked between the two of them from the corner of the room.

"I really wouldn't recomme-"

The cold glare she cut him silenced him.

Turning back to Cade, she raised an eyebrow at him, daring him to refuse her again.

"Fine. But I'm taking you to her." His face was just as determined.

Deianira wanted to argue but she just didn't have the energy, so she conceded.

"Let's go."

Chapter Thirty

Cade was still shaken up as he sat on Salem's sofa waiting for Deianira to start speaking.

When she'd dropped in the training room, he'd nearly had a heart attack. Then, she started shaking, and screaming. Cade had no idea what to do so he picked her up and ran to the infirmary. It was pure luck that Mikhael was already there, but he didn't know what to do either. Cade had never felt so helpless. He didn't move an inch from her bedside until she woke.

What did she mean by 'it happens all the time'?

Cade would've liked to think that he would've noticed something like that, but being completely uninformed on the matter, he sat back and listened.

Deianira remained standing and flicked a glance his way before beginning.

"Remember when you told me that compulsion has to be undone to prevent side effects?"

"Yes," Salem said from her chair opposite Cade, eyeing him, probably trying to figure out why he was there.

She didn't look annoyed in particular, but something told him that she didn't want him there.

Deianira's eyes flicked down. "I think someone might have done that to me."

"Done what?" Salem asked, her face blank.

"Compelled me... And whatever they did, they didn't take it away."

"How long have you known about this?" Salem inquired.

"The headaches only started a couple of weeks ago but I wasn't sure until the flashbacks started. Like you said."

So these aren't just little headaches.

Salem's expression didn't change in the slightest. "Why didn't you tell me at The Haven?"

"What do you think?" Deianira raised her voice defensively. "I'd be saying that someone *compelled* me to do something very, very bad. That is a *huge* claim to make and I still haven't gotten the full picture yet."

Salem blinked. "That's understandable but this is quite dangerous. The longer you leave it unattended, the worse the symptoms get. You could lose your actual mind." she said evenly.

What?!

His shock aside, Cade was perturbed by the way that Salem spoke. Her tone was so conversational. She was just reciting information with no emotional resonance. Not even a flicker in her tone.

"Okay, Gods, I get it," Deianira declared, tired. "I'm asking you now. Can you help me?"

She blinked. "How?"

"By undoing it."

"Undoing what?" she asked.

Deianira sighed. "The compulsion, Salem."

"Oh. I don't even know what the memory is."

Deianira flicked her eyes to Cade again. Whatever the memory was, she didn't want him to know.

Standing from his seat, he spoke to her softly. "It's okay. I'll wait outside."

Her gaze followed him until he was at the door.

"No," he heard from behind him.

He turned back toward her.

"Stay."

Hiding his approval, Cade nodded briefly.

He walked back to her but before he took his seat, he guided her, with a hand at the small of her back, onto the sofa, then took the seat next to her. Surprisingly, he was met with little resistance but when he looked up, Salem's raised eyebrows showed that she'd witnessed the whole exchange.

Feeling awkward, Cade motioned to Deianira.

She took a shaky breath.

"The night my family died... I don't think it was an accident."

Cade tensed.

"I think someone compelled me to... kill them, then tried to make me forget. It's not all back yet but I remember them telling me-" She grew so quiet, Cade only just about heard her. "They said to start with my father, then my mom, then Cal."

He wanted the floor to swallow him up. Cade remembered the day he'd thrown that in her face and if he thought that he felt as guilty as he could back then, he was grossly underestimating himself. Deianira had been bearing that day on her conscience for over a hundred years only to find out that someone had made her do it.

"After all this time, I thought I had lost control and lashed out. If someone else is responsible, I want to know who it is, so please, undo it."

Cade examined her closely but he couldn't decipher what Salem was about to say for the life of him. She assessed Deianira's words, responding with only sharp nods and head tilts.

"I apologize. I didn't explain properly," Salem started. "You misunderstand. I can't take something that I didn't put there."

Sensing her annoyance and desperation, Cade wanted so badly to console Deianira, but he doubted she would be so welcoming to his affection at that moment.

"No! The first thing you said earlier was that you didn't know what the memory was. That means that there is a way."

She took a moment to recall before nodding. "Technically speaking, there's always a way, but it's not worth the damage I could do."

At Deianira's defiant look, Salem let her eyes stray around the room before landing on the coffee mug on the rack in her small kitchen. Gesturing to it, she started.

"Imagine that mug is the false memory and you hid it in a pitch-black house rigged with almost a hundred billion tripwires. Every time I trip a wire, a neuron in your brain dies. The information you've given me is as good as telling me what room it's in. I've never been in the house before and I didn't see the person responsible plant the mug, so I don't know where it is or where the wires are. Every move I made would put you at risk of irreversible brain damage." She nodded to herself, looking proud of her explanation. "So, yes. I can walk in and blindly reach for it, but there is a 98.6% chance that it would result in brain death." Sitting back in her seat, she looked at Deianira. "Does that help?"

Cade could barely believe what he was hearing.

No, it doesn't help! He wanted to shout. But this wasn't about him. He watched the hope drain from Deianira and be replaced with irritation.

"So what do I do?"

"Whoever planted it is responsible for your family's deaths and I doubt they would step forward, therefore, you won't know until the memory unravels. So you have to let it."

"What's going to happen to her?" Cade asked tersely, no longer able to just observe.

Deianira rolled her eyes while Salem narrowed hers before responding. "The speed of her progression depends on how strong her mind is. She's very powerful so it should unravel fairly quickly but the episodes will continue, they'll be more painful, and she might lose time. But it should all stop altogether when she gets the full picture though."

Cade stared at Salem, horrified.

Deianira would have to go through that all over again.

Chapter Thirty-One

Deianira called a meeting to review the last of the plans for the Prima Ball. She'd had little to do with it so far and wanted to make sure that things were ready for tomorrow.

"We've double security at both entrances and I have a witch on standby just in case there's a malfunction with the wall," Hewn explained.

"Good. I also want scouts on the outside. If anyone crosses the border I want to know about it," Deianira said.

"Of course," he nodded.

"Going off RSVP alone, 83% of civilians will be in attendance and the palace's lockdown procedures are ready if necessary," Jude presented.

"Thank you."

Everyone had pulled their weight in the planning of the Prima Ball. It allowed Deianira to rest easy knowing that everything was being taken care of.

As Jude and Hewn started up a new conversation, Salem took a seat uncomfortably close next to Deianira.

"Are you sure we should be moving forward with plans considering the circumstances?" she tried to whisper, but it sounded more like a mumble.

"The people have been preparing for this for months. It's Prima Day. I won't let my personal issues rob them of their celebration."

Salem nodded respectfully. "Okay. Have you had any more episodes?"

"Nope," Deianira told her truthfully.

Trying to appear casual, Salem settled back into her seat, moving even closer to Deianira.

"So... Do you want to talk about what's going on with you and Alden?"

Deianira continued staring straight ahead. "Nope."

"Are you positive?"

"Yep."

"Well, I think he has romantic feelings for you. His pupils dilate when he sees you," she started listing. "It's evident that he's concerned for your health, and he doesn't seem aware of it, but he's constantly trying to be in close proximity to you-"

"You're in close proximity to me." Deianira snapped. "And I said I didn't want to talk about it."

Salem assessed the space between them as if seeing it for the first time. "Oh. I apologize." She scooted halfway down the sofa.

Deianira sighed. Salem was one of the most perceptive people she knew but socially, some things slipped her mind. It wasn't intentional. "No, it's okay. I'm sorry, I'm just tired. I'm going to head to bed," she lied as she stood and started making her way to the door. "See you on Prima Day."

"Good night," Salem responded.

As Deianira opened the study door, Cade stood right outside, hand raised to knock.

She jumped. "Shit!"

Looking back to make sure no one had witnessed her outburst, she pushed at his chest, followed him out, and shut the door behind her.

"Sorry, I didn't mean to sca-"

"What the hell are you doing here? You can't just knock on the door, my whole council's in there," she hissed.

"I just wanted to check on you," he whispered.

The guilt wasted no time in washing over her.

"It's okay," he said before she could apologize. "You're busy."

"No," she replied way too enthusiastically. "I mean, I'm not busy. I was just heading out," she blurted and instantly regretted it.

"Where?"

She studied him for a while before shaking her head. Why not?

"The woodlands."

Cade frowned. She couldn't tell if he didn't believe her or if he was just worried about why she was going there.

Deianira sighed. It had been a long day and she could let loose for just a minute. As much as her stupid heart jumped at the thought, she had to force her next words out.

"Do you want to come with me?"

She could see the surprise flash across his face before he schooled his expression.

He nodded. "Yeah, sure."

She turned in the direction of the east stairwell, expecting him to follow.

"Uh, those don't go to the ground floor," he called.

She scoffed. As if she didn't know that.

"We're making a pit stop."

There was a moment of silence before she heard his footsteps thudding behind her and soon, he was at her side again.

As they continued walking, Cade broke the peaceful silence. "Have you had any more episodes?"

Rolling her eyes, Deianira groaned. "Why does everyone keep asking me that? No, I haven't."

Cade stopped walking and Deianira turned to him, waiting.

His face was straight, eyes were hard. "Deianira, you scared the shit out of me that day. You might not think that it's a big deal, but I was the one carrying your body to the infirmary, and if I have to see you like that again, Mikhael's gonna need an extra bed for me." He stepped forward. "So, I'll ask you every five minutes if it means I'll be better prepared to help you."

Deianira's breath caught in her throat, she hadn't thought about that. She'd been so focused on being resistant toward him that she ignored what he had done for her. The fact that he even cared so much made her feel uncomfortable.

She flicked her gaze away before fixing him with a stare of her own. "Well, as I said, I haven't had any and I've been managing fine. It's your hovering that'll send me over the edge," she griped.

Cade didn't cower away from her hard look. "Cry about it."

For the hundredth time in the past few weeks, she stared at Cade, stunned.

Wanting to change the subject, she grasped at random thoughts until a question struck her.

Placing her hands on her hips, she narrowed her eyes at him. "Cade, where are your guards?"

A mischievous smile spread across his lips as he began walking again. "No clue."

"You do realize that they are for your protection as well, right?" she shook her head with disbelief and caught up with him.

This was the second time he'd slipped his detail.

He shrugged "I don't need protection. I have you."

"I wouldn't count on it. I'm probably the one you need protection from." She had meant it as a joke, but she couldn't help but notice the small hint of truth that it held.

"Somehow, I doubt that."

"Either way, I'm upping your security, first thing after the ball." As they reached a small supply closet, Cade shot her a confused look.

She just brushed past him and walked into the room to collect what she came for.

To his credit, Cade didn't ask too many questions as they trekked through the trees. It allowed Deianira to breathe in the cold air, to listen to the icy leaves crunching beneath her boots.

Almost there.

"Are we just walking or are we going somewhere?"

So much for silence.

Deianira ignored him as she picked up her pace. She couldn't help but smile as she reached her destination. It had been too long since she'd last been here. As much as she liked to train or spar with Jude to clear her mind, this topped it, no questions.

Cade finally caught up to her as she set her bag down on the ground. "Deianira, wh-"

"Shh!" she hushed him as she stared out onto the frozen lake. Reaching into her bag, she pulled out her pair before pulling out a second. She wasn't sure what Cade's size was but they were the only pair she could find that seemed big enough.

"Put these on." She handed them to him.

Cade stared at the strange shoes.

He'd never seen anything like them.

They looked like boots but they had a long blade running along the bottom.

He carefully took them from Deianira's hands.

"Am I allowed to talk now?" he asked.

She stared at him, bored, before nodding.

"What are these?"

Deianira took a seat on the ground and started pulling off her boots. "They're called ice skates."

When he only blinked at her, she rolled her eyes. "You put them on your feet."

Cade shrugged. Why not?

Copying Deianira, he took a seat next to her and took off his boots before slipping them on and tying up the laces. Not too tight though, they were already a smidge on the small side.

He didn't want to ask any more questions about what they were doing so he just waited for her to explain.

After a few seconds of watching her struggle, Cade rolled onto his knees and scooted in front of her, gently grabbing her leg.

"What are you-"

"I got it." He waved her off as he started to loop the lace through the hole before giving them both a firm tug. Cade smiled to himself as he started to fold them over one another and cross them. For such a small person, she had quite big feet. He tied a second knot and pulled it tightly, then he tucked the extra length into the sides of the boot.

"There."

Cade looked up to find Deianira staring at him.

Her gaze took in his whole face. His eyes, his nose, his lips.

"What?" he asked, nervous.

He wasn't always sure if he was doing something that was annoying her. He was still trying to learn her quirks.

Deianira blinked and shook her head.

"Nothing. Let's go."

He caved. "Go where?"

Deianira granted him a rare smile when she gestured towards the lake as she stood. For someone that looked beautiful with a scowl, a smile on her lips was nothing short of enchanting. It transformed her whole face. He had to look away before she caught him staring.

Cade's stand wasn't nearly as graceful as Deianira's.

She stomped up to the lake before holding onto a low-hanging tree branch as she took a step onto the ice.

He stilled.

"Deianira."

She snorted as she put her other foot down.

Cade started stomping towards the lake after her.

"Deianira, get off the ice!"

She turned to him, walking backward across the ice. "No," she smiled.

He stopped his advance.

She wasn't walking, she was gliding.

It was... beautiful.

Cade wasn't sure what she was doing or how, but his heart still raced at all the thoughts of what could go wrong.

"Deianira, I'm not kidding! It could break."

She rolled her eyes as she spun in a circle and made her way back to the edge before stopping and spraying ice from her feet.

"It won't. I come here every year. Trust me." She gave the ice two hard stomps making Cade's heart leap. "It's solid."

He wasn't so sure. He just wanted her back on solid ground.

Deianira tilted her head. "Come on," she said, hands in her jacket pockets.

Cade chewed on his lip. She was obviously fine and he did trust her. Shaking his head, he marched towards the edge and grabbed the same tree branch.

The second his 'ice skate' touched the ice, he went flying.

Cade didn't even know where his feet went as he skidded several feet forward.

He'd barely managed to feel the dull pain that sprouted in his knee when a captivating sound filled the air. He lifted his head and squinted his eyes to find Deianira, hands on her knees, laughing her head off.

It only got louder as she caught Cade's expression. She began wheezing.

It was all Cade could do not to smile. He couldn't even feel the ache in his knee anymore. He couldn't focus on anything but that beautiful sound.

He did his best to feign annoyance. "Something funny?"

She slapped her hands over her mouth with a loud snort as she shook her head.

Cade tried to get back to his feet but found himself on his knees again. It really did hurt, but he would throw himself off the top floor of the palace if it meant that she would keep making that sound.

In his attempts to stand, he'd gotten closer and closer to her. Deianira didn't seem to realize what he was doing before he grabbed her around her knees and brought a hand up to cradle her head as he yanked her down to the ice.

She squealed and locked her arms around his neck, still racked with laughter. Cade joined her this time.

Deianira giggled as she tried to squirm out of his hold but every time she made headway, he grabbed her again. Cade wasn't stupid. He knew that she was stronger than him. She could've knocked him out and escaped his hold if she wanted to, but she was having fun. He could tell because he was having fun too.

Eventually, he rolled on top of her and as she kicked out, he landed right between her thighs. Their laughter quickly sobered.

He could see their breaths mingling in the frosty air but neither of them said anything.

His eyes dipped to her lips. They were right there. So close. He could've just…

Well, whatever it was, it can't happen again.

Cade pulled back and sat on his haunches. She had boundaries. He needed to respect them.

Preparing himself to give an awkward apology, he was surprised to see Deianira stand, seemingly unruffled.

"Come on." She held a hand out. "I'll help you."

Cade learned a few things over the next hour.

First, 'ice skates' were meant for 'ice skating'. As in literally skating across the ice. Cade couldn't count the number of times he'd fallen. He was definitely going to be sore in the morning, but it was okay because she found him hilarious.

Second, Deianira was good at just about everything. He couldn't get over the way she moved. She was powerful but elegant. Strong but graceful. He could've watched her forever.

"How do you just do that?" he asked as she landed a jump and skated a circle around him.

"I don't know. A hundred years of practice kinda helps you to just *do* things."

Fair enough.

"Jude brought me out here a lot."

He steadied himself, arms out as he looked at her wistful smile.

"After it happened," She didn't need to elaborate. "I couldn't go to school anymore. I couldn't see my friends. Well, they weren't my friends anymore at that point." She sighed. "I don't blame their parents though. I wouldn't let my kid hang out with a killer," she said lightly, but Cade could see the pain beneath the surface. "There's an ice rink in the city that I used to go to, but I'm sure you can imagine that it wasn't as appealing when the whole Dome wanted me dead."

Unsteadily, Cade skated towards her. She reached for him as he came close, hands grabbing his biceps as he held her arms.

"My parents were loved. Truly adored. And-" She took a deep breath seeming more annoyed than upset. "Jude still wanted me to have a life outside of the palace, so he found this trench and had it dug out and filled." Her smile peeked out again. "Now it's a lake, but my very own ice rink in Prima season."

He didn't know what to say.

She'd been a child. Not only had she just lost her parents but the nation she was set to rule had hated her. That wasn't something that a thirteen-year-old should have had to deal with.

He'd never seen her as at peace as she was when she was skating, so he wordlessly turned her in his arms and grabbed her hand as he started to push off his back foot. Deianira followed him seamlessly. She kept at his slow pace and held onto his hand as they rounded the rink. They kept going around, lap after lap, and Cade's chest slowly eased as he watched her face soften a fraction every time her foot hit the ice.

Chapter Thirty-Two

"How come we never got any of this in the program?" Cade asked, biting into his pastry.

After a painful walk back to the palace, on which Cade incessantly complained about his bruised ankles, Deianira surprised herself by suggesting that they get something to eat. That was the second time today that she'd asked him to hang out with her. She should've been telling herself to rein it in but she was enjoying herself too much.

They sat side by side on the counter, the stove on to warm the room up.

"Because it's a disciplinary program. For criminals. It's not supposed to be nice," Deianira drawled.

"Fair poi-" He cut himself off and hopped off the counter.

Deianira turned to see what had caught his attention.

Reaching above the cupboard, Cade picked something up and turned to Deianira with a questioning smile on his face.

"No," she said instantly.

Cade's smile dropped as he held up the bottle of whiskey.

"It'll warm you up," he said, gesturing to her red hands.

"No."

"You didn't even think about it."

"I don't need to. It's late."

"What does that have to do with anything?"

"Tomorrow's Prima Day. It's called being responsible."

"Wow," Cade cocked his head at her. "I always thought you were hard-headed but I didn't know you had a stick up your ass too."

Frowning at him, she said, "I know what you're doing."

He shrugged, trying to hide his smile. "I'm not doing anything. That's just your subconscious agreeing with me."

"Uh-huh. Sure it is."

"I mean, this is your palace, your alcohol and you're gonna let the time of day dicta-"

Deianira rolled her eyes.

"Oh my Gods!" she grumbled as she snatched the bottle from his hands, removed the cap, and poured back a shot.

Cade roared with laughter, clapping as she winced from the burn.

"Will you shut up now?"

He took the bottle back from her and took a swig.

"I don't remember agreeing to those terms," he smirked, coughing into his fist.

Then the night really started.

Deianira didn't remember the last time she'd enjoyed being around someone so much. Starting her reign at the age of thirteen didn't leave much time for fun. Being young, female, and in power, everyone expected her to lead armies, but they also expected her to fail or fall short. With the amount of work she had to put in to prove herself, fun wasn't a factor. So she was cruel when she had to be, heartless when the occasion called for it. But after years of earning the respect of her people, she realized that that was all they saw. No one looked further to see what was behind the mask. Except for Cade. He'd seen her from the very beginning. She'd been about to kill him that day in the city square and he still saw her.

"What even happens at a ball anyway?" Cade slurred, way past tipsy. She cocked her head at him, then remembered.

"Oh, outsider. You can eat, drink, dance, it's basically just a fancy party for Prima Day."

"Sounds nice." He nodded, looking at the ground as he leaned back on the counter.

She narrowed her eyes. "What, too pretentious for you?"

"No, it's not that. Things are just very different here," he said quietly, blinking slowly.

"You don't have parties on the outside?" Deianira mumbled, stumbling over her words.

"We do, actually. I-, I meant that you guys have a lot that we don't." Cade huffed. "You know before I got arrested, I was a carpenter. I didn't even really like it but I didn't have options. Not many of us did. And you were considered lucky if you could get a contract with a trading official here, only to get paid less and less each season. But at least you could eat." He paused for a moment, thoughtful. "When I turned sixteen, I became an apprentice and learned woodcraft. Even though it wasn't the best, I'm glad I did because if I didn't, I would've been on the streets by now."

"Why?" she asked curiously.

Cade blew out a breath and began fiddling with his hands.

"My father. Now, he was a man with options, but he chose to make my life a living hell."

He didn't elaborate but Deianira had an idea. It was the last thing she wanted to think about. Knowing that she had a part to play in- She stopped those thoughts as her mood soured.

Crossing her legs onto the counter, she averted her eyes. "I can't do anything about that. They're not my people, Cade."

Cade rolled his head to the side to look at her. "They *were* though. At one point. We all live in Terra."

Those words struck her harder than expected. It was true. There wasn't always a Dome. Those people were cast out to suffer and even if it wasn't by her own hand, she had to take some responsibility. Her heart felt too heavy.

Lazily blinking up through her lashes, she asked Cade a question that she'd never cared to ask anyone before. "Do you think I'm a bad person?"

He looked at her for a while before trying his best to articulate his words.

"No, I don't. I think that it's real easy to hate you for making the hard choices but what some people fail to realize is that you're making them so that they don't have to. So, no. I don't think you're a bad person. Hard choice or easy, I know you'll do what's best for your people. All of them." he added intentionally.

Deianira sat still, shocked. He got it. He understood.

That familiar feeling that she got around him settled over her. The one that felt too warm, too close. As much as she hated to ruin what they had started tonight, she needed space.

"Really? Or is that what you tell yourself to assuage your guilt for sitting here, drinking with the Evil Queen while your people starve." she spat bitterly. "Don't kiss my ass to cover up your self-serving bullshit," she slurred.

Cade cocked his head at her, narrowing his eyes. "Stop doing that."

"Doing what?" she retorted defensively.

His eyes lowered to the floor before answering. "Trying to make me go away. You choked me out on my first day in the program and I'm still here with you. I think it's safe to say that I'm not leaving anytime soon," he said, giving her a fake tight-lipped smile.

Deianira remembered that day clearly. She had been so angry, so confused, and she took it out on him.

She tried to tamp down her breathing. "I think that speaks more to your lack of intelligence than your resilience."

Cade shrugged, facing forward to look at the wall. "Entirely possible. But you should know that it'll take a little more than a few drunk words to make me hate you."

Deianira stared at his profile for a while before trying to change the subject.

"So, will you be joining us tomorrow?"

Cade thought about it for a moment.

"I don't know. Maybe."

"Well, it's up to you." Deianira shrugged, hiding how much that disappointed her, *hating* how much that disappointed her. "Uh, I should probably go. It's getting late." There was an uncomfortable tension in the room now.

Cade didn't look at her as he nodded. "Yeah, me too."

Suddenly feeling awkward, Deianira slid off the counter and headed to the door, but not before turning back and saying, "Goodnight."

"Night." she heard echoed back as she closed the door.

Chapter Thirty-Three

Cade had lain awake with his thoughts most of the night.
In all honesty, he wasn't sure whether he wanted to attend the ball or not. He was telling the truth when he said that they did have parties outside of The Dome, he just hadn't been to any. Large groups weren't his thing but he would've said yes in a heartbeat if Deianira had expressed any interest in his attendance. His feelings for her had only doubled after last night. Cade knew that it must not have been easy for her to ask him to come to the lake. It was obviously special to her.
After much deliberation, he decided that if she could step out of her comfort zone, so could he.
He was going to the ball.
First though, he needed something to wear.
Cade had barely left the palace since his arrival. He had no idea where to start but what he did know was that he wanted to impress Deianira.
Getting an idea, Cade ran up to Jude's study, first thing in the morning and knocked.

"Come in," he answered promptly.

Nervous, Cade opened the door and stepped in.

He hadn't spoken to Jude much during his time in the palace but he knew that he'd practically raised Deianira. That was reason enough for Cade to be scared.

"Good Morning, sir," Cade said respectfully.

Jude snorted. "Way to make a guy feel old. Jude, please."

Cade nodded emphatically. "Jude. Right. I, uh, wanted to ask you a favor."

"Go on."

Cade rubbed his shaky hands together. "So, the ball is tonight and I was wondering if I could borrow a suit. I didn't exactly pack to come here and I don't know where to get one or..." he trailed off as he caught Jude's amused expression.

He sat back in his chair, lips tipping up. "Someone to impress?"

"No, sir," he replied, way too fast. "Jude."

Jude laughed and stood, already moving to his adjoining bedroom. "I should have a couple lying around."

"Thank you." Cade released a sigh.

"No problem." Jude stopped and turned back to Cade with a sentimental look. "For the record, I think you're good for her."

Cade wasn't sure what to say, so he just inclined his head.

"Wake up!"

Cassian jolted awake and rolled off the side of the bed, hitting the floor with a not-so-graceful thud.

"What the fuck was that for?!" he yelled, glaring daggers at Eulalia.

"I need you to do something for me."

"Oh yeah, I would love to after the sweet way woke me up." he hissed as he got back into bed.

She shook her head. "So dramatic. But seriously, I need you to cover for me tonight."

"For what?" he asked, words muffled by the pillow.

"I'm going somewhere I can't take my guards," she said casually.

He lifted his head from the pillow. "Where?"

"None of your business. I just need you to say that I'm in here sleeping if anyone asks."

"No," he said, pulling the covers over his head.

The covers were quickly yanked back down.

"Why?" she whined.

Cassian looked at her like she was out of her mind. She probably was.

"You do know that if something happens to you and Cade finds out that I lied and let you go off into the night, he might *actually* kill me."

"No, he wouldn't..." she said, narrowing her eyes before rolling them. "Okay, maybe, but that's beside the point. This is really important." she pleaded.

Cassian leaned up on his elbows. "Eulalia, what could be that important?"

She watched him for what felt like an eternity before quickly saying, "I think my mother is here but I need to look for my birth records in the queen's study to be sure."

Oh.

Cassian wasn't sure about the specifics but he knew that Eulalia didn't grow up with parents. She'd lived in the school for most of her life.

He was young when his mother died and if he had the opportunity to see her again or even learn more about her, he'd take it. Her curiosity was understandable.

"Fine," he huffed before rolling over.

"Thank you!" she squealed, throwing herself on top of him in a very uncomfortable hug.

He elbowed her off him and readjusted the covers. "You have until three to do whatever you need to do and I swear to the Gods if you're not back by then, I'll rat myself out to Cade."

"Aww," she cooed, climbing off the bed.

"What now?"

She turned back toward him. "You care about me."

She wasn't wrong but he wasn't going to admit it.

⟠

Deianira sat on her bed and stared at her dress.

The truth was, she'd found the Prima Ball almost unbearable each year. There honestly wasn't much to enjoy.

She got to watch others sing, dance, and enjoy themselves whilst she sat and watched, pretending not to notice how her people gasped or flinched when they moved too close to her. But that was the reality of ruling. Though Deianira hadn't signed up for it, she knew that fear was the only way to keep order.

As much as she didn't want to admit it to herself, that was why she wanted Cade there. Having one person in the room that didn't fear her or wasn't bound by duty would've made the night just a bit more tolerable. But she understood his objection. His words from the night before had been playing on her mind.

Of course, she knew of the history behind the divide in Terra. Even before her reign began, she was schooled by the best teachers in The Dome. Knowing and hearing it first-hand was different though. Deianira couldn't even imagine how the people outside were living, but she swore an oath to protect hers.

But does it have to be one or the other?

Cade was right about everyone being 'one people' at a time. But that was hundreds of years ago. Deianira was nothing like her ancestors before her, who created the Prima Act, but that didn't mean that she had to be the one to rectify their wrong-doings.

Did it?

Chapter Thirty-Four

Cade was already regretting this as he stood in the corner, back facing the wall.

He shouldn't have come. It wasn't just the crowds. It was the looks. How Cade ended up in The Dome was no secret. After all, most of these people were in the city center that day. The same people that cheered on his death now watched him with pure disdain. They looked at him like he was an outsider, a murderer, a thief. He didn't blame them, but he didn't have to like it either.

"Where did you get *that*?" Lia strutted up to Cade, waving her hand around him.

He looked down at his black tux with silver trimmings and subtle accents, his black dress shirt with a sharp lapel, his bowtie that he spent an hour trying to figure out how to tie.

Cade cringed and ran a hand over the hair pulled back on top of his head. "From Jude. Why? Is it not-"

"You look amazing." She beamed.

"Oh. Thank you," he said, releasing a sigh of relief.

Cade then looked Lia up and down, blinked, then did it again.

She was in a knee-length, silk, purple slip dress that complimented her almond skin perfectly. It was strange seeing her in anything other than her mesh gear and muddy boots.

"Since when did you wear dresses?"

She looked down at herself and smirked. "Since I found one in the armoire. Pretty, right?" she giggled giving him a twirl.

"Very," he laughed. "You look good."

Something over Cade's shoulder caught her eye and she let out an awe-struck laugh.

"Not as good as your girl."

Cade's cheeks flushed. "My girl? Who's my g-"

"Oh, shut up and turn around." she cackled, already grabbing a hold of his shoulders and rotating him.

Cade turned as the room quieted. He looked from the double doors to the stained glass windows, to the high ceilings.

Where is she?

He knew she was close. He could practically feel her. If only he cou-

There.

The stairs.

The click of her heels were all that could be heard in the silent ballroom as she descended the center staircase.

Cade's breath left him.

Time didn't just slow.

It stopped.

The sleeves of her midnight dress started just off her shoulders while the hem of the bodice danced across her collarbone. The slits, lined with silver accents, went all the way up to her hips but were held together by crisscrossed strings on each thigh, leaving a long trail of material between her legs.

The band of the silver crown that sat on her forehead, dipping into a small 'V' above her brows, was concealed by her hair. Her shiny, pin-straight hair that swished with every step, free of its usual restrictions, ran down her shoulders and past the small of her back. As Cade met her eyes, he realized that even if the night ended right now, it was worth attending the ball just to see her like this.

Deianira tried to calm her nerves and she waited at the top of the staircase.
What was wrong with her? She did this every year.
"It's time," Salem said.
She took her place behind Deianira, next to Jude.
Deianira took several deep breaths as they walked to the head of the staircase, the room going silent.
As she slowly began to descend, she found herself searching the crowd for a certain someone.
She tried to stop herself considering the fact that he didn't promise he'd be in attendance but she couldn't stop her eyes from scanning the room, full of hope.
Partway down the stairs, Deianira had been close to giving up her search when she caught a glimpse of those beautiful green eyes in the corner of the room.
And they were looking right at her.
Her heart swelled.

That same warm feeling in her stomach came back and increased tenfold. She did her best to hold back her smile at his parted lips and wide eyes.

Deianira didn't take her eyes off him as she sauntered down the remaining steps and through the parted crowd in the middle of the room. Not even as she stepped up onto the platform where her throne was sitting. She only looked away to turn and take her seat where she was finally able to take a full breath as the violinists resumed.

That breath was quickly lodged in her throat when Deianira looked up to find Cade missing from where she had seen him last.

Scanning the surrounding area, she still couldn't find him.

Did he leave?

Had she been seeing things?

Maybe she just wanted to see him so much that-

"Your Majesty,"

That voice.

Standing at the foot of the platform, Cade stood with a face of wonderment, hand held out in Deianira's direction.

There is no way he's going to ask me t-

"Will you dance with me?"

Cade didn't even seem to notice the murmurs and gasps around him. He was just looking at Deianira as if the rest of the world had disappeared, an amused smile gracing his lips.

Her heart raced. She'd never been asked to dance before.

Who would ask that of the queen?

Evidently, Cade would.

With him though, she wasn't the queen. She was Deianira.

That was all she thought about as she stood from her throne and took his hand.

She distinctly heard Salem call from behind her but she was too focused on Cade as he walked her to the middle of the ballroom.

As Cade slowed, he turned with her hand still clutched in his and placed the other around her waist. He splayed out his fingers across her back pulling a shiver from Deianira.

Looking into his eyes, they began moving.

"I thought you wouldn't show," she whispered as she absently toyed with the hair dangling at the back of his head.

"Why?" he asked, brows drawn.

Taking a deep breath, she said, "Things don't usually turn out the way I want them to."

It was clear that Cade understood the meaning behind her words because a warm smile spread across his face.

"Well, I'm glad I did. You look gorgeous."

She could feel herself softening in his arms. So she tried to rein it in. "Shut up!" she hissed.

Cade let out a loud snort. "I can take it back if you want," he said cheekily.

She rolled her eyes. "Thank you."

Deianira looked him up and down wondering whether she should compliment him back when she noticed something.

She narrowed her eyes and cocked her head at Cade. "We're matching," she said warily. "Did you see my dress?"

Cade looked down, apparently, only just noticing the same thing.

"No, I-" he stopped before he let out a small laugh. "Your uncle."

Huh?

"Jude gave you that?" she asked, surprised. "I always thought he didn't like you."

All the humor drained from Cade's face. "Did he tell you that?" he rushed out, his grip on her hand tightening.

Deianira tried her best but she couldn't help the giggle that burst from her throat. She hadn't been lying, she didn't think that Jude liked him. But seeing Cade so flustered at the idea that her uncle might not be a fan was hilarious.

As she sobered, she realized that most of the room was staring at her. But the only pair of eyes that looked at her with awe were Cade's.

"You should laugh more," he told her with all seriousness. Then he delivered a soft pinch to the side of her waist.

"Cade!" she half-snorted.

"But not at me," he said with amused eyes.

She scoffed as she drew back her foot to kick him in his ankle. There was no doubt they were still sore from yesterday.

"Don't you dare…" he smiled, stepping back but keeping his hold on her.

Deianira narrowed her eyes in challenge. "You're only making me want to do it more."

Cade abruptly tugged her body tight against his, pulling a squeak from Deianira.

His lips brushed the shell of her ear. "Behave."

At a time, she might have been angered by his instruction, but her whole body shuddered at his deep rumble. "Fine line, Cade," she said in a breathy whisper. "I've killed men for less."

He drew his head back to stare deep into her eyes. "Yeah?" he asked, breath fanning over her lips. "Yet I'm still here."

He was right. He was still here. After every word he'd said or infraction of his, he was still here.

Deianira thought about his words for a while but no matter how much she tried, she couldn't find it in herself to regret anything that led them here.

I am no slave to compassion.

Maybe, she was.

Spotting the queen at the top of the stairs and knowing that everyone's attention would be on her, Lia slipped through the side entrance of the ballroom and jogged down the hall, silently cheering when she waited and realized that no one had followed. As quickly as she could, she took the service stairwell back upstairs to Deianira's study.

Standing outside, she did another quick survey of her surroundings. She was still alone.

Lia cursed as she tried the handle.

Locked.

She momentarily thought about breaking in. There was no way she slipped away just to go back. Then, she remembered that the bedrooms were connected to the studies.

Walking further down the hall, Lia sent up a quick prayer before trying the door. It opened.

Thank the Gods.

Finding the internal study door locked as well, Lia searched for a key. No, not a key.

It had a digital pad, no keyhole.

Lia sat down on the bed, wanting to cry. She wouldn't be getting any answers tonight.

"Ugh!" she groaned.

As if responding to her outburst, a soft ping sounded from across the room.

Standing up abruptly, Lia walked in the direction of the sound when she caught sight of a small light coming from the queen's vanity.

Pulling the first drawer open, Lia found the source of the light. The queen's bracelet. The one that opened all of the doors in the entire palace.

Lia couldn't believe her luck.

Choosing not to waste any more time, she grabbed the bracelet and ran back to unlock the study.

Stepping inside, she saw that she had her work cut out for her. Bookshelves lined the high walls around all four lengths of the room. She first went to the section titled 'Birth Certificates'.

Lia searched through the year she was born but when she found nothing, she looked a few years out on either end, just in case she had the dates mixed up. But still, she found nothing.

Getting another idea, she moved on to hospital records. Her birth might not have been registered but if she was born in a hospital or clinic, it would have been recorded.

She was skimming through the names on the list of recorded births when she caught something. Flicking back to check again, she thought she was seeing things.

'SAMBOR, GRACE'

She was looking for births that were recorded and not registered but she didn't expect to see her last name on a file, clear as day.

When she was found behind the school as a baby, the name 'Eulalia Sambor' was stitched into the bottom of her blanket so she knew that this meant something.

Taking the file into the bedroom, Lia separated all the attachments and extra pieces of paper on the desk when she came across a picture.

If there was any doubt in her mind that this woman might have been her mother, it was gone now. She felt the sting of tears behind her eyes as she looked at the picture. The most beautiful brown eyes stared back at her. From her dark bronze skin to her curly, black, voluminous hair, Lia saw herself.

It was her.

Putting the image down, she wiped her eyes as she skimmed the patient information for anything recent.

Delusions.

Paranoia.

Involuntary hold.

The Haven.

That last one was updated only months ago.

That was it. Lia would go to The Haven.

She would meet her mother.

Chapter Thirty-Five

As one of the last songs drew to an end, Deianira reluctantly removed her hand from Cade's shoulder.

People were around them singing and dancing, evidently over the fact that Cade had asked Deianira to dance. But she didn't want to leave the bubble. Not yet, maybe not ever.

They had eaten, danced, and laughed.

Really laughed.

The ball would be over soon but Deianira wanted more time. She wanted something else too. Something that had been brewing from the beginning of the night. From the moment she saw Cade.

If there was ever a time to let go, it was tonight.

Turning to find Salem by her throne, Deianira signaled to her. At her sentinel's nod of understanding, she made for the side exit, but not before grabbing Cade's hand and hauling him behind her.

As soon as they made it into the hallway and rounded the corner, Deianira whirled on Cade, ignoring his expression of concern.

"Is it an episode? Are you ok-"

She cut him off with her lips, both hands holding either side of his head, pulling him to her. His answering groan was like music to her ears as he wrapped his large hands around her waist and opened his mouth. Pulling her tighter against his body, Cade walked her back to the wall as his tongue delved into her mouth. Deianira moaned against his lips as his hands slid lower, cupping her ass.

Instinctively, she hopped up and wrapped her legs around his waist. Cade didn't even pause for a beat as he cradled her behind and she shuddered as she felt his length press against that perfect spot.

"You have no idea how badly I've wanted you like this," he groaned, pressing another kiss to her lips. "What I want to do to you."

"Show me," she whispered into his mouth.

He didn't need to be told twice. Tightening his grip on her, he marched through the halls and up the stairwell, all while giving her his full attention. Deianira was impressed.

Cade walked backward through her bedroom door, still holding her against him. Wiggling out of his hold, she turned and pulled her hair over her shoulder. He already knew what to do. Pressing a soft kiss to her nape, he slowly pulled at the zipper, his lips following the trail down her back.

⌒▽⌒

Cade had no idea what had caused Deianira's change in behavior but he would take whatever she was willing to give him.

When he saw her walk down those stairs, he thought his heart might beat out of his chest. She was bewitching.

He was surprised that he'd managed to make it through the night without pushing his luck, but he was still content with just being in her presence. That was until she attacked him in the hallway, Cade wasn't complaining though.

As he swiftly removed his clothes, Deianira turned to face him and let her dress fall to her ankles. He was speechless.

He'd never seen someone so...

"So perfect..." he whispered, drawing her back in.

He kissed her like a man starved. Moving from her lips to her jaw, he threaded his fingers into her hair above her nape and tugged.

He'd always wanted to do that.

Deianira's answering gasp was everything. Using his left hand to tilt her head back, he kissed his way down her neck. His right hand glided down her soft skin, sliding over her pert breasts, down her tight stomach, slowing when he reached between her legs.

Cade knew what she wanted and her desperate moan as he rubbed his thumb over that sensitive spot attested to that. He circled her clit slowly while kissing his way down the other side of her neck.

"Cade," Deianira breathed. He couldn't deny her anything when she said his name like that.

Speeding up his movements with his thumb, he slid a finger into her slick entrance. When he withdrew it, Deianira began to protest before he returned with a second. He thrust his fingers faster, deeper, until she was panting. As her breaths quickened and he felt her begin to tighten around his fingers, he slowed, much to her disapproval. He repeated the movements over and over before he removed them altogether.

The little growl that Deianira let out would've been cute had she not shoved at his chest while using her ankle to drag his knee from beneath him. Cade nearly yelped as his back collided with the bed. *Damn.*

Leaning up on his elbows and scooting back, he watched as Deianira crawled towards him.

Reaching him, she gave him a chaste kiss, whispering against his lips. "Hands at your sides."

Cade complied without a second thought. He kept his hands to himself and watched as Deianira moved closer and closer to where he needed her.

Deianira sat back on her knees and took Cade's impressive length in her hand. As she gave him a gentle stroke, she smirked when she was rewarded with his sharp intake of breath. Leaning down, she made sure to keep her eyes on him as she licked up the underside of his shaft.

"Deianira…" he groaned.

Hearing her name on his lips only encouraged her, so she went a step further and took the tip into her mouth, swirling her tongue around him while slowly pumping with her hand. She could see his hands shakily grasping at the bedsheets, just wanting to move, to touch her, so she took him deeper. Hollowing her cheeks, she sucked, gently squeezing his length as she pumped her hand up and down a little faster.

"Oh, Gods!" he choked out.

The rise and fall of Cade's chest quickened as his head fell back, exposing the strained veins in his neck. Taking him as deep as she could, Deianira's eyes began to water but she didn't let up, even as she felt him begin to twitch at the back of her throat.

"Deianira! Gods I'm gonna-" he gasped, but she released him at the last second.

Without giving Cade a second to catch his breath, Deianira climbed over him, aligning her center on his tip, and lowered herself onto him.

Their simultaneous moans filled the room.

Deianira had to pause for a moment. She was so full. It was almost too much.

"Fuck..." he hissed, his hands automatically coming to her hips as she tried to adjust to his size.

Taking a deep breath, Deianira summoned two shadows to grab both of Cade's arms and hold them to the pillows.

"What the-"

She gave him a smug smile. "I said, hands at your sides."

Then, she began moving. With her hands on his chest, she rode him, rising and falling on his length.

It was euphoric.

As Cade's groans grew louder, she picked up her pace, grinding her pelvis to his on each fall.

Feeling her release gradually build, she kept going until the only sound in the room were their labored breaths and the slap of their flesh.

Abruptly, Cade thrust his hips upwards and reached a spot so deep, he almost threw her over the edge. Deianira's eyes fluttered as a loud moan tore itself from her throat, her focus interrupted.

Before she could protest, she was falling onto the mattress and Cade was looming above her with a smug smile that rivaled her own.

"I tried," he panted before his eyes darkened. "My turn."

As she opened her palm to bring another shadow, he thrust forward with so much force that the headboard slammed against the back wall. Deianira cried out as her release hit her on impact, sending her into sweet bliss. All she could do was hold onto him as he rode her through her climax while she writhed beneath him. As she came to, she looked up and locked eyes with Cade.

There was so much she wanted to say, so much that she felt. It soon left her mind though when Cade wrapped one of her legs around his waist and leaned down, bringing them chest to chest, deepening his thrusts.

"Cade, Gods!" she squealed, as he hit that sweet spot over and over again.

She didn't even realize that she had closed her eyes until he spoke. "Look at me."

Deianira blinked up, her vision hazy as she began clenching around him, her release building again.

Keeping her eyes on him, she drew her hand over her head and placed it flat on the headboard as his thrusts became punishing. He was frenzied, relentless.

As he pushed into her again and again, Deianira's eyes caught the small ring on a chain around his neck. It swung over her forehead, jostling in time with his thrusts. It was hypnotizing.

Her climax came over her in intoxicating waves, each one more powerful than the last. It was all she could do not to scream as she bit her lip to muffle her cries. Being with him like this made her feel exposed, like she was breaking before him. That voice in the back of her mind was there again, telling her to rein it in.

Defiantly, she closed her eyes again and tried to tamp down her breathing.

"Deianira..." Cade sighed as he slowed his pace, his own release not far off.

He could tell that she was holding back but she couldn't help it. It felt like an invasion.

"No," she gasped at his silent request, still riding out her pleasure. The next thing Deianira knew, she was on her stomach. Cade, kneeling behind her, quickly drew her up bringing her back to his chest as he entered her again.

"Let go." Cade rasped into her ear, locking a hand around her neck.

"Please." With his free hand, he dragged his fingers between her folds.

Grabbing onto the headboard again and placing a hand on his thigh, Deianira couldn't contain her moan as he stroked her clit in time with his thrusts, gently squeezing her throat.

She gritted her teeth and hissed at the intensity.

Deianira was only half aware of the lewd sounds coming out of her as she growled and gasped. She wasn't sure how much more she could take.

"Deianira..." he said more sternly. "Let. Go." His thrusts were hard, deep, meaningful.

Her third climax was dragged out of her almost painfully. Deianira screamed out, unabashed by the possibility that someone might hear. She didn't care. There was only Cade.

"That's it," he groaned in praise. "Just like that."

Picking up his pace enough to make the bed shake, Cade found his release, spilling into her while grunting into the crook of her neck. It only drew out her pleasure as she shook against his chest, hands frantically grabbing at his arm.

Eventually, he slowed to a stop, pressing sweet kisses onto her shoulder as she pulsed around him.

The room was silent, save for their tired breaths.

"You're so fucking beautiful," he whispered into her ear making her heart warm.

As they both dropped back onto the sheets, uncertainty filled Deianira's veins. She felt bare, revealed.

Will he leave?

Should I leave?

No, this is my room.

A hand around her waist drew her from her warring thoughts. Cade silently pulled Deianira into his chest. Suddenly, she didn't feel so vulnerable.

She melted into his arms as three words swirled around in her head, but sleep took her before they could leave her lips.

Chapter Thirty-Six

Standing at the entrance of The Haven, Lia tried to get a hold of herself. She had no idea what state she'd find her mother in.

Why was she in assisted living?

Lia hadn't fully read the file. When she found out where her mother was, she was off without looking back.

Walking up to the reception desk, she steeled her spine and took a deep breath. There was only one lady behind the desk, which made sense considering the day.

"Hi," Lia said a little bit too loud.

The woman quickly looked up from her computer. "Hello, how can I help you?"

Lia froze for a second.

This might actually be it.

"Uh, I'm here to see Grace Sambor." she managed to spit out.

The woman's brows lowered. "First, Her Majesty, now you? That's the second this week. What's your name?"

"Lia." she blurted before she could stop herself. She should've used a fake name.

"Liaaaa..." she drawled as the typed. "You're not on the visitors' list, sweetie."

Of course, I'm not.

She sprung for the first thing that came to mind. "Oh, yeah, I know. Her Majesty actually sent me to conduct a welfare check."

Her eyes narrowed. "You expect me to believe that Her Majesty sent *you* here?"

"Yes," Lia responded, starting to sweat. She pushed down the slight offense that nibbled at her at the lady's disbelief that the queen would send *someone like her* to The Haven.

The woman didn't appear convinced.

Improvising, Lia pretended to fiddle with the digital bracelet on her wrist.

"Listen," She looked at her badge. "Marta. I'm on a tight schedule and if I have to tell Her Majesty that I couldn't complete this one task, on Prima Day of all days, who do you really think she'll rain down on? Her devoted assistant who sacrificed her one night off to work or the receptionist who thinks she's the high gatekeeper to *The Haven*?"

Lia tried to keep a straight face as Marta blanched. "Room B-06" she whispered.

"Thank you." Lia smiled sweetly. "And Happy Prima Day."

As soon as she passed the double doors and turned left, Lia ran up the stairs for fear that the lady might realize she was an imposter and seek her out.

Standing outside B-06, she squared her shoulders and knocked. Then she remembered what time it was and figured that whoever was behind the door would be asleep. She considered just walking in when the door creaked open.

Lia stood in place as it opened wider.

She couldn't move.

It was her.

It was really her.

"Yes?" her mother said.

Lia couldn't speak. She just stared as tears brimmed in her eyes. That must've hinted something because in the next second her mother's face contorted into one of surprise, happiness, longing, and grief, all at once.

"Eulalia?"

Lia choked on a sob and nodded.

The next thing she knew, she was in her mother's arms. She squeezed Lia so hard, she struggled to breathe. But Lia didn't care.

I found her.

After settling into the room Lia's apprehension rose. Of course, she was happy to have found her mother but she had questions.

"I'm sure that you have questions." Grace started.

Lia smiled despite her nerves.

"I do," she replied, sitting on her hands. Lia took a calming breath. "Okay. I had a vision a couple of days ago… A woman paid some officials to take me to the western sector when I was a baby." She peeked up at her through damp lashes. "Was that you?" Lia asked, her voice breaking at the end.

"Yes." her mother responded solemnly.

That wasn't what Lia wanted to hear. On her way over, she'd half convinced herself that she was kidnapped or taken from her birth mother. But her mother was the one who gave her up.

"Why?" Lia asked in a pained whisper.

Grace's eyes never left Lia's. "It was the only way to protect you."

Annoyance rose in Lia. "I heard you say that in the vision, but what does it even mean? Right now, it sounds like an excuse."

"He would've killed you if he found out about you." Grace cast her eyes to the ground.

"Who?" Lia almost shouted before she remembered that it was late and she wasn't supposed to be there.

Her mother didn't speak for a while.

Lia just wanted an explanation.

She was about to prompt her mother again when she finally spoke.

"Your father," Grace whispered.

Lia reared back. "My father? Why would my father want to hurt me?"

Grace shook her head grimly. "He's not the man I would've chosen. I was in a bad place. I had no idea what he was until it was too late."

"Answer the question. Why would he want me dead?" Lia urged.

The look Grace gave her was one of pure misery and hopelessness. "My poor child. You shouldn't have come here."

She might as well have been speaking in riddles. Lia just wanted a straight answer. "Why?!"

"Because if he succeeds tonight, you will be the only thing standing between him and the throne."

Chapter Thirty-Seven

Deianira woke up a few hours later to an empty bed.
Instantly, her heart sank.
She didn't think that he'd actually leave. Not after what they'd just done.
Maybe, it didn't mean that much to him, her mind told her.
She didn't know why that thought hurt so much, only that it made her feel like she couldn't breathe. She wanted to scold herself for being so pathetic.
Sitting up, she clutched the sheets to her chest, a sob readied in her throat, when she saw Cade standing at her desk. Donned in his slacks, his was back to her.
Her heart unclenched.
That was until he turned around and she caught the look on his face. Those shimmery green eyes were dull and red, filled with unshed tears. That cheeky smile was nowhere to be found.
He looked distraught. No, broken.
Concerned, Deianira wrapped the covers around herself and ran to him. She had something special in store for whoever put that look on

his face. As soon as she raised a hand to his cheek, he stepped out of her embrace.

A cold shot of rejection shot through Deianira.

What the hell happened?

He was fine only hours ago.

Or maybe he wasn't fine before. Maybe it was all an act.

That thought had ice threatening to fill her veins.

Would he really-

Her eyes caught something on her desk.

'SAMBOR, GRACE'

'HADRICK, ELIZA'

Deianira closed her eyes before she could read any further.

I should've told him.

The guilt and the memories had been eating away at her for years and she just wasn't ready to see Cade look at her like she was a monster. She wanted to live in the fantasy for a little longer.

Deianira knew it was wrong. She knew it wasn't fair, but sometimes when Cade looked at her, she felt weightless. She didn't want to come down yet.

Opening her eyes, she realized that the Cade standing in front of her was one she'd never seen before. The anguish and despair were gone and replaced by pure, hot rage.

When he spoke, it was so quiet and so low that she almost didn't recognize his voice. She was almost afraid.

Cade took a step forward, leaning close. "Why do you have a picture of my mother under the name Eliza Hadrick, and who the hell is Grace Sambor?"

There was no more waiting. She had to tell him the truth. The whole truth.

So she did.

"Eliza Hadrick was her name before she met your father," Deianira whispered, not meeting his eyes.

When all she heard was the hitch in his breath, she continued.

"A very long time ago, I had a servant named Grace. She was much more to me though, she became one of my closest friends. One night, just like you did, she came to me, hysterical, and told me that her wife had died in their home. She wasn't sick, it was an accident. Unexpected. Her wife was an empath named Eliza Hadrick and I had met her on a few occasions. She was a wonderful lady, a teacher, but none of that mattered," Deianira hiccupped. "Because at the moment, I couldn't say no to Grace. I had never restored anybody until that day and..." Her voice broke with a sob. "I- I tried my best, I swear to the Gods, Cade, I did. But restoration is unstable and when she woke up, she didn't remember a thing about her life." Her eyes fell closed again as she shook her head. "Not her wife, not her job, not even parts of herself." She inhaled. "Grace was heartbroken. She tried to keep it together but Eliza must've been overwhelmed because she ran away some time later. From that day, it was like Grace became a ghost."

Risking a glance at Cade, those glaring eyes were still on her. He hadn't moved an inch. He didn't even try to speak to her, to embrace her.

Oh, Gods...

She'd ruined it. Deianira didn't even try to tamp down her cries as she told him the rest.

"She wouldn't eat, wouldn't sleep. I only managed to keep tabs on Eliza for a few years. Then, she just disappeared." Her voice was so quiet, it was only for the silence in the room that he could hear her.

"Grace quit her job here and started spiraling. She wasn't herself, she started drinking. I had to pull rank to get her out of trouble with the law countless times. Eventually, she fell pregnant. A baby girl. She wouldn't tell me who the father was, wouldn't let me help her. She started getting visions that someone was going to hurt her baby and she was becoming paranoid. I knew it was Eliza's absence that pushed her off the edge so I had her admitted to The Haven just before she gave birth. I just didn't want her to hurt her baby or herself." Deianira's chest heaved. This was the part she blamed herself for the most. "About a week after she gave birth, the baby went missing. Grace wouldn't tell me what she'd done, only that she'd protected her, and I had no idea what had happened until Eulalia showed up here with your brother."

Deianira's shoulders silently shook as she waited for Cade to speak. She stood there, raw and open.

"I wanted to tell you-" Deianira started only to be cut off.

"Then why didn't you?" The thick rasp in his voice startled her.

"I..." she shook her head. He wouldn't get it.

"So, you knew I was gifted too?"

"I'm sorry..." she gasped and apparently, that was all Cade needed. His laugh was empty and harsh as he aggressively swiped a hand over his eyes.

"My mother died in my arms, ten years ago. She'd just given birth to my baby brother, who never even got the chance to live. Stillborn." He shook his head cruelly. "In my head, she's already gone. She has been for a long time. But Lia's mother is alive. She's been here for weeks and you've said *nothing*."

"I'm so sorry..."

That only seemed to anger Cade more as he brought his face closer to hers.

"Stop it!" he bellowed, hands shaking. "You don't get to be sorry!"

He turned away from her for a second and came roaring back.

"She was three weeks old!" Deianira flinched. "She lived in a crappy building for fifteen years, surviving off of whatever scraps my mother could sneak to her. And she never once complained. I may have had a crappy father, but she had nothing. Absolutely nothing!" Cade shook his head, chest rising and falling. "This would've been everything to her." He backed up slightly. "I might be able to forgive you for keeping this memory of my mother from me. But I will *never* forgive you for taking this from her." He gestured to the files.

Cade backed up and she watched as he grabbed his shirt off the floor before slipping it on.

Deianira had fought men, beasts, looked into the eyes of death itself, but she had never been more scared than she was right now.

Please, don't leave.

That's what she wanted to say. But the next words that came out of her mouth were more selfish than any she'd ever muttered.

"Do you love her?" she rasped into the dead room.

She didn't need to elaborate. He knew she was talking about Lia.

Cade stopped and turned to look at her. Very slowly.

His lips were parted with shock.

"Are you seriously *that* stupid?" he asked, shaking his head with utter disbelief.

Deianira didn't know whether to be offended or confused.

He advanced towards her. "No, seriously, are you that blinded by your own deception that you can't see what's right in front of you?"

he said, his hands forward and pressed flat together, voice growing louder.

She remained silent, still not understanding.

What am I meant to see?

"DEIANIRA, I LOVE YOU!" he bellowed.

Her blood stilled.

"I came to this stupid ball and borrowed your scary uncle's suit FOR YOU! I dragged myself out of bed at three in the morning every day so you could kick my ass, just to spend time WITH YOU! I am here, right now, because I LOVE YOU!" Every word was laced with hurt.

"But you couldn't even..." He sounded like he was in physical pain.

"She was my mom, Deianira..." he choked out quietly.

She wanted to crumble just watching how much her actions had hurt.

Eliza wasn't just Grace's wife to him, she was his mom. If Deianira could learn more about her parents, she'd jump at the chance. She hadn't seen them in over a hundred years. But Cade's wound was fresh. She could've given him something beautiful but she kept it to herself out of selfishness, because she wanted to keep him.

Cade must've mistook her silence for lack of caring because he watched her, standing still for a few more moments, before shaking his head and making for the door.

He loved her.

The possibility hadn't even crossed Deianira's mind.

Well, whatever he'd previously felt for her was gone now.

She'd done it. Cade was right, it did take more than a few drunk words to make him hate her. She just didn't know that it would happen so soon, that it would hurt this bad. That it would feel like her heart was trying to crawl out of her chest.

Each step that he took away from her felt like a punch to the gut. She wanted to stop him, to tell him that she loved him too, that she'd never loved anyone like she loved him. But the second, she stepped out from her spot, a crippling bolt of pain brought her to her knees and she watched him walk out of the door without a backward glance.

Blood.
Cade! She tried to shout.
So much blood.
No, no, no, not now.
"*What have you done?*"
Gods, please, not now.

Chapter Thirty-Eight

Cade felt dizzy as he stumbled through the hallways to get back to his room.

She knew. This whole time she knew.

The pieces began to fall into place leaving him winded.

He wanted to hate her. He really did, but every cell in his body was so ridiculously in love with her. There was no easing the vice grip that she had on his heart.

It hurt, really hurt.

Why wouldn't she just tell him? Did she think that he'd be angry at her for the restoration?

His mother was who she was talking about before she restored Devin. The one that went wrong.

But how could she possibly think that he'd blame her for that? All he would've wanted was the truth.

And Lia.

Despite Cade's struggles growing up in the western sector, he knew that Lia had it harder. Not only did she start out alone, but she grew up to be ostracized, bullied, and cast out. All for things that she couldn't control.

Deianira wasn't to blame for her upbringing but she could've given Lia the only thing that she'd ever wanted. She could've given Cade a fraction of the person that he'd missed for ten years. But instead, she kept it from him, from them.

Does she really care that little?

As much as that thought made him want to tear his heart out, he didn't regret a second with her. She gave him something to live for a short while. He couldn't take that from her.

Cade just needed some time. Some space.

He was just entering the guest wing when he heard it.

BOOM!

The whole palace shook.

Startled, Cade ran to the closest window and looked out. Like a light in the dark, flames raged from the side of the palace. Only seconds later, the lights in the hallways went out and were replaced with a red hue.

Lockdown Procedure.

Cade should have been running to the arena but that was the last thing on his mind.

Deianira.

That was all he could think of.

It was just cruel that he still couldn't escape her after everything that had happened tonight. That his first instinct was to go to her, to make sure she was safe.

Cade cursed. With Deianira on his mind, he ran back in the direction he came. He was almost at the stairwell when he heard the familiar beat of boots marching behind him.

Enforcers.

He turned, hoping to see someone he recognized, to ask what was going on.

As he passed the staircase entrance and the enforcer in the lead came into view, Cade felt a shiver up his spine.

He couldn't quite put his finger on it but *something* wasn't right. Trusting his intuition, Cade backtracked toward the stairwell as casually as he could. As soon as he reached it, he threw himself through the doors to the staircase, just before the shooting started. He didn't even give himself a second to breathe as he bolted into the stairwell.

Why in Terra were enforcers shooting at *him*?

"*Listen to me.*"

Deianira nodded.

"*You will kill them. Tonight. Start with your father, he is the strongest.*" When she shook her head, he snapped at her. "*Deianira, look at me! Then your mother, she will try to protect your sister but she won't be able to hurt you. Then Calliope. Make it quick.*"

Deianira nodded again, her mind cloudy.

Blood.

So much blood.

"*We never have this conversation. This is all your fault. You lost control and you did this.*"

"Yes, Uncle Jude."

Deianira jolted awake, coughing. Trying to come out of her haze, she fluttered her eyes expecting them to have to adjust to the light when she noticed the red tint of everything in her room. Everything was red.

Lockdown Procedure.

No.

This couldn't be happening, they'd planned for this. Jude was supposed to-

Jude.

The flashback.

The mole.

The attempt.

Deianira's mind was moving too fast for her to keep up.

Cade was a liability. If he'd known enough about his father's plans, he could've outed Jude. So Jude tried to get rid of him.

Cut the problem at the root.

Cade.

Deianira tried to get to her feet but her knees gave out.

What's wrong with me?

She didn't have to look far to find the problem because if the blood on her white carpet was anything to go by, she was too weak. That flashback had really taken it out of her. She could just about move, everything ached.

Thud! Thud! Thud!

The door.

She was in no condition to handle an intruder.

Using her elbows, she dragged herself to the right side of the bed to conceal herself just as the door burst open. She held her breath, not even making a peep.

In an invasion, she would be a target and her condition made her even more vulnerable. If she was going to live, fighting wasn't the solution. She needed to hide.

Dull footsteps thudded on the carpet. Deianira tried to quietly drag herself under the bed when she heard the voice.

"Deianira."

She could've cried from relief.

Salem.

"I'm here," she rasped.

Salem rounded the bed.

"What happened?" She crouched beside Deianira, assessing her condition.

"I saw him." Deianira tried to explain as Salem helped her sit up.

"Saw who?"

"Jude. It was him." Tears sprang to her eyes at the memories. "He was there that night. I think he's the mole."

Salem, true to form, only allowed herself a moment to think over it before reverting to action mode. Standing, she jogged to the armoire and pulled out the first few things in there. A pair of shorts and a training top. She threw them at Deianira.

"Put those on. We need to go."

Deianira began tugging the clothes on as best as she could. "What about Cade? Did you see him?"

"No, I didn't. Lockdown has been in progress for two hours so he could already be in the arena." Salem lowered her brows thoughtfully. "That may be a bad thing considering Jude is the one who implemented the security measures for tonight. It's probably a trap."

Deianira's lips parted. She wanted to be sick. "Salem he was alone when he left." She ignored her sentinel's raised eyebrows. "He'll kill him."

"I doubt he's still alone. Before I came here, I helped Hewn get the remaining civilians out of the building." She paused. "Hewn doesn't know. His unit is headed to the arena with hundreds of people. If it's a trap, it's unlikely that he can protect that many people."

"Salem, we need to-" Deianira tried to say.

"I should've seen this coming. Maybe, he won't kill them. If he killed your family and he's leading an invasion on The Dome, he probably wants to overthrow you."

"Salem."

"But he can't be king if there's no kingdom. Though, that's assuming he wants to rule The Dome. With all the sectors supporting him, he wouldn't need *this* kingdom to-"

"Salem!"

Salem quieted and blinked. "I apologize. I was thinking out loud."

Deianira sighed. "You can think all you want but as you said, we need to go."

"Where?" Salem asked.

"The arena." Deianira sluggishly laced up her boot.

Salem's brows drew together. "But it's a trap-"

"I know it's a trap!" she exclaimed. "Even if Jude's waiting for me with a gun cocked, I'm not just going to leave him." She panted, lowering her voice. "Trap or no trap, I'm going. You can join me if you feel like it."

Chapter Thirty-Nine

BOOM!

Cassian was startled out of his sleep.

What the hell was that?

Was it some part of the Prima Day celebration?

Cassian wouldn't know. He opted out of going to the ball. It didn't feel right to him to be enjoying himself when he'd caused so many problems for his family. Although Cade had forgiven him, he found it hard to be in the same room as him with his whirling guilt. Even as Cassian thought of his father, shame overrode his senses.

What would his father think of him now?

Cassian didn't want to care, but he did. It wasn't easy to hate the man that had raised him despite his shortcomings.

Throwing back the covers, he swung his legs over the side of the bed when the lights flicked to red.

Okay, maybe not fireworks.

Lockdown Procedure.

Cassian was sure that he had given the queen all the right information, so how could this have-

The informant.

He only spoke to the queen about his intel. Whoever the mole was, they had to be close to her. With his information, it should've been impossible to infiltrate The Dome, let alone the palace. They changed their plans. They were tipped off.

Lockdown procedure stated that he should go to the arena but that didn't seem like a good idea anymore. Besides, if they were in the palace, there was no way he could get out unscathed. He wasn't gifted like everyone else.

Cassian took a moment to think.

Eulalia still hadn't checked in with him. Maybe she was still out. As much as he didn't like the thought of her being alone, outside was probably safer at that moment. She just needed to stay wherever she was. Cade didn't come back last night either. Cassian assumed he was with the queen, those two weren't subtle. If they were together, they'd have no trouble getting out.

He paced around his room as he ran through the structure of the palace in his head. He just needed a weapon and a way out but he doubted that he could get up to the training room without being noticed.

Cassian threw on a shirt and a pair of boots before striding over to his door. Opening it, he looked both ways and when he saw no one, he jogged down the hall to the room that he hoped would still be occupied.

First, a weapon.

He knocked and waited.

No answer.

Bouncing from heel to heel, he knocked again.

Come on...

Still no answer.

Taking a chance, he pressed on the handle and it opened. He sighed with relief but almost pulled it back shut as he saw Devin standing right behind the door, his hand pulled back and ready to fire.

"Oh, it's you," Devin said as he looked Cassian up and down.

"Yeah, it's me, so put your freaking hand down before you hurt somebody," Cassian hissed, covering his face.

"Oh, sure." Devin lowered his hand.

A thought occurred to Cassian. "Wait, were you just going to stay in here the whole time?" he asked, narrowing his eyes.

Devin cocked his head to the side. "The door opens from the outside and the room dampens my gifts, smartass."

"Oh."

"Yeah, oh. What do you want?"

"I think the palace is under attack but I can't get out of here alone."

Devin finally seemed to show a sense of urgency as he looked out into the hall. "Shit. Are you sure?"

"Yes, and I need your help to get out."

Devin paused for a moment. "One condition."

"Are you serious right now? You're in danger too, you know."

"Do you want my help or not?" Devin shot back, crossing his arms.

Oh my Gods.

"Fine." Cassian seethed.

He responded immediately. "We go to the staff quarters first."

"Why-? Actually, I don't care as long as you're quick. Let's go."

"Sweet." He grinned. "Now, get out of my way."

Cassian rolled his eyes, allowing Devin to pass by and they set out into the hallway, keeping their footsteps light. Well, Cassian kept his footsteps light. Devin didn't seem to have a care in the world as he strolled down the halls behind him.

The quickest way to the ground floor would be through the main stairs in the guest wing but Cassian was quickly stopped when trying to enter the service stairwell.

"Hey," Devin called quietly from behind him.

Cassian turned with his hand on the pull bar.

Devin shook his head vehemently. "We can't take those stairs."

"Why?" he asked, his brows creased.

"I can hear something." He started to walk backward. "We gotta go. Like, right now," he urged.

"Go where?" Cassian argued, stepping back from the door. "The east stairs don't stop on the ground floor." He knew the palace's plans like the back of his hand.

Devin was growing more skittish. "Then we go through the sub-level bu-"

The door to the stairwell burst open, enforcers spilling out of it. Cassian leaped to the left and just about made it out of the line of fire, covering his head before they started shooting.

Before he could even take his next breath, the shooting abruptly stopped. Carefully removing his arm from his face, he looked up to see Devin standing front and center, eyes closed, murmuring quietly. The rest were frozen in place.

Simultaneously, all the guns lowered and the enforcers began clutching their throats, gasping for breath. Cassian watched with wide eyes as they dropped to the floor and began seizing violently before slowing to a stop. He turned his eyes to Devin who still stood, unmoved.

"Devin?"

Devin opened his eyes and pinned Cassian with a smug look. "Now, will you listen to me?"

Cassian was still in shock. It was a good thing he went back for Devin.

"Let's go."

"Wait," Cassian called. "Grab a gun."

"Sometimes, she'd stay," Lia said with a nostalgic smile. "She'd sit with me and we'd talk about absolutely everything."

Grace hung onto her every word.

Lia giggled as she remembered. "At one point, she was convinced that I had a crush on Cade. She would make googly eyes at me whenever he was around." She snorted. "She couldn't have been more wrong." Lia quieted for a moment. "I just wished I'd told her why. I knew at the back of my mind that it wouldn't change how she saw me, but there was already so much that set me apart. People were already shying away from her because of how much time she spent with me and I guess I didn't want to make her look bad." Lia shrugged. "If I'd known about you guys-"

BOOM!

Lia's head spun in the direction of the closest window. She couldn't see the palace from the room she was in, but she could make out the smoke rising from the center of the city.

"It's started," Grace whispered.

Lia turned back to her mother. "What's started?"

At her mother's silence, Lia grew suspicious.

"What's started?" she repeated.

Grace turned to look out of the window. "I tried to warn them. Just like I told them that you were in danger, but it was no use. I'm in here after all. Nobody listens to the mad."

As much as Lia wanted to cry for her, she didn't have time for tears. Cade and Cassian were still inside the palace.

"I need to go. My friends are there." Lia said, getting to her feet. "I promise, I'll come back."

To her surprise, Grace didn't try to stop her. "I'll be here." she nodded solemnly.

Lia started for the door when she called. "Eulalia."

She turned back to her mother.

"Don't tell her."

Huh? "Don't tell who what?"

"Just don't tell her." She didn't explain further.

Lia nodded but in truth, she had no idea what Grace was talking about. Who was she talking about and what did Lia have to tell? Taking the stairs three at a time, she made her way out of the building without looking back.

It was much darker now than when she'd left but thanks to her great sense of direction, it didn't take much longer to reach the palace.

Lia was approaching the corner leading to the main entrance when she heard him.

"They're in lockdown. Jude says this is the only exit available so if she's inside, we'll flush her out through here. All of them. First group, with me!"

Lia almost tripped over her feet as she skidded to a halt. She knew that voice.

Hated that voice.

Drake Alden.

Leaning around the corner, she spotted him. Just the sight of him was enough to make her blood run cold, but it was his clothes that had her pausing the most.

Why was he dressed like an enforcer?

They all were. Hundreds of them. Dressed in full gear, from a helmet and goggles down to their boots. If she hadn't heard his voice, she wouldn't have thought to stay back.

That's the point, she concluded.

All the information that she and Cassian had given to the queen was null and void. With Jude on their side, all they needed to do was alter their plans. They didn't need to attack at the ball if they could just initiate a lockdown and let the queen come to them.

Lia needed to get in and warn them.

Warn them of what exactly?

She was torn. It wasn't like there was any other way out. There were fake enforcers inside so they'd need to come out either way. She needed a diversion. A way inside without drawing attention.

She scanned her surroundings and it only took her a second to find it.

Digging the knife out of her boot and palming it, Lia checked to make sure that no one was watching as she approached the 'enforcer' that stood alone by a truck, facing away from her.

The lack of daylight came in handy.

As swiftly and quietly as she could, she brought the knife to his throat from behind him.

She spoke quietly into his ear. "Breathe too loud and I will cut you from ear to ear. Nod if you understand."

The truth was, Lia had never killed anyone before and she wasn't sure if she even had it in her right now, so she just held her breath and prayed that he wouldn't call her bluff.

After a few seconds of angst, he nodded.

An easy smile fell over Lia's face as she walked him back into the shadows. She kept her hold on him, even when they were completely out of view.

"Give me your gun."

He didn't even try to fight. Just pulled the strap off his shoulder and passed it behind him. Lia could feel him shaking and she almost felt bad. He must have been young. Untrained. She could tell that he didn't know what he was getting himself into.

Carefully putting her knife away and holding up his gun she stepped back.

As he turned, she raised an eyebrow at him, daring him to run.

Once sure he'd stay put, she cocked the gun and said one word.

"Strip."

Chapter Forty

Up or down?
The enforcers were getting closer but Cade didn't know which way to go.
Going upstairs would be trapping himself, but Deianira could've still been up there. Downstairs is the only way to the arena but if intruders were coming in, they'd be coming up. He was trapped either way. But at least one way, he'd be with Deianira.
Just before the door burst inwards, Cade set off, sprinting up the steps. The gunshots that followed had him sticking to the outer walls of the square-spiraling stairs.
As he reached his floor, he practically fell through the doors. Shutting them behind him, he quickly looked around for anything to secure the doors. If they got onto the floor, running would've been pointless.
Spotting a pot of bo staffs at the entrance of the training room, he made a break for it. Grabbing an armful of staffs, he sprinted back to the door just as an enforcer came into view through the small

window. Cade slotted the staffs through the handlebars as the door jolted forward.

It held.

He didn't take a break yet though. Jogging back to the training room, he looked for anything and everything he could arm himself with. Grabbing a utility belt and vest, he strapped them into place over his dress shirt and slacks before stepping into a pair of boots. Running to the shelves, he brought down a specific box and checked inside.

Deianira's throwing knives.

After loading as many as he could into his belt, there was one left in the box. As if sending him a sign, the knife slipped through his fingers and landed next to his foot.

"What's the point if you can't even reach for it?" Cade asked, tilting his head at Lia as he kicked at the tent pegs.

She rolled her eyes as she poked the fire. "You shouldn't have to reach for it. It's a backup." She patted her boot. "Fail to prepare, prepare to fail."

Cade quickly picked up the knife and tucked it into the sole of his boot.

He looked for a firearm but, of course, his luck didn't stretch that far. Loud banging echoed from the hallway and Cade knew he was running out of time. Those wooden staffs wouldn't hold them forever. He couldn't fight them all either. Or run, he needed to find Deianira. He was about to leave the training room when something caught his eye.

Oh, hell yeah.

After setting up as fast as he could, Cade hid behind the planks of wood and waited. He knew that the enforcers had seen him go into the training room. It would be the first place they would look.

He was counting on it.

On cue, he heard a loud crash signaling that they had breached the door. It only took them seconds to start filling up the gym, but Cade still waited. He waited until the last enforcer stepped into the room before he pressed the remote.

At the sound of the mechanical whirring, Cade finally took a breath.

It's working.

Seconds later, hundreds of steel arrows flew across the room, raining down on the enforcers. Cade still didn't move. He listened to the shouts, the screams, the cries.

Only when the room stilled did he step out from behind the boards to see bodies littering the training room floor.

For a moment, he stilled. He knew what he was doing when he loaded the arrow launcher, but nothing could've prepared him for what he saw. There were so many.

As much as he tried to block it out, he couldn't pretend that he didn't hear a few faint wheezes around the room. Some of them were still alive.

When he was brought to The Dome and convicted of murder, he was innocent. But now?

Deianira.

That was the only thought that brought him out of that hole.

He just needed to get to her and it would all be fine.

Leaving the training room, he started towards Deianira's room. Just as he rounded the corner, he caught a figure moving down the hall.

Quickly moving back around the corner, he closed his eyes and leaned back against the wall, praying that they hadn't seen him.

"Come on out, Cade."

He stopped breathing.

Cade didn't fear his father, but as he heard the quiet footsteps approaching around the corner, he was petrified. Not for himself, but for what might happen to Deianira if he couldn't get back to her. It was only because of his gift that he was able to detect that there were imposters in the palace. No one else would know. They'd be handing themselves over.

"We're not here for you. We just want the girl."

The girl.

Cade could've laughed at Drake's reference to Deianira. That girl was the queen. That girl was the woman who held his heart in her very palm. That girl was the reason he'd make it out of this.

His father had already seen him. Cade wasn't stupid enough to try and run, they'd gun him down before he made it to the end of the hall. So he stepped out from around the corner, hands held up, and faced Drake Alden. But not before reaching for the chain around his neck to leave a little message.

I came back for you.

Growing up, he'd always seen his father as this big brute. This man who inspired fear in people.

The Head Councilman, Drake Alden.

But the man that Cade stared at, head-on? The one that stood back with a gut-churning smirk as enforcers advanced on him, grabbing his arms, hauling him into the stairwell? He was nothing but an insecure little boy on a power trip. There was nothing note-worthy about him.

Deianira was practically dragging herself through the halls behind Salem. She was drained, physically and emotionally. Her strength was wavering with each step, even her senses seemed to evade her. That's why she didn't hear the footsteps when Salem did.

"Deianira," Salem called quietly.

She squinted at her through blurry vision.

"They're downstairs. I can't make out what they're saying but we need to skip that floor. We should take east."

"That'll take too long and Cade can't wait. We'll be fine," Deianira panted.

Salem kept on. "Deianira, you're too weak right now. It's my job to protect you and I can't do that while trying to fight off a group of intruders. Our odds aren't great either way but at least we'll be alive to find him if we take the east stairwell."

Deianira thought about it. Salem had a point, but she just hated that Cade would be in danger for longer.

"Okay," she breathed.

Salem slung Deianira's arm around her shoulder.

Starting towards the stairwell, they passed the entrance of the training room before seeing something and backtracking. It looked like a scene out of a nightmare. Bodies surrounded by blood littered the floor. Steel arrows were sticking up in every direction in the room.

Deianira had to hold back a scream of anger.

These were enforcers.

Her men.

All dead.

Deianira yanked her arm out of Salem's grip and stumbled towards the first body, falling to her knees beside him. Breathing heavily, she lifted his mask, praying that it wasn't Hewn or Finch, and she paused. She didn't recognize this man. She'd never seen him in her life. Confused, Deianira tried the next. Then the next. She didn't know any of these men. But they were wearing standard issue enforcer gear down to the make of the guns they were equipped with.

The raids.

The raids had started months back and Deianira was convinced that they were connected, but they were too spread out, they were happening in different sectors. That must have been a ploy to cover their tracks. They were biding their time. No one in the palace would be able to tell the difference.

"Deianira," Salem called, urgency leaking into her voice.

Boots. They were loud. Loud enough for her to hear, so they had to be close.

Her head spun to the service stairwell. She would've run towards that sound a minute ago but after seeing these imposters, she wasn't taking that chance. If Jude wanted her, he'd have to come in and get her himself.

Salem picked her back up and they headed towards the east stairwell when Deianira's eyes caught a small object on the floor. It was shiny.

"Wait," she rasped.

Deianira pulled herself out of Salem's hold to take a step closer.

The second she recognized it, hope ignited in her chest.

The ring.

Cade's ring.

"He was here," she told Salem as she grabbed it. "It's his. He left it here on purpose."

"It could've fallen off."

"No, he wears it on a chain. It couldn't have. He left this here for a reason."

He was here.

He came back for me.

Salem tensed. "We're too late," she whispered.

The disorganized footsteps were coming from the east stairwell too. They were lighter, fewer, but they were still coming in fast.

<hr />

The sub-level was pitch black.

Cassian slowly followed the sound of Devin's footsteps, careful not to trip.

"How can you even see anything?" Cassian whispered to Devin.

"I can't."

Cassian's brows lowered.

"I've been down here a few times. From the stairs, it's twenty-six steps, left, twelve steps, left, seventeen steps, right, eight steps, up."

He frowned in confusion. "Up?"

Devin snapped his fingers and a small flame appeared in his hand.

"Up," he repeated with a smile on his face as he pointed upwards.
Cassian followed his eyes to find a grate on the low ceiling.
"This leads to the utility room in the staff quarters," Devin explained as he lifted the grate and shifted it onto the side. "I'll be back in a sec."
Huh? "Back? What are you-"
Devin didn't hear the rest of Cassian's question because he was already lifting himself through the gap in the ceiling.
Cassian silently fumed. He had no idea how Cade managed to live with Devin for so long without throttling him.
With nothing better to do, he leaned back against the wall and waited. About a minute later, light shone through the opening. Stepping towards the gap, he looked up.
"Hey, Cass. Catch." was the only warning he got before a small object struck him in the nose.
"Ow!" he exclaimed before bending to pick it up.
A flashlight.
At least it was something useful.
Devin came flying through the opening, landing perfectly on two feet.
Finally.
"Can we go now? There isn't much ti-"
A second pair of legs appeared.
Instantly on defense, Cassian lifted his gun and took several steps back. But then, Devin stepped towards the opening, grabbing onto the hips of the person coming through and gently lowering them.
Cassian was beyond confused.
A girl.
A short girl with bright red hair covering most of her face.

Tilting her head gently, Devin brushed her hair out of her face, revealing a striking set of red eyes. That wasn't what stood out most to Cassian though. It was the jagged scar across her neck, spanning from ear to ear. It looked old but it was deep. He'd never seen a wound that bad before.

"Now, we can go," Devin announced, holding her hand.

Cassian stared at them. "You're not going to introduce me?" He pointed to the girl.

"Oh yeah. Cass, this is my girlfriend, Emori. Emori, this is Cass."

"Cassian," he corrected.

"Right," Devin smirked. "Let's go."

Cassian stood still for a moment before shaking his head and following Devin and the mysterious girl through the sub-level. Though it hadn't been long, he noticed that she was very quiet. She hadn't spoken aloud once, but he saw her whisper into Devin's ear every so often. What surprised him, even more, was the change in Devin's demeanor. Gone was the sarcastic, goofy boy. He barely took his eyes off her and kept her hand in his at all times, looking from left to right.

Abruptly, Emori stopped walking. Devin stopped right after. "What's wrong?" he said as he leaned down for her to whisper into his ear.

Their dynamic confused Cassian, but he kept silent.

Devin turned to him, looking slightly more uneasy than before.

"They're waiting by the exit. Hundreds of them. We can't go out this way."

"This is the only way out. We're in lockdown," Cassian argued.

"I think that's the point..."

It made sense, but Cassian was still doubtful. He needed to get outside to see if Eulalia was out there. It was way past three and he wasn't even sure if she was in the palace when the lockdown started.

"How do you know?" Cassian asked Emori. There was no way he was turning back now for anything short of sure.

The glare that Devin shot him had him backing up as he put himself between Cassian and Emori.

"She said it's a trap, so it's a trap. We're going back upstairs," Devin said slowly.

He wasn't sure where that had come from but he wasn't looking to get into it with Devin right now. Holding his hands up in surrender, Cassian conceded. "Fine."

Leading Devin by his hand, Emori walked ahead of them as they started back in the direction that they came.

Chapter Forty-One

Lia's height had always set her apart growing up, but she quite liked it. It suited her. However, she'd never been more grateful for it than she was right now.

After changing into the lone enforcer's gear and hogtying him behind an armored truck, she'd manage to slip into a group that was just heading into the palace. She didn't recognize any of the men as people from her sector, but she knew that they must've been from the outside. They were untrained and disorganized. It made her job of fitting in so much easier.

All she had left to do was to separate from her group without drawing any attention.

Heading through corridors, Lia's anxiety rose. The palace looked deserted. She just hoped that Cade and Cassian had managed to hide somewhere.

As they turned right to ascend the service stairwell, Lia saw her opportunity and began slowly to lag in order to fall to the back of the group. Just as the last enforcer passed through into the stairwell, she turned out of the way of the door as it closed behind them. She waited a few seconds to see if anyone would come back before she made a break for it, running towards the north stairwell. The enforcers were moving quite fast but if she could make it up to the floor of the guest wing before them, she might be able to find someone.

Pumping her arms as fast as she could, her gun bobbing at her hip, Lia sprinted up the stairwell.

On arrival, she practically flung the door open. Cade's room was the first she went to. She shoved at the door and tumbled in.

No one was in the room. The bed was perfectly made.

Stepping outside momentarily, she checked to make sure that she was in the right room.

She was.

Heart rate rising, Lia jogged across the hall to Cassian's room and her heart almost stopped as she saw the door standing open.

Lia immediately raised her gun. Coming up to the doorway, she looked inside cautiously.

Again, it was empty.

After sweeping the room as thoroughly as she could, she began rummaging through his room. She didn't know where else to look. She ran to the closet, then the bathroom only to find nothing. She was spinning in circles, looking for some hint of where they might have gone.

Noise on the other side of the floor told her that the enforcers had arrived. She might've gotten up quicker but they wouldn't be far behind.

Her search grew more frantic as she looked for anything, a hint, a message, even blood. Cassian was the one she was meant to check in with when she got back. Why wouldn't he leave her a note or something?

Heading out of the room, she ran towards the stairwell exit, only to trip on something.

Ruffled, Lia picked herself up and was stopped dead at the sight. The enforcers, the whole group that she had come in with. They were all on the floor. She couldn't tell if they were dead or unconscious, but she didn't want to find out.

Who did this?

If there was someone in the palace that was still on their side, Lia needed to find them.

Scrambling back, she took a quick mental list of all the places she had checked. Maybe Cade was on the top floor.

Lia had seen the signs. She knew he had feelings for Deianira. Thinking about it, Deianira would probably be the first person he'd look for.

Decided, Lia headed to the east stairs.

Pulling the handlebar, she tip-toed into the stairwell and paused to listen.

Incoming.

Backing up to the wall she waited to see if they would exit on the floor below. They didn't.

Lia grasped her gun. Leaning over the railing, she aimed at the wall on the lower flight of stairs and waited for the first person to come into view. She felt the sweat dripping down her forehead, her palms clamming up. All she could do was hold her breath and wait as a familiar blonde head staggered into her eye-line.

Cassian?

She let her gun lower, lightly tapping against the railing, and let out a sigh of relief. That was all it took for Cassian to look up and see her. Lia smiled down at him before she realized that he was lifting his gun and aiming at her.

Belatedly, Lia remembered what she looked like and ducked, throwing herself backward, just before the first of many bullets hit the wall behind her.

"CASSIAN, STOP! DON'T SHOOT! IT'S ME!" she screamed at the top of her lungs.

The bullets stopped.

"Eulalia?!" Cassian shouted up.

Lia slumped as she huffed. "Yes, you idiot! You almost took my fucking head off!"

"Shit!" Several footsteps pelted up the stairs.

Lia scooted back on her bottom as Cassian, Devin and a girl she'd never seen before came up the steps.

"Sorry about that." Cassian offered her a hand to help her up.

She smacked his hand. "Yeah, you should be, asshole."

"What was I supposed to do when you're dressed like that? Why *are* you dressed like that?" He tilted his head.

"It was the only way I could get in. The whole lockdown was a ruse, they wanted us to come out of the front entrance. They're waiting for us. Something's going on," Lia panted.

"Told you, dumbass." Devin smiled smugly as he squeezed the hand of the girl next to him.

Cassian rolled his eyes but Lia's attention turned to her.

"Who's this?" she asked Cassian.

Devin answered for him. "Emori."

Lia watched them all for a second. Deciding that she didn't care enough to ask any more questions, she shrugged and turned back to the others.

"They're sending more in every thirty minutes to flush us out. We need to find Cade and find another way out. Fast."

At their nods, Lia took off, leading them up to the top floor.

Cade stared at his father as he twisted his wrists behind his back, the rope digging into his skin. He hadn't said a word since he'd been dragged into the kitchen and tied to a small wooden chair. His father, however, wouldn't stop talking.

"As you can see, my son here isn't a big talker," he said, laughing with the three other enforcers in the room.

Drake Alden was a narcissist. The worst kind too. He thought the world of himself, needed others to see how great he was. Unfortunately for young Cade though, the front only lasted so long. He knew what happened when the mask came off.

If he wasn't hellbent on getting out and finding Deianira, he would've taken the opportunity to embarrass his father, to see how he liked being tested. But that wasn't the goal. So Cade sat in his chair and waited for the real conversation to start.

"I just want to know where she is. I'll even let you go after. This doesn't need to be hard." Drake almost seemed genuine.

Even if Cade knew where she was, there wasn't a chance he'd tell his father.

"Why do you even care what happens to her?"

Cade recognized that tone. He was goading him. He'd done it a million times before but it never worked. Now though, his father was entering dangerous territory.

Drake let out a huffy laugh. "You know, when my little birdie told me that you were kicking it with the Evil Queen, I didn't believe it." He shook his head. "There was no way my boy was getting some action like that. With the Queen of the Dome, no less."

Cade cringed at the way his father said *'my boy'*. On multiple occasions, Drake had accused Cade's mother of infidelity. He said that he couldn't have produced an invalid, a child who couldn't speak. But now he was his son?

"I'll admit, you did well. But you can stop playing Kings and Queens now." His tone deepened. "Tell me where she is."

Cade said nothing.

Drake nodded. "Expected as much." He then inclined his head at one of the enforcers.

On cue, the enforcer stepped up to the stove and grasped the handle of a cleaver. Cade sucked in a breath.

They were going to cut him.

As he handed it to Drake, Cade noticed that what used to be a shiny silver was now a glowing red.

No, they were going to burn him.

Drake advanced on him slowly, menacingly.

He didn't move, only tensed as his father got closer. Cade leaned back as far as he could, trying to keep his distance from him.

Drake tilted his head thoughtfully as he bent down in front of Cade. "Are you actually going to make me do this?" he asked, feigning hurt. "Over some girl?"

Cade's chest rose and fell faster as he glared at his father.

He stepped back at Cade's expression. "Oh, son. Don't tell me you have feelings for her."

Cade cast his eyes to the ground. He couldn't look at him any longer.

"That's disappointing, Cade. That is really disappointing." Drake gave him a sad head shake before turning to one of the enforcers. "Take his shirt off."

Chapter Forty-Two

Cade's head lolled towards his shoulder as he panted.

"You can make all of this stop, Cade."

He was spent. Every breath he took agitated the seared skin on his chest. But he still held out, Cade could tell that his father was getting desperate. That was good. The longer he was focused on getting information out of Cade, the more time Deianira had to get out of the palace.

"Have it your way."

Drake removed a serrated knife from the set on the counter and approached him.

He could only heave as Drake drew closer.

The first time, he wasn't sure if his father would go through with it. He knew he was sick but he foolishly thought that there was a line that Drake wouldn't cross. Well, he was sadly mistaken.

Even in his condition, he strived to keep his head up, to look at the man who fathered him.

Positioning the point at Cade's collarbone, he pressed down and dragged the blade down his chest, uncaring of the other wounds.

Cade squirmed and grunted, did his best not to cry out. He just kept his focus on the counter next to the stove. It was where he and Deianira had been sitting the night before the ball. They'd talked, joked, and drank.

She's so beautiful.

He replayed that night in his head again and again. It was the only thing he could hold onto.

As he writhed, Drake angled the knife on its point and pushed in an inch causing an animalistic groan to pass his bloodied lips. Through the buzzing in his ears, Cade caught a small laugh before the knife went further. This time, he couldn't stop the gurgled cry that broke free. Drake pulled back the knife.

Cade wheezed as the cool air brushed his open flesh.

As he tossed the bloody knife onto the counter, Drake whirled on him with a punch to the gut. He immediately fell forward as his stomach turned. A few ribs had cracked on his father's third attempt to get him to talk and each hit was beginning to decrease in pain. He was going numb.

That's not good.

Blood and bile crawled up Cade's throat and spilled past his lips. Drake jumped backward and cringed. "Well, that's just nasty."

They'd been at this for over an hour. Cade had a feeling that his father knew he wouldn't tell him anything, knew that he didn't know where she was. That he just wanted to punish him, make him suffer. The possibility wasn't unrealistic. Drake was a twisted man.

"Are you still holding to your vow of silence?" he asked as he wiped the sleeve of his jacket with a cloth.

Cade spat out the remaining blood in his mouth and pushed his facial muscles to pry open his swollen eye and glare at his father. He was clearly enjoying this.

Not that it would've been an excuse, but Cade wasn't a bad child. He didn't misbehave, didn't talk back, did everything he was told. But it was never enough for Drake. There was always something he wasn't doing right. Cade would've liked to be able to say that he didn't care at all, but he did. He just wanted to know what he'd ever done.

Drake sighed. "I will kill her either way. If I really wanted to, we could just blow this place up with her inside." He leaned in again. "I'm trying to give you an out. To save your life despite all the trouble you've caused. Will you work with me?" he asked politely.

Cade's chest heaved with anger, with rage. He was going to kill Drake. One day, he'd kill him.

The sympathy drained from Drake's face. "Well, shit," he huffed. "I've tried just about everything. Maybe, I'm just not that convincing."

Cade continued glaring as his father nodded to the enforcers. "Follow me."

At that, they all trailed after him as he pushed through the kitchen door and left.

He's leaving?

Cade didn't know where he went but he had a feeling that he wouldn't be gone for long. He started throwing his head in each direction, taking stock of what he had at his disposal.

It was a large kitchen. He was in the middle of the aisle and the counters were too far apart for him to reach anything if he tried. His wrists were rubbed raw. Every move he made scraped his skin against the ropes.

The chair he was sitting in looked sturdy enough, but Cade figured that if he tried to stand and fell down hard enough, he could break it. Wasting no time, he stood at an angle and grunted as he dropped onto the chair as hard as he could.

It didn't break.

He tried again.

Nothing.

As he went to stand again, he heard faint footsteps outside.

They're coming back.

Cade's movements became urgent as he bent forward and stood before making small hurried steps toward the counter. He swung his body to the side, desperately trying to break the chair against the cupboards as the footsteps got louder. The chair was starting to chip at the legs. He was close. So close.

Before he could try one more time, the door swung open and all Cade's hope left him.

I can't do this again.

He just couldn't. All he wanted was to find her, to know that she was okay.

Cade was falling deeper and deeper into a dark hole of anguish when Jude quietly rushed into the room.

His heart lurched as he dropped to his knees, the remnants of the chair still attached to his arms. He was saved.

"Oh my Gods, Cade!" Jude exclaimed, his face twisted in horror. Cade knew what he probably looked like. There was no time to ponder over it.

"Jude," he wheezed. "Untie me."

Jude didn't waste another second. He ran behind him and got to work. Cade winced and cringed as he agitated his sore skin. As soon as the rope fell to the floor, Cade fell forward on his hands, gasping. Jude came to his side and carefully helped him up.

"What the hell happened?" Jude asked once he was on unsteady feet.

Cade held onto the counter as he tried to push the words past his lips. "Deianira..." he panted. "They're gonna kill her..."

Jude stood behind and placed a hand on his shoulder, his voice laced with desperation. "I know. I was looking for her. Where is she? Is she okay?"

He shook his head grimly. "I don't know," he said, pained. "I don't know where she is-"

Jude cut him off. "Think, Cade. Where did you last see her?"

He sputtered. "H-her room. A couple hours ago. I tried to go back but-"

Cade winced as Jude's grip on his shoulder tightened. "Come on. Where would she go?" He sighed. "I want to keep her safe. Just like you."

Cade's nose twitched. Even in his condition, through his pain, he could smell it. It was a scent he'd smelled before. It wasn't overbearing, it was just a hint of something.

What is that?

It was something... wrong. Something dark. Dishonest, deceitful. Cade almost choked.

He had no idea what was happening but he was almost sure that...

Jude just lied to me.

"I can't let them get her. She's all I have." Jude continued.

Lie.

He was lying.

Why?

Why wouldn't he want to keep her safe?

Cade's mind spun.

Of course.

It was all too convenient that Jude showed up the second his father left. They planned this.

The only thing Jude didn't know was that Cade had figured that much out.

That was his only advantage. So he used it.

He tried something. Something that he'd never done intentionally before. It was only because of what he'd learned about his mother's past that he took notice of it. It was a risk. If it failed, he'd be giving himself away. If it worked...

"Jude..." Cade muttered as he turned around slowly, eyes hopeful.

"Yes?" Jude answered quickly.

Summoning every memory, every moment, every touch that he had shared with Deianira, Cade projected his love for her. "You don't want to hurt Deianira..." he said carefully. "She's your niece. She's all you have left... You love her."

Cade didn't even breathe as he waited. He might have just signed his death warrant.

Jude's eyes glazed as he stared at Cade. "I don't want to hurt her. She's just my little girl."

Cade let out a sigh of relief but held on as he let images of her cloud his mind. "You want me to help her. You want to let me g-"

Click.

"I knew it... Just like your mother."

Cade froze as he felt the barrel press into the back of his head.

Like a switch flipped, Jude shook his head and glared at Cade, eyes clear.

"You son of a bitch," Jude whispered. "Did you know about this?" he asked Drake over Cade's shoulder.

"I had a feeling," he said regretfully.

Jude sneered at Cade. "Impressive. But do tell, what was that? I know compulsion and that wasn't it. I mean, I actually felt that," he said, shaking his head in disbelief. "I loved her. How did you make me do that?"

Rage. That was the only thing Cade could feel. Pure, unfiltered rage. Her own uncle. He was like a father to her, she adored him.

"Come on, son." Drake bumped the gun against the back of his head. "You were blabbing just a second ago."

Breathe in, breathe out.

"Fine. Don't tell me." Jude stepped up to Cade and gripped both sides of his head. "You're not the only one with tricks."

Cade felt the haze coming over him but quickly bent and ducked out of his grasp.

BANG!

The world went silent for a second as Jude fell to the ground in front of him. Then, the ringing in his ears started.

Shaking his head, he stood back up and twisted.

His vision didn't need to be clear to see that his father was scared. Taking advantage of his momentary shock, Cade grabbed the arm holding the gun and brought it down hard on his knee.

Drake cried out, instantly dropping the weapon. Cade ignored the burn on his chest as he dove for it. Before he could grab it, a weak arm pulled at his leg. He didn't hesitate as he pulled his foot back and kicked out with all his might.

A choked cough told him that he'd hit his target.

Grasping the gun, he rolled onto his back and tried to aim at his father. He was seeing two of him and no matter how much he shook his head or blinked, he couldn't get a lock on the target.

Cade pulled the trigger anyway.

BANG! BANG! BANG!

When Cade didn't hear a body hit the floor, he lowered the gun and squinted.

Drake was gone.

He'd fled.

Coward.

Cade struggled back to his feet, ready to pursue him when he noticed a red blotch in his field of vision.

But not a body.

Not Jude's body.

Just a trail of blood leading out of the back door. He was alive.

Cade roared out in anger before kicking the abandoned wooden chair, smashing it to pieces.

He couldn't go after them both.

He needed to pick one.

His father for himself, or Jude for Deianira.

Chapter Forty-Three

At the top of the stairs, Lia stood directly in front of the door and motioned for silence as she turned to the group. "Cassian, Devin, stand to the right of the door and be ready to follow me. I've got a vest so I'll stay in front just in case. Emori, when I say go, I need you to pull open the door as fast as you can and stay behind it."

Emori instantly tensed and looked up at Devin. In response, he pulled her closer and pressed a kiss to her forehead before whispering something in her ear. She nodded her head and turned back to Lia.

Lia assumed that meant she was ready so she awkwardly inclined her head at Emori.

Everyone got into position and waited for Lia's signal.

Three,

Two,

One.

"Go!" she whisper-shouted.

Emori swung the door open, keeping her body behind it as Lia advanced, gun first, through the exit, Devin and Cassian quickly flanking her. After panning out and seeing that no one was there, she turned back to Devin and gave him a nod.

Clear.

As if he had been held against his will, Devin sprinted back to the door and pulled Emori from behind it. He leaned down and said something to her prompting a wide smile in response.

Lia watched for a second, curious as to the nature of their relationship when the world disappeared around her.

Everything went black.

She blinked and shook her head.

"Cassian!" she called through her mask.

"What?" he responded, slightly startled.

"I can't see!"

Lia held her hands out in front of her and saw nothing. Gripping the edges of her mask, she tugged it off. Nothing changed.

"Cassian, I can't see!" She was panicking now.

She felt a hand touch her arm and instantly batted it away.

"It's me!" Cassian told her before grabbing her head and gently pulling apart her eyelids. "Hold still."

She could feel the air touching her naked eyes but she still saw nothing.

Distantly she heard a small raspy voice. "Salem, stop! It's Eulalia."

In the next second, the world reappeared.

Lia gasped and blinked rapidly, struggling out of Cassian's hold. As her eyes adjusted to the low light, she spotted the queen and her sentinel down the hall.

"I apologize," the sentinel said, not looking the least bit sorry. "I thought that you were an intruder."

Lia could've been angry but the only thing she felt was relief.

"It's fine. It wouldn't be the first time," she said, side-eyeing Cassian.

Then her attention was drawn back to the queen.

She looked terrible. Her strides were heavy, head was lowered, breaths were stifled. It even looked like there was dried blood on her face.

"What the hell happened to you?" Devin gasped.

Deianira cut him a dirty look before nodding her head to her sentinel.

The sentinel took her cue.

"We don't have time for me to give you a detailed explanation but Jude is the one who orchestrated the attack. He manipulated her mind which caused side effects resulting in her current condition. We can't go to the arena but we need to get out of the palace."

Lia already knew this. Well, the first part.

"And Cade," Deianira breathed.

"And find Cade." Salem nodded.

So they weren't together. A dark feeling crawled up Lia's spine.

"Do you know where he went?" Cassian asked.

Deianira responded before Salem could. "No, but he was here. I don't know when, but he was. He left this." She held up a ring.

Eliza's ring.

Lia had given that to him years ago. She had no idea he'd hung onto it this whole time.

Devin stepped forward. "But protocol states to go to the arena. If he's anywhere, it would be there."

Lia instantly disagreed, shaking her head. "No, he's not. I didn't see him out there and I know he wouldn't leave this building without her," she said, nodding in Deianira's direction.

Deianira's expression dimmed even more.

Shouldn't she be happy?

"Well even if he's inside, the palace is huge. He could be anywhere."

"Well, he isn't up here," Salem stated.

"We could split up and look for him," Cassian suggested.

Salem blinked at Cassian. "That would be the worst thing to do for a multitude of reasons. We are grossly outnumbered, we don't know which enforcers to trust, four out of six of us are untrained, and one out of the two that are is momentarily incapable of defending herself." She turned to the others. "Does anyone have any better ideas?"

Lia held back her snort but Devin didn't. To her surprise though, Cassian didn't look offended. He looked intrigued.

Everyone was silent as they all waited for someone else to make a suggestion when the door at the other side of the hall burst open.

"Shit!" Lia jumped.

"Don't run," Devin urged all of them. "Get behind me."

Deianira wasn't sure what his plan was but she didn't have anything better to offer, so they all scurried to get behind him.

He took a deep breath before clapping his hands twice and pulling them apart.

She was about to ask him what that was supposed to do when she noticed the slight shimmer of the air in front of her. Before she could make any other observations, at least fifty enforcers advanced from around the corner, headed right in their direction. They were looking right at them. But then, she noticed that they didn't pick up their speed as they started towards them.

They can't see us.

It was a cloaking spell.

As they got closer, Devin carefully took steps out of their path and the others matched him, slowly angling themselves out of their way. They were marching right in front of them.

As they passed, Deianira managed to pick up some of the conversation that a few in the front were having.

"This is the last floor. I'm telling you, she isn't here."

"Where else would she be? We would've seen her if she'd left."

"I don't know but if she's hiding somewhere, the boy ought to know."

"Well, Alden needs to hurry up and beat it out of him. I just want this to be over with so I can get my cut and go home."

Cade?

The first enforcer laughed. "That guy is a cold bastard. Cutting up his own son for a payout? Wish I had the stones."

Deianira sucked in a harsh breath.

"What was that?"

They have him.

The sharp glare that Devin shot her way should've told her to stay quiet but she couldn't.

Cutting up his own son for a payout.

Deianira's mind was set. She ignored everyone's objections as she stepped forward and dragged herself out of the cloak.

Grabbing the first enforcer to notice her by the neck, she summoned all her strength and dug her fingers into his nape. With a pained cry, she gripped the thick bone and screamed as she tore his spine from his back.

All the enforcers seemed to pause as they took in the sight before them with various looks of terror written on their faces.

Keeping his spine clutched in her right hand, she let his body fall and looked on at the large group of enforcers as blood dripped onto her foot.

"Where… is he?" she rasped, her breaths ragged.

Like a chain reaction, as one of the enforcers fired his gun in her direction, the rest followed.

"For fuck's sake!" Deianira heard from her right before Devin, Emori, Cassian, Eulalia, and Salem appeared out of thin air.

Devin immediately put up a shield as Lia and Cassian started firing back.

Deianira didn't want to be behind the shield. She wanted to find the man that had been speaking about Cade. She *needed* to find him.

Pushing through her fatigue, she grunted as she summoned shadows and lifted herself before flying over the shield and toward the front of the line.

As they noticed her above them, the enforcers started shooting upwards, but she paid little attention to them. She had her eye on the enforcer at the front.

Before she could reach him, a bullet grazed her arm. She cried out as she spiraled to the ground with a sickening crunch.

Looking up, surrounded by enforcers, she locked eyes with the one who had shot her as he brought his gun up again.

Deianira growled. She didn't have time for this.

Stretching her arm out, a shadow swooped in and swirled around his head like a tornado before she heard a satisfying crack.

As she struggled to her feet, hobbling slightly, she looked out to the rest of the group. Lia and Cassian were still firing into the crowd while Salem was using one enforcer as a human shield as she advanced on two more, spraying bullets with his gun. Devin was no longer holding up a shield, he was standing in front of Emori hurling fire at the enforcers.

Every time he brought his hand back, flames would appear in his palm and grow before he'd throw it into the sea of enforcers.

Deianira didn't have time to be impressed though as she was body-slammed from behind.

As her head hit the ground in front of her, everything went hazy, even more than before. She was expecting to feel the impact of a bullet when the enforcer unexpectedly grabbed her hips and turned her over beneath him. This one wasn't wearing a mask but she couldn't even make out a feature on his face as her eyes fluttered.

"I've always wanted to get up close and personal with the queen," he whispered in her ear, his voice full of venom.

Deianira almost threw up in her mouth as his hand made its way up her hip and into her shorts.

She started to struggle, to push him away, but there was no give, he was too close.

Reaching to the side, she stretched her fingers across the floor trying to grasp something, anything.

As he grabbed her rear, Deianira choked out a cry out of disgust. Then her hand locked around it.

She wasted no time in grabbing the spine that she'd dropped and plunging the jagged edge into the side of his neck. He choked for a few seconds, stilled, then fell on top of her.

She pushed and kicked to wriggle out from beneath him as blood from his mouth started to drip onto her face.

Deianira gasped as she got back to her feet and wiped the blood from her eyes with the back of her hand. She did her best to clear her vision as she searched for the man again.

There.

He was keeping low, hiding behind his comrades. For some reason, that angered her even more.

Cade.

That name was all she needed to call forth the power to take flight once more. As she approached, she adjusted her position and flew into him, feet first, knocking him to the ground. She didn't give him a second to recover before she threw her body onto his and grabbed both sides of his head.

"Where is he?" she demanded ruggedly. She didn't even recognize her own voice.

She saw the moment that the man realized who she was and watched the fear enter his body. If she hadn't been on a mission, she would've laughed at his expression.

"Who?" he whispered.

"Where is he?" she repeated, her voice much quieter, much more sinister.

She could feel his heart pound faster in his chest as he said, "Arena." Deianira took a deep breath and leaned in closer, tightening her grip on his head. "That is the second time you've insulted my

intelligence," she gritted out before trying to steady her voice.
"Don't make it a third."
Now he was shaking.
"K-kitchen."
He's in the kitchen.
"Thank you," Deianira said earnestly.
Pressing her hands together, she let out a strained cry as she pushed.
"Please!" the man gasped.
Deianira grunted and kept pushing until his skull gave way between her hands and he stilled, releasing a final breath.
She stood shakily and turned back.
There were only a few enforcers left and she took the liberty of sending them flying into the wall with shadows before she dropped to one knee, breaths labored.
Salem rushed over to her.
"That was incredibly stupid."
"Bite me," Deianira breathed as the others gathered around. "He's in the kitchen. His father has him."

No.
Cassian froze as the words left Deianira's lips.
His father was in the palace.
Drake Alden.

He was the last person Cassian wanted to see right now. After his time spent in the palace, his eyes were opened to a lot of things. What Eulalia had said to him that night in the forest had stuck. But that didn't mean that he was ready to face him. Not now.

But Cade. Cade was down there.

Cassian tried not to even let himself think about the things that his father was going to do to Cade. He'd seen what he did when he didn't get his way. With the pressure even higher than usual, Drake would be on a rampage.

He stepped forward. "We need to-"

Before he could finish his sentence, the lights flicked back on. Cassian squinted his eyes against the white light.

Lockdown's over?

Why would they end the lockdown when they hadn't found Deianira yet?

Krrr. "We're sending backup to the top floor. Are you sure you've got her? Over."

Nobody moved.

Krrr. "Unit Twelve? Do you copy? Over."

Nobody spoke.

Krrr. "We're coming up."

Eulalia turned her wide eyes to Cassian.

There was no way they could take on any more of them. They didn't have the manpower or the energy.

Salem's head popped up.

"They're getting closer." That should've been their cue to leave but nobody seemed to be able to move.

A few seconds of silence followed before Salem tilted her head. "They're here."

As if on cue, the door to the east stairwell swung open, right in front of them.

Cassian watched as Devin's head spun towards the enforcers that poured into the hall, then turned to Emori, a desperate look on his face.

At her nod, he turned back to the group and bellowed, "Cover your ears!"

Cassian didn't know why Devin said that, but he'd already learned to listen to him first and ask questions later, so he dropped his gun and covered his ears. As did the others while Salem only closed her eyes and placed her hands over Deianira's ears where she was kneeling, half-conscious.

Just as the enforcers started running, Cassian vaguely heard Devin's roar. "EMORI! NOW!"

As soon as the words ceased, a piercing scream filled the air.

The ground shook.

Cassian didn't dare to remove his hands as he turned to Emori. He watched her as she stood with her hands thrown out, mouth open wide.

That sound was actually coming out of her.

In unison, the enforcers grabbed their ears and cried out, but their screams didn't rival Emori's.

One by one they dropped, clutching their heads and writhing on the floor. It didn't take much longer for them to stop moving.

Then, it stopped.

Cassian hesitantly lowered his hands from his head as Emori gasped for breath before settling and righting her stance.

The others followed suit and stared at her in shock.

"Guys. Kitchen." Devin said, pulling their attention from her.

So they weren't going to get an explanation.

Cassian patted the side of his head and gnawed at his jaw to get his ears to pop as he started moving. They had almost reached the stairwell when he noticed that they were fewer.

Turning back, he spotted Salem, passed out on the floor.

He didn't even hesitate to rush over and fall to his knees beside her. Moments later, Deianira was at his side.

"Salem." He picked up her head and shook her gently. She stirred but didn't wake. "Salem," he said a little louder as he jostled her shoulder.

She jolted and turned her head in his palm, trying to sit up. But her movements were awkward, jittery.

"Salem," Deianira called from right next to her, but Salem didn't even look at her.

She was looking at Cassian's lips.

"Salem, are you okay?" he said slowly.

She watched his mouth move before responding. "Yes, I'm okay."

Cassian let out a pent-up breath. "But I can't hear anything."

He winced as he remembered.

She didn't cover her ears. She was protecting Deianira.

"Shit," Deianira breathed as she leaned into Salem's eye-line. "I'll get you to a healer as soon as this is over."

Salem watched her, then nodded. "Okay." She calmly pried Cassian's hand off of her and stood on unsteady legs.

Chapter Forty-Four

Lia was shaken. Not because of what Emori had just done, as unexpected as it was, but because she was frightened for what they were about to find.

She and Cade had grown up attached at the hip. Lia had seen the effect that Drake had on the people that she loved, and unless he'd had a change of heart in the weeks that she'd been in The Dome, Cade wouldn't be in good condition when they found him.

As they grew closer and closer to the floor that the kitchen was on, her fear only grew.

She just hoped that he could hold on long enough for them to find him.

They'd only just made it onto the floor when Emori and Devin halted simultaneously.

The rest stopped as they noticed.

Devin motioned for them to stay back and slipped his hand from Emori's as he lifted his gun, carefully stepping up to the turn at the end of the hall.

No one tried to stop him. He was the most capable at that moment.

He kept his back to the wall as he subtly peered around the bend. Then his gun lowered. Devin stepped out into the corridor, his eyes unreadable as he stared down the hallway.

He hadn't told them that it was safe to follow but Lia wanted to see what he was seeing. Apparently, the others did too because they all followed as she walked closer to him.

At first, she wasn't sure what she was looking at. Even with the lights on, it was hard to make out the figure from the distance. It was definitely a person, but they weren't walking.

They were crawling.

The others seemed to have noticed the same thing as the atmosphere shifted.

Squinting her eyes, she could see that it wasn't an enforcer, they weren't wearing a uniform. It wasn't Cade either.

Only when she heard the voice did her blood run cold.

"Deianira…"

Jude.

Lia stopped dead as she watched Jude Ivar drag himself along the floor toward them, leaving a trail of blood in his path.

She felt nothing. Absolutely nothing.

She expected to be scared or enraged coming face to face with him, but not numb. It was as if she was looking at a stranger. Lia might have had fifty percent of his DNA but this man wasn't her father. That thought was strangely comforting. She *felt* nothing for him because he *was* nothing to her.

"Deianira, help me…" he begged as he drew closer. "He's gone crazy. He's trying to kill me"

Who?

Lia looked over at Deianira. Her face had completely fallen, she didn't even look angry. Just sad.

While Jude wasn't Lia's father, he was Deianira's. In the sense that mattered anyway. He raised her, she looked up to him. Maybe, it would've made more sense for Lia to be jealous of her. Jealous that her actual father was in The Dome raising Deianira when she was a street kid on the outside, but Lia could only feel sorry for her. She never had a father but Deianira was losing hers.

Jude reached out a hand as he drew closer. "Help me..."

"I know," Deianira whispered as he struggled to his knees.

And just like that, his mask fell.

"You rotten bitch," he spat.

Deianira physically flinched at his tone while the rest of them took a step back.

"This was never supposed to be yours..." he panted as he clutched his shoulder and stood. There was a hole in his polo neck, he must've been shot. "None of it. I was the firstborn."

"What are you talking about?" Deianira asked, defeated.

"I was born first!" he roared, striding forward. "The throne was supposed to be mine! She only got it because she presented first but that's not the way it works." he shook his head manically. "No, they took it from me."

"My mother? What does that have to do with me?"

"Everything! You were never even supposed to be an heir!"

Lia gently laid a hand on Deianira's shoulder to urge her backward as Jude continued his advance.

She sniffed. "Why didn't you just kill me that night?"

Lia wasn't sure what she was talking about but getting away from him seemed more important.

Jude's lips split into a cruel smile. "You don't think I tried?" He laughed humorlessly. "That was the whole plan until you snapped out of it. You were too powerful for your own good. The best I could do was make you forget."

Some ice returned to Deianira's voice as she yanked her arm away from Lia. "Well, I didn't forget."

"I see that," Jude retorted dryly.

Deianira stared at him for a while. She looked like her whole world was crumbling.

Lia was so busy watching her face that she didn't see her reach for her gun. Deianira snatched the gun out of Lia's grip and pointed it at Jude.

He tilted his head and slowed. "You're going to shoot me?" He narrowed his eyes. "Come on, sweetheart, you're better than that." He took a slow step forward.

Deianira gritted her teeth and shook her head. "Stop that!"

Another step. "Whatever happened to honor?"

She grunted as she rubbed her ear against her shoulder. "Get out of my head..."

One more step. "I've seen you fight looking more dead than you do right now. Why don't you put the gun down and come here? We both know you're not-"

Jude flinched, froze, then coughed, blood spotting on the ground in front of him.

What the-

Before Lia could even finish that thought, Jude fell to his knees revealing a figure several feet behind him, hand pointed straight out. As they lowered their hand and stepped into view, Lia's heart almost stopped in her chest.

Chapter Forty-Five

Cade?

Deianira held her breath as he stepped forward.

He was only in his slacks from the night before, though those were almost torn to shreds as he limped up to Jude's shaking body. His chest was a mix of dark and bright reds. Burns, cuts, blood.

And his face.

His beautiful face was almost unrecognizable. Through his one good eye, she could only just see that pop of green that she loved so much while one side of his lip was twice the size of the other.

Deianira slapped a hand over her mouth to stifle her cry.

What did they do to him?

She stepped away from the group to run to him when she realized that he wasn't looking at her. He was looking at Jude.

She watched as Cade staggered over to him. He put a knee to Jude's shoulder and pulled something out of his back pulling a shrill cry from him. And he didn't stop there.

It was like he couldn't see the rest of them standing there. Like Jude was his sole focus.

Cade kneeled down behind Jude and grunted as he flipped onto his back.

Deianira was convinced that she heard a faint "Please..." before Cade pulled his arm back and buried the knife in Jude's chest, forcing a gurgled cry out of him.

Her whole body went still.

Despite what she'd learned in the last hour, her heart lurched. The man she loved just put a knife through the chest of the man that raised her.

Then Cade did it again. And again. And again. He wouldn't stop. After a while, she couldn't even see the shine of the dagger, just the blood and Cade's arm pulling back and plunging repeatedly as she stared on in horror. She was sure that Jude was already dead but Cade wouldn't stop stabbing him, even as the blood splattered across his own face.

That didn't deter Deianira from taking small, unsteady steps in his direction. She wasn't afraid of him.

"Cade..." she softly called as she came up to his side.

It was as if he hadn't even heard her.

"Cade," she called again, placing a hand on his shoulder.

He jumped and whirled on her, knife pulled back.

She froze.

He was covered in blood, it even dripped from his sweaty locs of golden hair. Even his gaze was punishing.

"Cade, enough," she whispered. "Please."

Then his face changed.

All the anger, the pain, the rage. It doubled.

"Deianira..." he breathed.

She shakily nodded.

That was all it took for him to drop the knife and grip her throat with both hands.

"Cade!" she gasped.

"She betrayed you. She used you. You mean absolutely nothing to her. The second you see Deianira Rikar, you will end her and watch the light go out in her eyes. You will not remember this. Only your own rage. Kill her."

Cade quickly bent and ducked out of Jude's grasp before the gun went off above his head.

"Cade!" Deianira gasped.

Kill her.

Cade could distantly hear voices in the background, but he blocked them out.

She betrayed me.

"You betrayed me," he whispered as he watched her eyes go wide.

"No!" she screamed, grasping at his hands. "Don't hurt him."

She used me.

"You used me."

"Salem, no! He's... compelled!" she choked out before meeting Cade's eyes. "I'm sorry..."

Cade felt his hands loosening before he shook his head and retightened his grip.

"I mean absolutely nothing to you..." he said through gritted teeth as he shoved her into the wall, releasing her neck.

She hit the wall and fell to the ground, gasping and wheezing.

Cade was hit with a pounding sensation in his head. It got more and more intense with each breath he took until he had to grab both sides of his head, grunting in pain.

On her hands and knees, she raised a pleading arm. "I can take it! Devin, make her stop!" she yelled. "Please, stop, I can take it!!" she cried.

His whole being was throbbing. He could barely breathe.

Then in the next second, the pain disappeared, finally allowing Cade to take a breath.

Deianira's sigh of relief reminded him of his task. He drew a leg back and sent it into ribs. She screamed as she dropped back onto the ground. The voices around them got louder but she still pushed back up.

"Salem, I swear to the Gods, if you hurt him, I'll kill you!" she growled with tears streaming down her face.

She's protecting me-

No.

She used me.

Before Deianira could turn back to him, he backhanded her with as much force as he could deliver. He couldn't even feel the pain anymore. It was all numb.

"I can take it... I can take it..." she chanted over and over again. When she finally caught his eyes, she tried to reach him. "Cade, listen to me-" He fell to his knees on top of her, cutting her off.

"I want to kill you," he seethed in her face before picking the knife back up and bringing it to her throat.

"I know..." she whispered as tears rolled down the sides of her face. Cade shook his head, blinking.

Kill her.

I want to kill her.

"I'm so sorry I didn't tell you," she hiccupped.

"Shut up..."

"I was just scared that you would see what I am. That you'd hate me," she whispered.

Oh, Deianira-

No.

I want to kill her.

"Stop! Talking!"

He pressed the blade more firmly against her skin.

"You're so good, Cade." She was shaking beneath him. "You make me wish I was too, but I'm not." She winced as the blade nicked her under the chin. "I ruined their lives," she whispered. "They were so happy and I tore them apart. I was the reason your mother left The Dome." She blinked slowly.

Cade jerked his head away.

"Stop!" he barked.

"When I realized who you were, I was convinced I was being punished. That the Gods wanted me to suffer for my sins. But you weren't a punishment." she breathed, shaking her head. "You saved me."

Cade's mind pulsed. "No, no, no..."

"Not just physically, but in every way you could possibly imagine. I couldn't see you hurt after everything you'd done for me. And... and I just wanted you to look at me like I was a good person for a little longer, but it was wrong."

Cade groaned as a sharp sting ran through his temple.

"I shouldn't have taken that from you, either of you."

Kill her.

He shakily dragged the blade an inch across her throat.

Deianira gasped. "I know that now. If you want to kill me, I won't stop you." A few shouts of outrage sounded behind him but Cade tried to focus. "But you should know that I love you too."

Kill her.

Kill her.

Kill her.

She smiled at him, wincing as her split lip stretched. "I love you so much."

"Deianira, I can't..." Cade stressed, his heart racing. "Run."

She shook her head.

"Hit me."

Again, she refused.

"I'll kill you," he growled.

"I know." She nodded before straining to lift her head and press a soft kiss to his lips. As she pulled back, a small stream of blood seeping from the side of her neck, she closed her eyes and released a breath.

Kill h-

Cade gasped and choked as his mind flipped inside of his head.

Deianira closed her eyes, content. After pouring her heart out like that, she should've felt vulnerable, but she was at peace. She'd never been in love before but she was just glad that she got to experience it before she left. Nothing she'd done before had ever made her feel so fulfilled.

Any second now, he'd take the kill. And she was ready.

"Deianira?..."

She opened her eyes warily.

Cade blinked through wide, teary eyes before he jumped off her. Spotting the knife in his hand, he threw it like it was on fire.

"Cade?"

Deianira took her eyes off him for a second to see Lia and the rest of the group sag with relief.

"Did I just..."

She struggled up onto her knees, ignoring the burn in her ribs and the bruises on her limbs.

"It's okay," she said as softly as she could.

Cade scrambled away from her on the floor. "No! Don't come closer!"

"Cade, you broke the compulsion, you're not going to hurt me," she tried to reassure him.

"You don't know that!" he yelled before his bewildered eyes darted around the hall. "I'm sorry," he rasped, eyes red, face crumbling. "I didn't mean to, I swear."

She followed him and took his arm. "I know. I'm okay," she sniffled as she climbed into his lap and buried her head in the crook of his neck.

He cautiously wrapped his arms around her, his hand coming up to stroke her head as his body shook with tears.

"I'm sorry, I'm sorry..." he said over and over again as he rocked her back and forth.

"It's okay…"

Chapter Forty-Six

Lia sat by the window in Deianira's room, her blood boiling.
She thought she'd seen Cade in bad condition many times but those incidents didn't have a touch on how he looked now. If it weren't for Deianira approaching him outside the kitchen, she probably wouldn't have even known it was Cade. He was beaten, bloodied, and burned.
Drake, his own father, had done that to him.
Lia looked away from the window, turning to Cade where he lay on the bed, head cradled in Deianira's lap as she ran her fingers through his hair.
She stood and went to sit on the side of the bed when something vibrated on her wrist. The room was practically silent before so all heads turned in her direction.
Deianira's bracelet.
"Why do you have that?" Deianira whispered in an effort not to wake Cade.
Lia's mouth opened and closed. Deianira didn't necessarily look angry. She guessed that was a good sign.

Considering there was a possibility that they wouldn't make it through the night, now was as good a time as any to come clean. "I-uh, I took it earlier," she admitted, casting her eyes to Cade. "I know about my mother," she said, keeping her voice down. "All I wanted was to meet her."

Deianira's face was frozen, so Lia continued. "I found her at The Haven... she told me everything. About giving me away, about Cade's mother-"

"I'm sorry," Deianira interrupted.

Lia looked up, confused.

Why was *she* apologizing?

"It was an accident," she said, her eyes filling with tears.

"I know," Lia said slowly. "She knows that too."

That didn't seem to assuage Deianira in the slightest. Lia moved closer and sat next to her.

"I don't blame you for what happened to them and I don't blame you for not telling me. I was a stranger. I barged into your home and started making demands. You didn't owe me anything. I might not have had Grace, but I had a mother," she whispered, looking down at Cade again. "A wonderful mother. If you hadn't restored her, I wouldn't have. So, thank you."

Deianira just watched Lia for a moment before nodding stiffly.

Lia wondered if she should tell Deianira about Jude's history with her mother, but something told her not to. She was going through enough. She didn't need any more to think about.

The bracelet buzzed on her wrist again and Lia stifled a snort before Deianira reached out and grabbed her arm. She flinched, wondering if she was mad after all when Deianira swiped her index finger across the bracelet. Lia almost jumped back as a small screen came out of it and Hewn's face appeared.

"Your Majesty, if you're watching this, we need an extraction team and quick. The arena was a trap. Finch and I managed to get most of us out but we have at least twenty injured."

Lia stared at the screen in awe as the others gathered around to see the message. She even tried to touch it but was astonished when her hand went right through it.

"Stop that." Devin smacked her offending hand and she glared at him before looking back at it.

"It's quiet now but I don't know if it's clear so I'm keeping the cloak up. We're in the woodlands. Head east at the gate and give us the passcode so we know it's safe." He took a deep breath. "I don't know how much longer I can hold it."

As the message cut out, Deianira dropped her head in guilt. She had completely forgotten about her people. She was so focused on finding Cade, she'd forgotten that Hewn was out trying to save them. She was still focused on Cade, she didn't want to leave his side.

She opened her mouth to speak but Lia spoke for her. "It's okay. I'll go."

"No," Deianira protested. "He'll want you here when he wakes up."

She flicked her gaze to the corner of the room where her sentinel sat on the floor, gnawing at the side of her jaw.

"Salem-" she started before she remembered.

Salem couldn't go. She was the most skilled person Deianira knew but she was too vulnerable right now.

"No, I'm not." Salem turned to her before uncrossing her legs and standing. "I can go. I'll suit up and take one of the guys."

Of course, she'd been reading them the whole time. "Salem, no. You can't-"

"Yes, I can," she said plainly as she turned to Devin. "Can you shoot an M-"

"I'll come with you." Cassian stepped forward.

Deianira was surprised to hear him talk, surprised to hear him offer his help.

Doesn't he want to stay with Cade?

"Let's go," he repeated, looking at Salem.

Deianira noticed a small smirk on Devin's face before she turned back to Salem who looked Cassian up and down.

She looked between them for a moment before sighing. "Fine. Be careful."

Chapter Forty-Seven

Cassian fiddled with his vest as they padded to the main exit. Salem stopped and turned to him. "Are you sure you want to join me? You don't have any training and-"
"I'm sure," Cassian said clearly.
As she lifted her gaze from his lips, she narrowed her eyes. "Okay." He flinched as she grabbed both sides of his vest and jerked it forward before pulling at the straps, tightening it to his chest. A shiver went through him when her hands moved to the front of his belt and adjusted the strap there. He quickly averted his eyes, trying not to choke as her small fingers worked deftly in righting his pack and securing the straps before she stepped back and turned again. Lips parted, Cassian watched as she started walking towards the exit.
"Thanks," he managed to get out, then shook his head.
Moving to catch up, he kept stride with her as they approached the exit.
"I don't know how many are left so expect an ambush. They're waiting for us but they don't know that we know they're out there so

we have an advantage, barring the fact that we're outnumbered. Stay behind me, keep your mask on and your gun down. If we can convince them that we're one of them, we won't have to shoot our way out."

Taken aback by her authoritativeness, he nodded jerkily.

"Good."

Cassian did his best to act normal as they approached the exit, the large doors were wide open. From what he could see, there were a few dozen enforcers at the entrance. Some milled around, some sat on the ground just outside the door. A group sat on the hood of an armored truck, one tossing his radio around in his hands.

They were just waiting.

One foot in front of the other, he walked through the doors behind Salem, keeping his head straight forward. Even though they couldn't see behind his mask, he didn't move his eyes from the spot on the back of her head as they stepped down onto the grass and passed the first of many trucks outside.

"Hold up."

Cassian cringed as he slowed to a stop.

But Salem didn't stop at all.

"Hey!"

She continued walking.

Shit. She can't hear them.

Cassian knew that he'd blow his cover if he tried to run after her or made any odd movements. With her back facing him, there was no way to alert her.

Stop, stop, stop, stop... he begged over and over again in his head.

"Stop right there!"

Turn around, Salem. Come on...

Salem stopped walking, turned, and faced him, her hand coming to rest on her gun. Cassian huffed with relief.

That was close.

"Where's your unit?" The one sitting on the hood of the truck slid off and palmed his radio as he approached Cassian.

Cassian flicked his eyes to Salem. She said to follow her lead but if she spoke, they'd realize she was a woman.

Clearing his throat, he spoke up.

"We lost them on the top floor. We were with the backup team but we had to retreat," he said as steadily as he could.

"Well, where's she now?" the enforcer questioned as others in the area started to tune into their conversation.

Cassian quickly thought of a lie to tell them. A lie that wouldn't put the others in danger. "I think they got out. We were going to do a quick sweep of the training fields and report back." That wasn't the best thing to say. If they searched outside, they would be more likely to find Hewn and the civilians.

The enforcer tilted his head. "Under whose orders? Ivar made it clear that we weren't to move from our posts. Next unit every thirty. That's it."

They didn't know.

They didn't know that Jude was dead.

"He was the one that sent us. You can ask him when he comes down." As he finished speaking, Cassian tried to turn around and keep walking when the enforcer pushed.

"Oh. Then you won't mind me sending a few with you? You know, for safety."

No.

If Cassian said no, they'd be suspicious. If he allowed them to follow, he'd lead them right to Hewn and the civilians. He just needed to stall, he could do that.

"Yeah, sure," he nodded before turning to Salem. She probably had no clue what was happening. Cassian just hoped that she could read the atmosphere and go along with it.

"Connor, Luca, and Tag. Go!"

Tag?

Cassian didn't recognize any of the other names, but he knew Tag. They'd worked together for his father. They weren't close by any standards but they'd grown up together. All it would take was one slip-up.

Cassian led them out of the palace gardens as he tried to think of a way to lose them. They couldn't walk around forever but he couldn't take them to the woodlands either.

On the bright side though, he was grateful that Salem wasn't acting out of the ordinary.

"So,"

Tag.

"What sector are you guys from?" he asked conversationally as they walked along the perimeter.

Cassian cleared his throat trying to make his voice deeper.

"Southern sector," he said gruffly.

"Oh. Connor, aren't you from the southern sector?"

"Yeah, I am," Connor responded cautiously. "Hey, what's your name?"

Think, think, think.

Duck...

Cassian whipped his head around and in all directions as the voice whispered in his ear.

None of the guys seemed to have heard it. They just watched and waited for him to answer the question.

"Uh- It's-"

Duck!

The voice was louder now.

Cassian turned again and slapped his right ear.

Was he hearing things?

Tag looked at Connor, then back at Cassian.

Cassian, DUCK!

Cassian startled at the volume and instinctively ducked.

As he bent, Salem sprang into action. She moved so quickly. Using the butt of her gun, she knocked Connor clean out. Holding onto both ends of the gun, she looped her arms around Luca's neck and pulled the barrel, bringing his head down on her knee. Tag seemed to catch on as he tackled Cassian to the ground. He quickly reached for his knife but before he could pull back his arm, Cassian lifted his hips and they rolled.

On top of Tag, he twisted his arm until he dropped the knife before striking him in the temple. Tag's movements slowed. He used the opportunity to pull the handgun off his belt and press it to Tag's head.

"No," Salem was at his side in an instant, covering his hand with hers. "Too loud."

Placing a hand on the side of Tag's head, she lowered her voice to a whisper and looked into his eyes. "Sleep…"

Cassian watched her eyes closely as her pupils contracted before swinging his gaze to Tag.

His eyes fluttered before his head lolled to the side.

Salem stood as if it was nothing while Cassian stumbled to his feet, both awed and off-kilter.

He moved to stand directly in front of her before speaking slowly, lips moving clearly. "That voice in my head. Was that you?"

She blinked at him before furrowing her eyebrows. "You don't have to speak to me like I'm stupid. And yes, it was me." Her eyes flitted between his. "Maybe, you're the stupid one considering it took three tries to get you to listen." There was no bite to her tone. Just her making an observation.

She turned and started walking in the direction of the woodlands. "We need to move. Hewn won't be able to hold the cloak for much longer."

Chapter Forty-Eight

Deianira was starting to worry.

He still hadn't woken up.

Since she'd managed to convince him that he wasn't going to hurt her and get him into the room, he'd passed out and had been down ever since. It was like his body just gave out after he'd found her. Like he was waiting to find her before he allowed himself to rest. With his injuries, she expected as much. But it had been hours. They wouldn't be able to get a healer until Salem and Cassian got back but Cade's breaths were becoming labored. He needed help now.

"Devin," she called.

Devin looked up from where he'd been sitting on the sofa, holding Emori while she slept.

"Can you help me with something?"

He looked cautious, but he gently removed Emori's head from his chest before laying her on the sofa.

Deianira looked up at him as he approached. "I need you to heal him," she said as she ran her fingers through Cade's hair.

He tensed.

"I- I can't do that."

"Devin, you're the only warlock here. There are a lot of things you can do now that you couldn't before."

"Yes, but I'd seen those things done. I'd learned them but got better after the incident." He looked down at Cade and shook his head. "I wouldn't even know where to start."

"Try," Eulalia said from across the room as she walked up to sit beside Deianira.

Devin turned to her, the pressure evidently making him nervous. "I literally set a napkin on fire on top of your head and you want me to try something new on him. He doesn't look like he could take a strong wind right now," he said through gritted teeth.

"I understand, but he can't wait," Deianira whispered. "Please."

It wasn't a word that she used much. She had never needed to before, but if there was a chance it could save Cade, she'd say anything.

Devin stared at her, conflicted, before sighing and moving around the bed.

"I'll help," she told him as she lifted Cade's head from her lap and let him rest back on the bed.

Kneeling beside him, she reached out her hands to Devin and he put his palms in hers.

"Start with what you can see and work your way in." She placed his hands, faced down, onto Cade's chest.

Devin cringed as his hands rub against the seared skin, but he held on.

"If you don't know a general healing spell, you can try to locate and rectify the damage. One injury at a time."

Devin nodded stiffly. His hands were shaking.

"Devin," Eulalia called. He looked up. "He trusts you. You're not going to hurt him."

He nodded again before closing his eyes. He started mumbling under his breath as Deianira held hers.

After a few moments, the burns started to slowly fade. She huffed out a relieved breath as the cuts began to close. His blackened eye began to lighten in color as the side of his lip shrunk.

It was working.

Then, Cade stiffened. His whole body went rigid, his chest stopped rising and falling.

"Something's wrong," Devin said quickly.

"What is it?" Deianira demanded as her eyes burned into Devin's closed lids.

"I-I don't know," he rushed out as his brows creased. "I can feel something."

Cade's chest bucked off the bed and he started seizing.

"Stop!" Deianira instructed Devin.

"No! I can feel it, just wait!" he yelled as he struggled to keep Cade in place. "Lia! Hold him down!"

Eulalia wasted no time in crawling past Deianira and pressing her hands down on Cade's shoulders as Devin started mumbling louder.

"What's happening?" Deianira asked, shaken, but no one responded and Cade started convulsing more violently.

"Oh, Gods..." she cried, hands over her mouth.

As she watched Eulalia and Devin bounce around, trying to keep Cade under control, Deianira thought back to how scared he was for her when she'd had that flashback that morning in the training room. If he felt even a fraction of what she was feeling now, she owed him an apology.

She didn't know how much longer she could watch. She considered forcing Devin to stop and wait for a healer when she noticed something moving under Cade's skin. She got closer to get a better look.

Eulalia voiced her thoughts. "What the fuck is that?"

Devin didn't respond. He removed his hands from Cade's chest and began raising them slowly.

Deianira watched as the small patch of skin raised even further before bursting. Eulalia screamed and Deianira gasped in horror as a bullet flew out of his abdomen and hit the ceiling. Then another. Devin placed his hands back on Cade's chest and the wound started to close.

"They must have gotten sealed in there when I closed his wounds," Devin whispered as he opened his lids and looked down, eyes wide. "There were so many..." His voice wavered. "Whoever did this is really fucked up," he said, voice thick.

Deianira stared at the two discarded bullets in the corner of the room.

His own father shot him. Twice.

That night in the kitchen, she had assumed his father was a bad man but nothing could've prepared her for this.

"Cade?"

Deianira flicked her gaze to Cade at Eulalia's voice.

His eyes were open.

She slid next to Eulalia. "Cade."

His eyes darted around the room before settling on her.

As they marched through the woodlands, Salem stopped and held a hand out before turning to Cassian and placing a finger on her lips.
Be quiet. Got it.
She tilted her head up to the sky and let out a strange whistle.
Cassian looked at her, then at the trees, then at her again.
Was something supposed to happen?
She did it again.
Still nothing.
"I can't give them the password," she whispered.
"What do you mean?" Cassian whispered back.
She started to back up. "I'm quite literally tone-deaf. I can't do it. We need to go back-"
"Show me," he said as he grabbed her hand. "Tell me in my head. Like how you spoke to me before."
Salem pulled her arm from him. "Close your eyes and listen."
Cassian obeyed.
He was expecting it this time so he wasn't as startled as the smooth rhythm echoed in his head. Despite the circumstances, Cassian felt a genuine smile touch his lips. It was amazing. He could hear her everywhere. Not just in his head, but in his whole body. Like a harmonious blanket.
She whistled the tune three times before she stopped. Cassian reluctantly opened his eyes and nodded.
He'd enjoyed that far too much.

Trying his best to replicate the tune, Cassian put his lips together and whistled. He even closed his eyes again to remember exactly how it felt when she told it to him.

Salem's tap on his arm had him stopping.

As he turned to the forest, he could see a slight shimmer several feet away before it faded, and there stood Hewn with hundreds of civilians around and behind him. He grasped his knees and took several breaths.

With the size of the wall he was holding and how long he kept it up, he must've been a very powerful warlock. Hewn wasn't a young man either.

Salem pulled off her mask, shaking her head from side to side, letting her wavy hair fall from the backstrap.

She brushed the coiled whisps out of her face and approached Hewn, apparently, uncaring of his condition. "Jude's the informant. There's no need to worry though, he's dead now. The intruders are still surrounding the exit but we can take them with this many people." She turned to the crowd. "Those of you who are armed, stay on the outside of the group. I'll take point. Hewn and Portan, pick a side and keep formation. Finch, at the back with Cassian. Move quickly, quietly and don't separate. No stragglers."

By the looks of the faces in front of them, Cassian wasn't the only person who thought that her words were blunt. She didn't even give Hewn a second to catch his breath.

Cassian didn't want to undermine her but he didn't think it was a good idea for her to be alone at the front.

"Ivar's dead?" Hewn asked behind her, as his face fell.

She didn't turn, just kept giving orders to the civilians.

This only proved Cassian's point.

"Salem," He went to place a hand on her shoulder but she quickly turned as he got within arm's reach.

"What?" she asked.

He lowered his voice. "Maybe, you shouldn't be alone on this one." Salem stared at him for a moment. "You're right," she concluded with a thoughtful expression. "You hold the front with Hewn. Finch and I will take the rear."

That wasn't what he had in mind but it was safer than the original plan. Nodding, he got into his position as they started to trek back towards the palace.

Chapter Forty-Nine

After about another hour, the sun made an appearance through the clouds.

Cassian turned to the group and held up his fist in a 'hold' motion as they neared the bend leading to the entrance. The footsteps began to slow as the message got passed down the line.

It was getting brighter and they wouldn't have cover for long.

Cassian peered around the corner, eyeing the entrance.

"What's taking them so long?" said the same enforcer that had questioned them.

"I don't know but I'm not going in when no one else has come out. I didn't sign up to be slaughtered."

"Well, if you want to go home, be my guest, but I'm not leaving without my cut."

Cassian jumped as Salem appeared at his side. "I'll take the ones on the truck. You stay back and cover me." She was ridiculously agile.

She turned and motioned some people forward.

Four girls and three guys.

Cassian frowned as she started giving them orders. These were teenagers. Kids.

"Understand?" They all nodded. "Take them out but don't kill them if you don't have to. Her Majesty will want them alive."

They broke apart and took their places.

As soon as Salem whisper-shouted "Go!", one of the girls closed her eyes and tilted her head to the sky. The sun that was peeking from the horizon darkened as a gray-tinted bubble encased everything in a hundred-foot radius. It looked like it was night again, but the sun was still up, just darker.

Taking the cue, Salem rounded the corner with the others and chaos erupted.

Some fell to the ground. A few went flying into the wall.

One of the girls stared down at an enforcer with a smile on her face as he picked his gun up. Cassian tensed but then, the enforcer's eyes went white and he backed away screaming, running from whatever he was seeing in his head.

Cassian was so entranced by the show that he almost didn't notice the enforcer dragging himself across the ground, one of his legs bent in the wrong direction. As he wheezed, he picked up his gun and pointed it at one of the girls who had her back to him.

No, not one of the girls.

Salem.

She was caught in the arms of one enforcer as another struck her across the face.

Cassian almost choked as he lifted his gun and fired a shot in the direction of the one on the floor. The man went limp. Swinging the gun back to the two on Salem, he tried to get a shot but they were moving too fast.

All of a sudden, she freed an arm and grabbed the head of the guy holding her. He went still, dropping her in the process. She didn't just fall though. She dropped and rolled, picking up his gun on her way. The second she was on one knee, she faced the second guy and sent two shots into each of his legs. He cried out in agony as Salem stood and walked to him, muttering something before he fell to the ground.

Cassian blew out a breath as the chaos began to cease. The surrounding area went quiet, light returned to the sky and the young girl opened her eyes.

Salem walked back to the group, using the back of her glove to wipe the blood off her brow. "Don't lower your guard now that we're in. There could be a few in the building."

Cassian stayed in line with Hewn as they crept through the palace. They hadn't said a word to each other the whole journey and Cassian preferred it that way. His whole presence was just a reminder of the reason he was here. He thought about how much worse that night at the lodge could've gone if he'd owned up. He would've been dead by now, but he still couldn't help but regret his decision. He could practically feel Hewn judging him.

They hadn't run into any enforcers yet but he still stayed alert. The civilians had significantly calmed since they arrived at the palace but they still had a long way to go before they made it to safety. Safety was the sub-level until they could clear out the rest of the intruders. The east stairwell would have been the most secure way down but it didn't stop at the ground floor. The quickest way down was up the grand staircase and back down at the other end of the first floor, so they started heading into the ballroom.

As their shoes tapped across the glossy marble floors of the dark ballroom, Cassian caught something moving in the corner of his eye. Turning his gaze, he looked closer and saw a shadowy figure retreat out of the side exit.

He quickly turned to Hewn to see if he had noticed, but he didn't appear disturbed.

There was something about the way that it moved, it was so familiar. It wasn't a warm familiar feeling though. It was a feeling that made his hairs stand on end.

"Hewn," Cassian whispered. "I'm gonna go check on Salem." he lied.

Hewn looked suspicious but he nodded anyway.

Cassian carefully distanced himself from the group. There were enough of them for him to sneak away unnoticed.

Making sure to stay out of Salem's eye-line, he walked backwards through the exit.

It led to the service stairwell and he knew that it didn't go to the sub-level. Whoever was there went up.

Cassian kept his breaths shallow as he took the steps two at a time, listening out for anything. As he reached the second floor, he noticed that the door was slightly ajar before it slowly drifted shut.

There.

Putting his gun strap back over his shoulder, he pulled his handgun out of his belt. He opened the door very slowly and pressed through the gap, both hands on his gun.

Cassian looked left and right before he crept through the hall. They could've been in any room. The second floor was mostly offices but there were still several doors.

Dum, dum. Dum, dum. Dum, dum.

At first, he thought he was hearing his own heartbeat in his head but as he walked further, the sound quietened.

Cassian furrowed his brows.

He turned back around and walked a few steps.

Dum, dum. Dum, dum. Dum, dum.

He kept in that direction and as he drew closer to the supply closet at the end of the hall, the sound got louder.

There was someone in there.

And he could hear them.

It was only then that Cassian started to second-guess himself.

Salem was right. He wasn't trained. The first time he'd shot a gun, he killed four innocent men and now he thought he could handle a solo mission?

What exactly was he going to do when he found them?

He didn't know but the door was calling to him. He needed to go in.

Standing outside, he opted to press his ear against the door first.

Dum, dum! Dum, dum! Dum, dum!

There was definitely someone in there.

Cassian stood back, hand on the knob, and took a deep breath.

Three, two, one...

He swung the door open and stood back, gun pointed into the room.

And he stopped dead in his tracks.

"Cassian, thank the Gods."

Dad.

"Cassian," he called, holding his right arm to his chest.

He didn't respond.

"Cassian, it's me."

No, it wasn't.

Cassian barely recognized the man that stood before him. His appearance hadn't changed, neither had his voice, but something was different about him. Darker.

The last thing Cassian wanted to do was speak to him but he had to ask.

"Why?" His voice was barely above a whisper.

"What do you mean why?" Drake looked utterly confused.

"Why?" he repeated. There was nothing else he could say.

"Cassian, I did this for you. For us." His eyes darkened. "I thought you were dead when that girl dragged you away in the middle of the night, but you were living here. With them." He shook his head. "It's okay, son, I forgive you. You made the best of a bad situation and-"

"That wasn't what I asked." Cassian spoke over him, gun still raised. Nerves crept in. "Why did you d-do that to him?" he stuttered.

Drake's mask slipped for a fraction of a second before he gave Cassian a sad look. "To who? Cade? Cassian he's sleeping with her. The Queen," he said quietly like he was telling him a dirty secret. "I did what I had to do. He's not on our side anymore." He shook his head, feigning disbelief. "I don't think he ever was."

Cassian grimaced. How had he not seen it?

He knew that Drake wasn't the best father but he'd always told himself that no one was perfect, that he had their best interest at heart in his own twisted way. But now? Cassian only felt shame for his oblivion.

"He's your son," he whispered. "He's my brother."

Drake shook his head grimly. "No, Cassian. Not anymore. Look what he's done," he said, holding up his arm. Cassian couldn't hold back his wince. His hand hung off his wrist at an awkward angle.

"Look what he's got you doing. You're pointing a gun at your own father. He's trying to tear us apart."

A thought occurred to Cassian. A very dangerous one. One that would tell him if his father was any bit of the man that he thought he was.

"Did you know I was still inside?" he whispered. It might have been selfish to ask about himself when Cade was the one wronged, but Cassian needed to know just how far Drake had gone.

Drake's mouth opened and closed multiple times before he sputtered a response. "W-what are you talking about?"

Cassian steeled his spine, even as his voice shook. "I'm talking about how you blew up the side of the palace and sent fake enforcers in here to shoot on sight." He felt the sting of tears behind his eyes, but he scrunched his nose and forced them down. When Drake didn't respond, he went on. "Do you know how many times I almost died today?"

"Cassian, I would never-"

"ANSWER THE QUESTION!" he roared manically. Drake flinched and took a step back. He lowered his voice as he tried to swallow down the painful lump in his throat. "Did you know I was still inside?"

"Cassian this is ridiculous, of course, I was gonna look for-"

"When?!"

Drake was silent.

"We're gonna look for my dead body, dad, is that it?"

Drake stared at Cassian before frowning, his face anguished. "What did he do to you?" he asked, shaking his head. "What did he put in your hea-"

"Stop blaming everything on Cade!" he bellowed as his breaths came quicker. He felt like he was going crazy. "What did *you* do to *him*?" he breathed with disgust. "I saw the cuts... the burns."

"Cassian, I did what I had to do. I'd do it again for you," he said solemnly.

He was so convincing.

Maybe, if Cassian hadn't witnessed what he had in the last few hours, he would've believed him. But he had witnessed it, and he didn't believe him.

Staring dead into Drake's eyes, Cassian lowered the gun a fraction. "You did what you had to do," he murmured.

Drake's face split into a sad smile. "Yes. You get it. This is why we always stick together. Because you and I do what it takes. We're the same." His stance relaxed. "Let's go home, son. We'll come up with a new plan and hit them back twice as hard next time."

Cassian nodded, resolving his decision in his mind. "You did what you had to do," he repeated softly.

"Exactly." Drake smiled warmly.

Cassian released a pent-up breath, guiltily relishing in the relief. "So did I."

He saw the moment his father's face fell. The minute he realized that Cassian wouldn't be coming home with him. The second he knew that he wouldn't be going home either.

BANG!

Cassian didn't move for a good minute as a single stream of smoke rose from the barrel of his gun. He just held it up, shaking from head to toe.

Drake was dead.

Gone.

Cassian would've done anything at that moment to be able to say that he hated his father. That he didn't regret it at all because he was an evil man. But he couldn't. He couldn't erase the good memories from his mind, he couldn't taint the image that his father had created for him. He knew that it was an act, a mask, but try as he might, he couldn't forget the Drake Alden that raised him.

The Drake Alden that lay slumped on the floor, a big red hole through his forehead.

Pulling himself out of his trance, Cassian finally looked down and let the tears fall.

It's not over yet, a voice whispered in the back of his mind.

His chest heaved and his hands shook as he reached down and grabbed the back of Drake's jacket. With a silenced sob, he tugged. He dragged and pulled. Cassian didn't stop as he made his way through the palace and headed in the direction of the kitchen. It didn't take him much time to find the last thing on his list and before long, he was approaching the main entrance of the palace.

As he stepped out into the light, he immediately spotted the tens of enforcers gathered outside. They must have been the ones in the building that came up empty, or they were the units from the arena. Cassian didn't care, it didn't make much of a difference now.

It took them a while to notice him. Really notice him. He still wore his enforcer gear, but he'd removed his helmet.

Silently, guns raised all around the gardens. Maybe it was because a few of them recognized him from the western sector, or it had something to do with the two bodies that he dragged behind him. Cassian wordlessly walked down the steps, feeling nothing as the bodies bumped on the concrete. Once on the grass, he stopped and released them.

He was mildly surprised that no one had taken a shot at him yet. He didn't want to die, but he wouldn't have made an effort to move if they did decide to open fire.

He took a step back and motioned to Drake and Jude's lifeless bodies. "It's over," he announced.

A few faces fell, but most just stared at him, not knowing what to do. That was expected. These were clueless young men who were promised a better future and manipulated into doing a job that they couldn't handle, and now their leaders were dead. They hadn't planned for this.

That was the only reason Cassian extended them a small mercy. The ones that had been incapacitated earlier were still down, but the remaining had a chance.

Cassian knew what would happen if Deianira got her hands on them, and she would've been justified. But he could just as easily have been one of them and now he stood with his hand on the radio in his belt.

He didn't pick it up.

"Run," he told them. "While you can."

Chapter Fifty

Cade lay awake in his infirmary bed.

The attack had ended days ago but in his head, he was still fighting. There was too much weighing on his mind. Too much that hadn't been addressed.

However, everyone around him seemed to be going on with their life, picking up where they left off.

Except for Cassian. Every time he came to visit Cade, his aura was suffocating, overwhelming. There was something seriously dark brewing in him but as guilty as it made Cade feel to admit, that wasn't what was weighing on his mind. The source of his inner turmoil was resting her head in her arms on the side of his bed.

They had talked over the past few days but the conversations were surface-level. They both knew that a bigger conversation needed to be had.

She shifted in her sleep before lifting her head and yawning.

Cade decided that today would be the day.

"Good morning," he said softly.

"Hi."

Cade might have been the empath but she could read him just as well as he could read her.

"Go ahead," she whispered.

He took a deep breath and willed his voice to stay steady.

"Did you mean it?" he said under his breath.

So much for steady.

"Did I mean what?" she asked as apprehension filled the room.

She was really going to make him say it.

"That day, when I-" He quickly stopped. Thinking about that day was physically painful. "Y-you said that you loved me." he choked as his voice became hoarse. "Did you mean it?... Or were you just trying to break the compulsion?"

Cade closed his eyes, head facing the ceiling, as he waited for her response. He felt that it would hurt more if he had to see the look of pity on her face.

It was strange how he'd never felt vulnerable all those times he'd put himself out there with her, all the times he'd given himself to her, but he did now. The possibility that she could feel the same way was far too sweet. He didn't know what he'd do if it turned out that she was just trying to wake him.

The waiting was agonizing too.

A soft palm on his face had his eyes peeling open. Deianira was standing, her face above his, looking into his eyes.

"I meant every single word," she said softly.

He felt as if an anchor had been lifted off his chest.

She went on. "I love you." Her eyes never strayed. "And I might have tried to ignore it for a while but I never lied to you, Cade."

He stared at her in awe.

She actually meant it.

Her lips split into a smile at his open-mouthed expression. "Do you need me to say it again?" she snorted. "I love you. There. You happ-"
He grabbed her face and brought her lips down on his. He held nothing back. Neither did she.
His tongue delved into her mouth as she massaged his scalp with her nails. He sucked gently on her bottom lip and she nipped at his as their hands explored each other.
Cade pulled back for a second with what he was sure was a goofy smile on his face. "Are you sure?" he asked her.
She giggled and rolled her eyes. "Yes, I'm sure."
His smile grew wider as he pulled her mouth back to his and dragged her waist closer to the bed.
Moving back again so that their lips were a breath apart, he asked her again. "Okay, but are you really su-"
"Has anyone ever told you, you talk too much?" she quipped.
That question gave him pause.
The answer was no.
No one had ever said that to him.
He'd grown up trying to take up as little space as possible, trying not to be heard. It was a defense mechanism, probably the reason he'd made it this far.
But with Deianira?
Cade didn't know what it was about her but she made him want to be the biggest and the loudest person in the room just to have a chance of being noticed by her.
He looked up at her warmly. "Never…"
With that, he rolled onto his side, grabbed her hips, and lifted her body onto his.

"Cade!" she squealed as she straddled him. "You're still healing and Mikhael said-"

He cut her off again with his mouth.

Pulling back he said, "I don't care." He kissed her again. "I want you."

Cade could feel her resolve wavering as he kissed his way up the side of her neck, pulling a moan from her.

"Cade, you need rest."

He pressed his hips up and as she moaned and rocked her center against his length, he knew he'd won.

"Fine," she hissed as if she was being greatly inconvenienced. Cade snorted. "But take it easy."

"Yes, boss," he murmured into her neck.

"Don't call me that," she breathed.

As she ground herself on him, Cade helped her as her hands made quick work of undoing his belt. Next to go were her pants as she wriggled out of them with ease. With a hand holding his length and one holding her, he nudged the tip at her entrance and slowly pulled her down, allowing her to feel every inch as he filled her.

Deianira shivered as he bottomed out and didn't wait to start moving. Hands on her hips, Cade groaned as he guided her up and down on his shaft.

She gripped him mercilessly.

He hissed blissfully as he ground her pelvis down onto his.

As they built up a slow and steady rhythm, Cade pulled her down so that they were chest to chest. He could never get close enough to her.

Placing one hand on her the small of her back and the other just below her head, he started thrusting up into her.

Her startled gasp tapered off into a deep moan.

Cade knew that she told him to take it easy but he couldn't resist. As gracefully as he could on the narrow bed, he held onto her as he rolled them over and entered her again.

This angle was even deeper, more intense.

"Cade…"

He would never get tired of hearing her say his name like that.

"I know," he whispered into the crook of her neck.

Cade interlaced his fingers with hers above her head as he deepened his thrusts, grinding his pelvis down against her clit.

Deianira's hips bucked as she squeezed his hand. "Gods,"

He groaned loudly as she wrapped her legs around him. He was close and the sounds she was making in his ear did nothing to help his stamina.

As he increased his pace a fraction, her channel gripped him tighter and Cade almost spilled right then and there.

"Deianira," he breathed but she clenched down even more.

Cade squeezed her hand before finding her lips again. He claimed her mouth, swallowing her moans. They came together as their rhythm became frantic. Deianira writhed and cried into Cade's mouth as he thrust into her relentlessly. With one final, forceful thrust, he shook as he spilled into her.

Their lips barely parted as they tried to catch their breaths.

Cade was so overwhelmed with emotion. It was something he should've been used to by now, but he couldn't stop his heart from speeding up every time he looked at her. Every time she spoke.

"I love you," she whispered against his lips.

There she goes again.

Epilogue

Seven years later...

Deianira secured her blindfold and stood in the center of the room. She had rolled out of bed just as Cade fell asleep to come to the training room.

It was where she was most at peace.

Since The Dome came down and the population almost quadrupled, she felt like she never got a second alone. There was always something going on.

It had been six years since she abolished the Prima Act and took down the wall but while most of her people adapted, some were still ignorant and couldn't see past their differences. At times, it made for a very hostile environment and came with a plethora of disputes for her to settle.

That was why Deianira cherished these few moments of silence. Tuning into the feeling of the mat beneath her bare feet, the slight breeze across her face, she raised the remote towards the arrow launcher, thumb over the button and ready to press.

"Absolutely fucking not!"

"Ughhhhh!" Deianira groaned as she tilted her head to the ceiling, ripping off her blindfold. "I just want to train!" she whined.

"Woman, I swear to the Gods, you're gonna give me a heart attack." Deianira rolled her eyes at his blatant exaggeration.

Cade stormed into the room, grasping the remote from her hand and shutting down the machine. "Baby, nobody's stopping you from working out," he said, bending down so they were at eye level, clasping his hands together in a pleading motion. "You have a room full of those wrist weights and yoga balls and-"

She glared at him and smacked his shoulder. "Are you trying to be funny? Yoga balls, Cade? I'm pregnant, not senile," she hissed as he rubbed his shoulder.

"I know that, but you can't keep sneaking off in the middle of the night by yourself. Next time, just wake me up and I'll come with you." He pulled her close and kissed her forehead. "I just don't want you getting hurt. Either of you."

Deianira softened at his tone.

"Fine," she mumbled. "But you can't just hover over me either."

"Got it. Just an observer," he smiled as he pressed a quick kiss on her lips.

Bzz. Bzz.

If Deianira rolled her eyes any further, they'd stick to the back of her lids. She just wanted a second of peace.

"We've been summoned," Cade said, looking down at his wrist.

Deianira quickly checked hers.

Emergency Meeting - High Council

"It's probably another dispute." She yawned. "Let's get it over with."

As Cade walked behind Deianira into the Council's study, he flicked his eyes over everyone there.

"Your Majesty. King Consort." His Head Enforcer nodded at them sarcastically. "Pleasure to have you finally join us. It's not like we have lives to get back to or anything."

Deianira didn't spare him a glance as she padded, barefoot, over to one of the two head chairs. "If my timeliness is an issue, Jacobs, I can easily demote you. Solve both of our problems."

Cade snorted as he took his seat beside her.

"What's the latest issue?" she asked promptly, simultaneously signing her question for Salem's benefit.

Most of them were still in their sleep clothes and it was obvious that they didn't want to be there any longer than necessary.

"I called the meeting," Lia said, her voice edgy, signing shakily.

The tone of the room seemed to shift.

"I was out scouting and I found something. It was washed up on shore, miles away from here. I would've brought it, but I doubt any of you would want to see that in person." She tapped the bracelet on her wrist and an image appeared.

Cade had to fight to not look away.

It was a head, and its eyes were gone. Not cut out, just gone.

"Who would do something like that?" Deianira asked, disgusted.

"Who could do something like that is the real question?" Cade retorted. "There's no blood, no scratch marks, no cuts. Look closer."

"No thanks," Deianira replied, a hand over her mouth.

Over the past few years, Cade had gotten even better at honing his abilities. He was able to distinguish an individual's specific emotions, even when he was around multiple people.

That's how he could see the waves of apprehension coming off his Head Enforcer.

"Devin," he called. Devin flinched and flicked his eyes up. "What is it?"

Cade had seen many sides to him but fear rarely ever made an appearance.

"Azraels," he said as if that explained it all.

Deianira's hand clutched her bump. "What do you mean azraels, Devin? There are no other azraels I don't remember decapitating that man," she said slowly.

He sighed. "There are no other azraels *here*," he stressed. "And these aren't the ones you're thinking about. These are... purebred."

Deianira was signing manically as she asked, "What do you mean purebred? And what do you mean 'here'? Devin, you're not making any sense!"

Cade rested a hand on her thigh and she took a deep breath. "Explain."

"Patriam," he started with his head down. "It's where we're really from. These Gods that we learned about in school, The God of Magic, God of Foresight," he said, turning to Lia, "God of Empathy," to Cade, "God of Psionicism," to Salem, "and the Angel of Death." His gaze landed on Deianira.

"Well, they weren't really Gods. They were immensely powerful beings called primas. Tens of thousands of years ago, primas and humans lived in Patriam, but the humans didn't live how they do now. They were like animals. Born to be hunted and slaughtered by the primas. Some primas didn't agree with this way of life so they started a resistance, took as many humans as they could, and fled overseas. To here. To Terra," he sighed as he carried on. "We were told that the gifted are at the top of the food chain, but we're basically a watered-down version compared to them. They're our ancestors." He pointed at the image still projected from Lia's wrist. "That's how the azraels hunt, how they feed. They suck the life out of you. Literally. Whatever did that, is the real deal. And if that washed up here, then they're not far behind."

Everyone sat still, open-mouthed at Devin's words.

Salem was the first to question him.

'Why is this the first time we're hearing of this?' she signed.

"The primas in the resistance wanted a fresh start. They wanted to integrate with humans but the actions of the primas in Patriam were so barbaric, it was bound to create problems, prejudices. So the resistance banned people in Terra from speaking about it. It was practically erased from history."

"Then how do you know about them?" Deianira demanded with a little more bite than she probably intended.

Devin's hands shook. He wouldn't get away with lying with Cade in the room but he was truly petrified now. So petrified that he opted to sign instead of speak.

'Because Emori's one of them.'

The End

Printed in Great Britain
by Amazon